"COUNSELOR TROI," TEVREN SAID SOFTLY. "TO WHAT DO I OWE THIS HONOR?"

"We're getting you out of here," Deanna said.

Tevren's attention was on Vaughn and the others. "I'm guessing you're with Starfleet," he said with some amusement. "Now, why would Starfleet be interested in me?"

Vaughn's eyes narrowed. "Don't flatter yourself."

Tevren chuckled, delighted. His eyes went back to Troi. "You look haggard, Deanna, and it's more than just the years, I suspect. War going badly, is it? Things unpleasant back home? Coming here when the place is infested with Jem'Hadar is quite a feat. Some might even call it an act of desperation."

"Tevren, we don't have time—"

"*Make* time," Tevren suggested. "This is all quite a fuss over someone no one ever wanted to see again. Unless, of course, I have something you want? That's it, isn't it?" And with that, his eyes gleamed. "They need me back home. They want to know what I know."

STAR TREK
THE NEXT GENERATION®

THE BATTLE OF BETAZED

Charlotte Douglas & Susan Kearney

**Based upon STAR TREK and
STAR TREK: THE NEXT GENERATION
created by Gene Roddenberry**

POCKET BOOKS
New York   London   Toronto   Sydney   Singapore   Betazed

This book is a work of fiction. Names, characters, places and incidents are products of the authors' imaginations or are used fictitiously. Any resemblance to actual events or locales or persons, living or dead, is entirely coincidental.

An *Original* Publication of POCKET BOOKS

POCKET BOOKS, a division of Simon & Schuster, Inc.
1230 Avenue of the Americas, New York, NY 10020

A VIACOM COMPANY

STAR TREK is a Registered Trademark of Paramount Pictures.

This book is published by Pocket Books, a division of Simon & Schuster, Inc., under exclusive license from Paramount Pictures.

ISBN: 0-7434-3434-X

First Pocket Books printing April 2002

10 9 8 7 6 5 4 3 2 1

POCKET and colophon are registered trademarks of Simon & Schuster, Inc.

For information regarding special discounts for bulk purchases, please contact Simon & Schuster Special Sales at 1-800-456-6798 or business@simonandschuster.com

Printed in the U.S.A.

To Marco Palmieri, who made this book possible;
with special thanks to Keith DeCandido

Historian's Note

This novel takes place approximately two months after the *Star Trek: Deep Space Nine* episode "Tears of the Prophets," and a few months before the events of *Star Trek: Insurrection.*

Prologue

SARK ENAREN HAD VOLUNTEERED for a suicide mission.

Scanning the heavens surrounding his homeworld, the scion of the Fourth House, Heir to the Blessed Books of Katara, and Holder of the Sacred Scepter of Betazed, experienced true fear for the first time in his adult life. Not the shiver of apprehension or the cold lump of dread he'd often felt before an unpleasant or mildly dangerous task. The sight of the massive armada of Dominion and Cardassian warships massed near Betazed filled him with a paralyzing terror that squeezed air from his lungs and slicked his palms with sweat.

Ironically, the intimidating size of the contingent also provided a glimmer of hope. While the enemy had kept ships in orbit since the invasion and fall of Betazed four months earlier, never had they amassed so many. The gathered forces implied that the rumor he had heard was true: the Federation was mounting an attack to free his homeworld.

If Starfleet forces succeeded in driving the invaders from Betazed, Sark's mission was superfluous. If their offensive was unsuccessful, however, the information he carried for the Federation became more important than ever.

Tearing his gaze from the enemy ships, he looked to the holo of his wife above his ship's flight control console. Holding their newborn son, Cort, Damira stared back at him with impish laughter in her black eyes, a smile lifting the corners of her lips, happiness radiating like a sun's corona. His hands hesitated above the controls. One simple command would turn the ship around, away from the Dominion forces, and send him fleeing back to the resistance stronghold in the Loneel Mountains. There he could hold Damira and his son in his arms again—

Until the Jem'Hadar came for them and all the other members of the resistance.

That chilling certainty overcame his terror, and with fresh resolve, Sark continued the shuttle on its heading and moved toward a break in the Dominion line.

Suddenly, proximity alarms screeched throughout his small craft. Sensors showed a Jem'Hadar attack ship bearing down on him. If he'd had a bank of photon torpedoes, he could have tried to blast his pursuer from space, but Sark's shuttle was no match for a ship designed strictly for warfare. Since he couldn't outgun the Jem'Hadar, he would have to outfly them. Steering a bob-and-weave evasive course that placed him always between a Dominion or Cardassian vessel and the determined attacker, Sark zigzagged his way through the enemy line. If the Jem'Hadar pilot fired on the runabout, he risked hitting one of his own battle cruisers.

With skill honed over years in the service of Betazed's homeguard, Sark burst through the armada with the Jem'Hadar attack ship still on his tail. He reached for the control to send the shuttle into warp, just as the Jem'Hadar's phased polaron weapons strafed his ship. His small craft shuddered violently.

Sark tapped the panel and sent his shuttle into warp drive. Glancing at his sensors, he saw that the Jem'Hadar attack ship had broken off, returning to its position in the Dominion line. With a sigh of relief, Sark assessed his damage. The hull had been blistered by the polaron beam, the vessel's pitching and yawing indicating severe damage to its stabilizers, and life support was barely functioning.

Damage to the ship paled into insignificance beside the loss of subspace communications. He had no way to transmit the contents of the datachip he carried. Turning back was no longer an option. He would have to deliver his intel personally to those who could make best use of it.

With the shuttle trailing a thin thread of plasma, he headed on an unsteady vector toward Starbase 19. The journey of only a few hours at warp speed seemed a lifetime in his badly damaged craft before he finally spotted his goal. Ahead, the graceful form of the starbase beckoned, and beyond, a bright cluster of blue-shifted points of light marked the approach of nearly fifty Federation starships.

Hope spread through him like a blessing. Help for Betazed was on the way.

When he glanced at the aft sensor display, however, Sark's optimism shattered. The Dominion and Cardassian fleet stretched behind him like a black cloud. With horror, he realized the armada had moved away from the Betazed system to engage the Federation forces here, at the starbase.

He ran a quick systems check. If his shuttle held together and his life support lasted long enough for him to reach Starbase 19, he could deliver the datachip to the station's commander, who could then forward it to Starfleet Command. With a swift prayer that the Federation ships protecting the starbase would allow him access, Sark stiffened his shoulders and coaxed more speed from his damaged engines. Failure was not an option. If Betazed was to throw off the Dominion's oppressive rule, Federation leaders *had* to receive his message.

Upon reaching the starbase, Sark tapped out a hail using the shuttle's outboard running lights, hoping his attempt to identify himself would be understood, praying his Betazoid biosignature would register on the base's sensors and that his ship wouldn't be fired upon for its unannounced approach.

Sark's ship was suddenly seized by a tractor beam and guided into a docking bay. A klaxon was blaring in the bay as he disembarked, and a Starfleet security detail with weapons drawn surrounded him. One of the guards pointed a tricorder at him, no doubt scanning for weapons.

"Identify yourself," the team leader, an Andorian lieutenant, demanded.

Sark fought to control his breathing and spoke rapidly, hands spread. "Sark Enaren, I'm with the Betazed resistance, and I have to speak to your C.O. immediately."

"That won't be possible," the lieutenant said. "The base is coming under attack. If you follow my men—"

"You don't understand," Sark interrupted, the deck suddenly shuddering beneath him with what had to be the first salvo of enemy fire. "What I have to tell him could make all the difference for Betazed. Please, just let him know I'm here. Tell him I'm with the resistance. Let him decide."

The guard with the tricorder held out his findings to the lieutenant. The Andorian took note of them and seemed to waver. Then abruptly he tapped his combadge. "Th'Vraas to ops," he said.

"Georgianos here," a gruff voice bellowed. *"Go ahead, Lieutenant."*

"Sir, I have the pilot of that shuttle we snagged. He claims to be with the Betazed resistance. He says he needs to speak with you urgently."

The deck shuddered again and Sark could hear a cacophony of activity over the lieutenant's combadge. After a moment it lessened, and the gruff voice returned. *"Haul his ass up here, and make it fast. Georgianos out."*

"Your lucky day," the lieutenant said to Sark. "Follow me." The Andorian turned and began marching out of the bay, Sark falling in behind. As they moved into a corridor bustling with rushing Starfleet personnel, waves of frenzied emotions assaulted Sark's Betazoid sensibilities and he attempted to shield his mind, but the feelings were too raw, too primal to block. Along with the strong determination and heightened excitement, he could almost smell the fear. With the size of the Dominion force bearing down on them, everyone on the station realized that within a matter of hours, they could all be dead.

An explosion cut through the corridor behind him, tearing into a knot of junior officers. One young man landed a few feet away from Sark, eyes glazed, his left arm missing. Smoke, choking dust, and the coppery stench of blood saturated the air. Sark reeled from the agonies of the wounded and dying that jammed his mind. A dusky blue hand suddenly gripped his arm. "You all right?" Lieutenant th'Vraas asked.

Steeling himself against the pain of those around him, Sark nodded once and let himself be led into a turbolift. The ride to the base's operations center was thankfully brief. As he entered, Sark suspected that the station's nerve center was being successfully targeted by the attacking ships. Damaged wires and conduits dangled overhead, flames licked the weapons console, and smoke dimmed the room, but the officers of Starbase 19 remained calm and focused, carrying out their duties as if the all-out attack were no more than a drill.

In the center of the room, a short, stocky man with blond hair, intense gray eyes, and the framed pips of an admiral on his collar snapped orders with precision.

"All phasers, fire," he directed the tactical officer, and on a large viewscreen, a Jem'Hadar battleship blossomed brilliantly as twin beams converged on its port engine nacelle. The admiral grunted in satisfaction before turning. "Commander Stein, get a team on those sensor arrays," he called out as his eyes settled on Sark. "I'm Admiral Georgianos. You have thirty seconds to tell me who the hell you are and what brought you here."

Quickly, Sark told him. And before his thirty seconds were up, Georgianos seemed to understand that the Betazoids' struggle to end the Dominion occupation of their planet had become desperate.

Before the admiral could respond, there was an announcement of incoming fire from tactical. An explosion ripped through ops and knocked Sark to the floor, causing his vision to fail momentarily. He struggled to his feet and saw Admiral Georgianos slumped against a railing, blood trickling from a gash on his forehead. Another officer sprawled dead across the weapons console. Georgianos pulled himself to his feet and wiped his face with his sleeve.

"Shields off-line," a young lieutenant reported in a shaking voice. "All communications are down, too, sir."

Her announcement stunned Sark. "Admiral, my message needs to get to Starfleet—"

"Jem'Hadar, Admiral!" a security officer yelled. "They're beaming in through weak spots in our scramble field."

Defeat flickered over Georgianos's square face, then disappeared in an instant. "Get those shields back up. We'll hold them off as long as we can. The Twelfth Fleet is almost in range." Georgianos turned to the Andorian security officer. "Th'Vraas, get this man to an escape pod." To Sark he said, "I can't spare anyone to go with you, so you're on your own. If the Jem'Hadar attack ships don't spot you, there's a good chance a Starfleet ship will pick you up. Good luck."

Georgianos was already bellowing new orders over the thunder of the Dominion barrage as Sark raced after th'Vraas again, this time down a narrow passage leading away from ops. The entire station shuddered spasmodically, and Sark wondered if he'd live long enough to reach the pod. Tamping down fear for his own survival, he silently repeated his mantra.

Failure is not an option.

Rage empowered his tired legs, but he wouldn't let his anger at the Jem'Hadar distract him from his purpose.

"We're here, sir." Th'Vraas tapped a control panel in the passage wall and popped open a hatch. He pointed inside to a contact near the pod's entrance. "As soon as you've secured the hatch, hit this and you're launched."

"Thank you." Sark avoided the gaze of the lieutenant and climbed inside, fearing for the safety of the Andorian and the others on the station. Sark had seen the size of the Dominion fleet. Starbase 19, he feared, didn't stand a chance.

Pushing the thought from his mind, he concentrated on his mission, secured the hatch, and tapped the launch control.

Nothing happened.

A nearby explosion must have jammed the mechanism. Sark tapped the contact repeatedly.

Still nothing.

The station rocked again. Sark searched wildly for a manual control, found a lever, and yanked on it, hard.

The force of the pod's ejection from the starbase slammed him back into the opposite wall of the compartment, temporarily dazing him. His senses returned, and he scrambled to his feet.

Wasting no time, he inserted the datachip with its encrypted message into the subspace transmitter and began sending. Someone on a Starfleet vessel had to receive it. If Starfleet's offensive didn't succeed, the contents of the datachip might be Betazed's only hope of throwing off the Dominion's yoke.

From the corner of his eye, through the starboard viewport, he caught the unmistakable outline of a Jem'Hadar attack ship.

He had time for only one thought.

Damira—

In an instant, the escape pod exploded in a burst of light, and Sark Enaren with it.

Chapter One

COMMANDER DEANNA TROI STARED out the wide expanse of windows in her quarters aboard the *U.S.S. Enterprise.* Sadness darkened her deep brown eyes, and worry etched the smooth perfection of her attractive face. Her long dark hair, usually sleek and shining, looked as if it had recently been attacked by a Myrmidon wind devil. She gazed at a cluster of stars that she knew included that of Betazed, her homeworld, shining through the spires of Starbase 133 as if mocking her with their peaceful glow. For once, the sight of home failed to brighten her spirits. If anything, it depressed her more.

"A fine state for a ship's counselor," she muttered, aware that her mood fluctuated between depression and anger but unable to throw off the negative emotions and provide for herself the cheer and encouragement she supplied so readily for the rest of the crew.

The Federation had been at war with the shape-shifting Founders of the Dominion, their genetically engineered soldier species, the Jem'Hadar, and their Cardassian allies for more than a year now. Four months ago, they had invaded and annexed Betazed, gaining a strategic hold in the very heart of the Federation. Starfleet's attempts to break that hold had so far failed disastrously. On every front, casualties were growing daily, with no end in sight. Too many ships lost, too many dead, too little hope of victory against an enemy that bred new soldiers faster than Starfleet could recruit and train cadets.

Deanna rubbed her burning eyes. Every bone in her body ached with fatigue. In less than two hours she had to report for duty, but she hadn't been able to sleep. How could anyone sleep, knowing what was happening out there? Every time she closed her eyes, she saw—

The chime on her door sounded.

She didn't answer, knowing who it was and hoping he would leave. The last thing she felt right now was sociable.

The chime sounded again. She flung herself down on the window seat and pulled a pillow over her head.

Imzadi?

She sensed Will Riker's presence, picking up telepathically his concern for her. Will had been her first true love and would always be her best friend, her *Imzadi*. But she was in no mood to face anyone now. Not even Will.

"Go away," she called.

For an instant there was quiet, and she was breathing a sigh of relief when the doors to her quarters slid open and Will stepped inside. He'd used his security override to enter.

She bolted upright. "What part of 'go away' don't you understand?" Anger filled her voice, but her more rational side realized it wasn't Will who angered her.

It was the damned war.

Will crossed the room and slid onto the window seat beside her. "I'm worried about you."

"You have a ship to run. Go worry about it."

He cocked his head in that little-boy gesture that always tugged at her heart because it seemed so at odds with the strength and maturity of the tall, seasoned Starfleet officer with his piercing eyes and regal beard.

"Maybe I should call Beverly," he suggested. "Have her look in on you."

"I don't need a doctor, Will," she snapped.

Will inclined his head toward the tabletop next to her. "You never met a chocolate you didn't like. And you're losing weight. I think Beverly should check you out."

Deanna glanced at the dish on the table that had once held a sinful concoction of chocolate ice cream, hot fudge sauce, whipped cream, and chocolate sprinkles. The bowl's untouched contents were now indistinguishable from a mud puddle.

"I'm all right," she insisted.

Will slid closer on the bench, draped his arm around her shoulders, and fixed her with a stare. "Try again."

Deanna couldn't help smiling. Will knew her better than anyone, and although she was the ship's counselor, he could give her a run for her money in the listening department any day.

Remembering the source of her depression, she let her smile fade. "You've heard the latest news?"

Sympathy filled his eyes, and he squeezed her shoulder gently. "I'm sorry."

Deanna snatched a padd from the table beside her and rattled off the information. "Thirty-six ships destroyed—hit before they could even enter the Betazed system! Starbase 19 practically obliterated."

She leaped to her feet and flung the padd across the room. It bounced off the far wall, barely missing a gilded Louis XIV mirror. Her reflection glared back at her, eyes flashing with rage, hair tousled, her cheeks sunken hollows from weight loss and worry.

She pivoted, all her anger and frustration focused on Will. "Thousands died. And for nothing! The Dominion's grip on Betazed is as strong as ever."

Will folded his arms across his chest and waited, as if sensing she needed to vent her frustrations without interruption. She wouldn't disappoint him. "And where were we? Sitting safely here at Starbase 133 while others did our dying for us!"

Unruffled by her heated display, Will rose to his feet and pulled her into his arms. He smoothed her hair and held her silently for a moment, as if trying to transfer his calm to her. "That's not fair, Deanna. There isn't one of us who wasn't itching to help, but the *Enterprise* wasn't battle-ready. The damage we took at Rigel still won't be repaired for a couple more weeks."

Her ragged breathing eased and her temper cooled.

Will offered her his hand and led her back to the window seat.

"Lwaxana?" he asked.

Deanna blinked back tears. "I've had no word from Mother, not from anyone on Betazed. With the Dominion's communication blackout, I have no way of knowing if Mother and my little brother are even still alive. No way of knowing how many on Betazed have died."

"Your mother is one of the most resourceful women I've ever met," Will assured her. "If anyone can outsmart the Jem'Hadar, it's Lwaxana."

Deanna stood up again and stomped across the floor. She didn't want comfort. "I want to *do* something."

"We all do." Will retrieved the padd from the floor on the other side of the room. Handing it to her, he raised an eyebrow. "No more throwing things, okay?"

"I can't agree to that."

"Why not?"

"Because throwing things can be very good therapy."

Will nodded toward the mirror she'd almost shattered. "Then use the holodeck next time you need a therapy session. You'll be less likely to destroy your prized possessions."

"Right now, possessions are the least of my worries."

"Picard to Troi." The captain's rich, crisp tones sounded over her combadge. *"Please report to the observation lounge. And bring Commander Riker with you."*

Deanna closed her eyes and sighed, got a grip on her emotions, and tapped her badge. "Acknowledged."

With Deanna at his side, Riker navigated the corridor toward the nearest turbolift. Although the interior of the ship was mostly deserted, Riker knew from the duty roster that work crews in environmental suits were swarming like ants over the port nacelle. The warp engine housing had been severely damaged by a disruptor wave cannon from a Cardassian *Galor*-class warship in a battle for the Rigel system two weeks earlier. The *Enterprise,* however, had been lucky. It had managed to limp back to Starbase 133. Four other ships and their crews hadn't returned at all.

"Those repairs should have been completed weeks ago," Riker said. The war had produced a critical shortage of resources and personnel needed for rebuilding, delaying La Forge's efforts to get the *Enterprise* back into the fight.

Deanna nodded. "Even Geordi is losing patience. He's barking orders like an Academy drill sergeant. After several scathing rebukes to members of his staff who weren't giving a hundred and fifty percent, he came to see me. He was mortified at his loss of control."

"I'm sure you gave him good advice."

"I told him to repair the *Enterprise* first and work on rebuilding rapport later."

Riker didn't blame the chief engineer for his impatience. The dismal progress of the war was affecting everyone, even Deanna. Although her mother was Betazoid, Deanna's late father, Ian Andrew Troi, had been human, a Starfleet officer. Given her genetic heritage, Deanna didn't possess the intense telepathic abilities of a full-blooded Betazoid. She was, however, a talented empath who could sense another's truthfulness and experience what others were feeling. That ability enhanced her effectiveness as a counselor, but at a time when so many suffered the fear, grief, and stress of war, her job was taking its toll on her usually sunny and optimistic nature.

They reached the turbolift. Riker followed Deanna inside.

"Observation lounge," he ordered.

While the lift moved soundlessly through multiple levels, Riker eyed the woman at his side. Before leaving her quarters, Deanna had changed into her uniform and brushed her hair, but she still wore the same exhausted expression, and her uniform hung loosely on her formerly curvaceous figure. She appeared to be wasting away before his eyes, and he felt helpless to comfort her. Since they'd lost all communication with Betazed four months ago when the Dominion invaded, no one knew what was really happening on her home planet. Not knowing freed the imagination to conjure the worst.

"Any idea why the captain wants us?" she asked.

"Someone docked in shuttlebay two while I was on my way to your quarters. Maybe there's news."

Her dark eyes clouded. "I don't think I can stand more bad news."

He started to reassure her that the news might be good, but held his tongue. Lately, good news had been scarcer than the grizzly bears that had once ranged his native Alaska.

The turbolift stopped and its door slid open. Riker motioned Deanna ahead and followed her into the observation lounge.

Captain Picard and an unfamiliar officer stood at the windows, their backs to the door. Admiration for his commanding officer flooded through Riker. He'd been offered his own command many times, but he hadn't wanted to leave the *Enterprise.* He loved the ship. His loyalty was to her captain, and it was difficult to imagine one without the other, or himself anywhere else.

"Ah, you're here," Picard said, tugging by habit at his jacket as he turned to greet them. His voice was warm, but his expression somber, and Riker feared Deanna was probably right about more bad news.

The unknown officer turned away from the window and faced them. He was a Starfleet commander, taller than Picard, with a full head of silver hair and a closely trimmed beard of the same color. Fine lines etched the corners of the stranger's serious blue eyes and the broad expanse of his tanned, high forehead. Riker noted that while he appeared relaxed, the man moved with a precision and economy that he'd seen before only in the most seasoned officers.

"Commander Elias Vaughn," Picard said, "my first officer, Commander William Riker. Commander Vaughn is attached to Starfleet special operations."

"Commander," Riker said. Vaughn nodded but said nothing as he gripped Riker's hand.

"And I believe you already know my counselor, Commander Troi," Picard went on, which puzzled Riker. He couldn't remember Deanna ever mentioning an Elias Vaughn. *Not that that means anything. There's probably a long list of people in our pasts that Deanna and I have never discussed.*

"Hello, Deanna, it's been a while." Vaughn shook her hand as well.

Troi nodded to him, though Riker could feel her

growing tense next to him. "It's good to see you, Elias," she said evenly.

"Now that everyone's acquainted," Picard said in a tone that inhibited further pleasantries, "let's begin. Commander Vaughn?"

Vaughn clasped his hands behind his back and eyed his fellow officers from beneath thick brows. "As I've already explained to Captain Picard, I'm here under orders from Starfleet Command to brief you on the *Enterprise*'s next assignment."

"Begging your pardon, Commander," Riker interrupted, "but our ship's in no condition—"

"She will be," Vaughn said. "Effective immediately, *Enterprise* is Starbase 133's top priority. Your ship will be mission-ready in less than four days."

"Everything Commander Vaughn is about to tell you is classified," Picard said as he took his place at the head of the table, "and not to be shared with anyone outside this room until I give you clearance. Is that understood?"

Riker watched Picard settle in his chair with the same air of undisputed command that he assumed on the bridge. Vaughn sat opposite Deanna with the easy grace of an athlete. Riker could sense Vaughn holding back and, from the grim set of Picard's face, guessed he wouldn't like what the senior commander was going to tell them.

"Yes, sir," Riker answered, and Deanna nodded.

Vaughn looked directly at Deanna. "As you know, last week's attempt by the Twelfth Fleet to retake Betazed was preempted by the Dominion's attack on Starbase 19, in which much of the force gathering there was wiped out."

Riker could sense Deanna tensing next to him.

"What you don't yet know," Vaughn went on, "is that Starfleet now believes that the recent battle actually was more disastrous to the Dominion forces stationed at Betazed than we previously believed. Recent reconnaissance indicates that only a dozen Jem'Hadar and Cardassian ships are left to defend the system. The diminished Dominion force gives us a new opportunity to retake Betazed," Vaughn explained, "if we act quickly before they can bring in reinforcements."

Deanna said, "That's excellent news."

"Save your enthusiasm," Vaughn said, not unkindly. "You may not like what else I have to say. The loss of the Twelfth Fleet has further diminished our already overextended resources. Simply stated, we're spread too thin to retake the planet with a full-scale assault before the Dominion's reinforcements get there."

Deanna's shoulders slumped, and resentment poured through Riker toward Vaughn, who had raised her hopes only to dash them again.

"How do we liberate an entire system without a full-scale assault?" Riker demanded, not even trying to keep the anger from his voice.

Vaughn's weathered face lost none of its seriousness. "A covert action. My specialty, which is why I've been assigned to help."

Deanna's stricken expression didn't change. "How can you expect to liberate Betazed with one covert action when an entire battle group couldn't do it?"

"During the last attempt," Vaughn said, "I was acting as tactical adviser to the fleet aboard the *U.S.S. Nau-*

tilus. Just before we engaged the enemy, we received an encrypted transmission from a member of the Betazed resistance."

Captain Picard gave Deanna a sympathetic glance. "The news, I'm afraid, isn't good."

"First," Vaughn explained, "the resistance has confirmed what our limited reconnaissance already suspected. The Cardassians have begun construction of a new space station in orbit around Betazed—Sentok Nor."

"So quickly?" Deanna asked. "They've been there only four months."

"For what it's worth, the station isn't quite complete, but it's already operational," Vaughn explained. "Apparently, the same resources the Dominion uses to rebuild their fleets so quickly were put to work prefabricating the key structural elements of Sentok Nor months ago, suggesting that the Betazed invasion was a long time in the planning. Cardassian and Dominion transports hauled the major components into the system right after it was secured. Betazoid slave labor has apparently been utilized nonstop to complete the construction as quickly as possible."

At the mention of slave labor, Deanna winced, then seemed to pull herself together. "Why even build a space station there?"

"Our information from the resistance suggests that the station is serving as a combined maintenance facility and Jem'Hadar hatchery. According to resistance estimates, almost fifty thousand Jem'Hadar are already serving in the occupation force on Betazed. Moreover, the station is the Dominion's strategic operations command post in this sector. Any attacks against Earth, Vulcan, or their nearest neighbors will be launched from Sentok Nor, sooner or later." Vaughn turned his gaze from one member of the group to the other. "That's where we come in. The destruction of Sentok Nor would severely weaken the Founders' hold on the system. The Eighth Fleet is already assembling to intercept a Dominion fleet we've detected leaving Cardassian space. While that's happening, the *Enterprise* will lead a smaller task force against Sentok Nor and the remaining ships in the Betazed system."

"'Weaken the Founders' hold,'" Deanna repeated. "How do we break it?"

"That, Commander Troi," Vaughn said, "is where you come in."

Deanna frowned. "I don't understand."

"The Betazoid resistance is led by some very clever people," Vaughn said. "They know Starfleet's forces are spread thin. They know it all too well, in fact, since it was that very handicap, along with Betazed's antiquated defense systems, that allowed the planet to be invaded in the first place. They've asked—*demanded* might be a better word—that if we can't help them retake their planet directly, we bring them someone who can."

"Someone?" Deanna wrinkled her brow in a frown. "Surely you're not talking about me?"

"No, not directly." Vaughn glanced at Picard, and Riker noted the captain's troubled look. Apparently the two shared differences of opinion on this part of the mission. Picard, however, gave a nod of assent to Vaughn, who continued. "While the *Enterprise* is carrying out the assault against Sentok Nor, Commander Troi will be joining an infiltration team, led by me, to Darona."

Early in his Starfleet career, Riker had been stationed on Betazed. He recalled that Darona was a small colony in the Betazed system known for its agricultural, medical, and scientific research facilities, but he'd never visited the place. "What's so important on Darona?"

Picard frowned, and Vaughn plunged ahead. "The man who's going to help a handful of resistance fighters rid Betazed of fifty thousand Jem'Hadar."

"That's impossible," Deanna said. "No one person can do that."

"According to the resistance," Vaughn said, "there is. His name is Hent Tevren."

"Tevren!" The color drained from Deanna's face.

"Who's Tevren?" Riker asked. "Some national hero? I've never heard of him."

"Hent Tevren," Troi explained, her voice shaking as she glared at Vaughn, "is a serial murderer, the worst Betazed has ever known. He kills with his mind."

Chapter Two

TROI'S OUTRAGE WAS PRECISELY the reaction Picard had expected it would be. He'd felt much the same when Vaughn first broached the mission with him. The captain had never considered himself a strictly-by-the-book officer. When the cause was noble or the stakes in lives high enough, he'd bent a few rules to achieve ends that were just, but Vaughn's scheme offended his moral sensibilities. If the commander's orders hadn't borne the imprimatur of Starfleet Command and the approval of the Federation Council, Picard would never have allowed Vaughn to suggest such a plan to his officers. In this case, however, the captain found himself uncomfortably without a choice.

"A killer?" Riker echoed Troi's description in disbelief. "The resistance wants us to provide them with a cold-blooded murderer? Why?"

Vaughn faced them with a frigid rationality, a mind-set Picard knew had served the commander well over the years.

"The Betazoids are a peaceful people." Vaughn fixed his attention on Troi. "They were protecting the planet with outdated defense systems when the Dominion arrived, and Betazed's offensive capabilities are almost nonexistent."

"My people detest violence," Troi said. "We gave up war centuries ago."

"Which is the other reason your planet fell almost without a fight," Vaughn said. "From the Dominion's standpoint, Betazed must have seemed an irresistible target, ripe for the picking. A weak spot. Don't take that personally, Counselor. The Federation suddenly seems full of similar weak spots these days. We're very quickly waking up to that. And so has the Betazoid resistance. Lacking sufficient weapons or skills to fight back effectively, they've realized they still have one untapped resource: the power of their own minds. If Tevren can teach them how he used his telepathic ability to kill—"

"That's absurd," Riker interrupted. "The Betazoids would never use their telepathic abilities for war. It goes against everything in their culture."

Vaughn set his mouth in a grim line, and his expression turned cold. "If they don't drive the Jem'Hadar from their world, Betazed will *have* no culture. Our informant stated that tens of thousands of Betazoids have already disappeared. At first, they were transported to Sentok Nor as laborers, but now that the station is nearing completion, some select groups of people are still being rounded up and taken away at an alarming rate.

No one knows why or what's happening to them, but the feeling within the resistance is that the Dominion's interest in Betazed extends beyond its strategic location."

Picard watched with sympathy as each of Vaughn's statements struck Troi like a blow.

"Tevren," Vaughn continued, "possesses knowledge no other living Betazoid is known to have. He knows how to employ his natural psionic talent as a lethal weapon. That knowledge can help the Betazoid population win back their planet."

"I won't be a part of this." Troi looked as if just hearing the scheme had made her physically ill.

"Well, that's unfortunate, Commander," Vaughn said, his eyes narrowed, "because we need you to make this work. You know Darona. You've lived there, and you know the people at the prison in charge of Tevren. You can convince them to release him to your custody. And, you know what to expect from the man himself. Don't you?"

Riker frowned. "Deanna, what's he talking about?"

Troi ignored him, glaring at Vaughn. "With all due respect," she said tightly, "I don't think you understand what you're asking of me."

"On the contrary," Vaughn replied evenly. "I'm asking you to do your duty as a Starfleet officer. To do your part to liberate your planet. Now, are you in or out?"

"Respectfully, Commander," Riker said, his temper rising, "just who the hell—"

"That's enough," Picard snapped, his limit reached. "I'm sure we all appreciate the gravity of the situation on Betazed, but I'll thank you not to forget you're a guest on my ship, Commander Vaughn, and that I expect you to conduct yourself as such." Without waiting for Vaughn to reply, the captain turned his attention to Troi. "I understand this is a difficult decision, Counselor. You needn't make it now. Take some time to think about it."

"But not too much time," Vaughn added. "Just remember that the longer you take, the harder this becomes."

Eyes on Vaughn, Riker stood, perhaps debating whether or not he and the elder commander should have a private conversation later. "Are we dismissed, sir?" he asked the captain.

Picard nodded as he and Vaughn stood also. "For now, Number One. But I'll expect you to meet with Commander Vaughn and me later to begin planning the assault on Sentok Nor."

"Very good, sir," Riker said tonelessly, then followed Troi out of the observation lounge.

As soon as the doors slid closed behind them, Picard turned to Vaughn. The commander's eyes seemed riveted for a moment to the just-vacated chairs across from him, then drifted to take in the entire conference table. Then, to Picard's surprise, Vaughn said, "I envy you, Jean-Luc."

"Me?" Picard said. "Why?"

Vaughn opened his mouth to elaborate, as if he were about to voice some long-festering frustration. Then just as suddenly, his mouth snapped shut and the wistfulness was gone, replaced by the grim resolve his voice usually carried. "Never mind. Best we stay focused on the issues at hand."

Picard had known Vaughn for over thirty years. On those rare occasions when circumstances had permitted, and usually over steaming cups of Earl Grey, they had spent hours discussing archaeology, history, philosophy, and Shakespeare. But never Vaughn's work in special operations. Picard knew some things—only a few scattered pages from the lengthy book of Vaughn's extensive career—but it was enough for him to suspect that those decades of service were beginning to weigh heavily on the man.

But neither their long acquaintance nor Picard's sensitivity to whatever personal issues Vaughn might have prevented the captain from voicing his concerns about Troi and the proposed mission. "Was that hardline approach necessary, Elias? Troi is obviously already distraught over what's happening on her homeworld."

Vaughn exhaled deeply. "Spare me the lecture, Jean-Luc. People are dying out there. We're losing this war. I can't go tiptoeing on eggshells to spare feelings when the stakes are too damned high."

"But training Betazoids to kill with their minds?" Picard shook his head. "Whether they succeed or not, this will change them fundamentally. Perhaps irrevocably."

"They're already changed," Vaughn pointed out. "This was their idea, not mine, and not Command's. This is what their desperation has brought them to. Starfleet isn't in any position to swoop in and save them, and they've figured that much out. The one thing we may be able to do is empower them according to their own wishes. And if we don't do something *now,* how long do you think it'll be before Andor or Tellar follow? How long before Alpha Centauri or Earth falls, when the Dominion has Betazed from which to launch an attack?" Vaughn leaned back against the viewport and folded his arms. "The ugly truth is, the clock is ticking for all of us."

"But how will the Betazoids ever put that genie back in the bottle?"

Vaughn shrugged. "They may not."

Picard yanked at his jacket and paced the floor of the observation lounge. "This damnable war has already affected the Federation way of life. It's changed how we think about ourselves, our neighbors, our very reasons for existing. I find myself wondering how we can fight for our beliefs when doing so forces us too often to compromise those very values we're willing to die for."

"Some would say we were overdue for a kick in our complacency. You'd think our contacts with the Borg would have done that, and that we'd have stopped taking the triumph of virtue for granted." Vaughn shook his head. "You know as well as I, Jean-Luc, that in times of crisis, difficult choices have to be made by good people willing to take on the burden, even if it means damning themselves in the process."

Picard eyed his old friend. "Are you one of them, Elias?"

"Let's just say I understand both sides of the argument. But I also know from bitter experience that making the right choice is seldom a question of black or white. Sometimes the right thing to do turns out to be merely the lesser of two evils." Vaughn straightened and started for the door.

"Is that what you believe in?" Picard called after him. "The lesser of evils?"

Vaughn didn't turn, but stopped long enough to say in a quiet voice, "I believe in the same thing you do, Jean-Luc. I believe in hope."

Without another word, he strode from the observation lounge, leaving Picard alone with his misgivings.

Chapter Three

RIKER WAS SEETHING. No small part of his anger was directed at Vaughn for the man's presumption and insensitivity, but he'd also reserved a good portion of his rage for himself. During the silent turbolift ride back to Troi's quarters, he'd had ample time to give more consideration to Vaughn's proposal. And to his chagrin, Riker had realized that in the larger strategic context of the Dominion War, arming Betazoids with the ability to fight telepathically wasn't such a bad idea. The plan had a potentially horrific downside, to be certain, but even Riker could see it had definite benefits, if they could pull it off.

The problem, he knew, was whether a culture as idyllic and peaceful as Betazed's could survive the transformation that might take place if the population's most cherished ability—to share their very thoughts—was turned into a means of waging war. Such abuse of their psionic talent was anathema to Betazoids, a corruption of their moral center.

It was these very issues, he knew, that Deanna was struggling with now. Even if he hadn't known her so well, Riker's heart would have gone out to her. Contemplating this decision might rip her apart. She had to make a desperate choice: go against the basic tenets of Betazoid society and her conscience—or resign herself to her world's loss of freedom.

Once again in the privacy of her quarters, he placed his hands on her shoulders and turned her to face him. "What are you going to do?"

She tilted her head with a defiant thrust of her chin and glared up at him. "What do you think I should do?"

He released her and shook his head. "You know I can't make this choice for you. The risks are astronomical at every level. But in the short term, you'll be behind enemy lines on a planet under Jem'Hadar control, trying to get off it with a dangerous prisoner who may not even want to cooperate."

"I've been in danger plenty of times before." She studied him with an intensity that made him struggle to keep from squirming. "The danger's not really what's bothering you, is it?"

"Damn it, Deanna, don't you dare turn counselor on me. This isn't a therapy session. I do worry about you—"

The smile he'd come to love played across her face, and she placed her hand on his sleeve. "I'm sorry, Will. I appreciate your concern. But we both know what the real issue is here."

Given the opening, Riker took the plunge. "What'll happen to Betazed if Vaughn's plan is successful?"

She folded her arms across her chest. "My home-world will be free."

"Free, yes," Riker agreed. "But adopting a serial murderer's abilities—"

Her temper flared and she held up her hands. "Stop it, Will. Please," she nearly shouted. "I understand that you want to make sure I've looked at it from every angle, but this isn't helping. I know the risks, and I know the stakes. I also know that ultimately, this is about more than just Betazed. The fate of the Federation could hang on whether or not we can force the Dominion out. And we both know that Betazed—*my* Betazed, the world I know and love—may need to pay the price for a Federation victory. I hate that, Will! I hate the fact that Starfleet can't do its job for Betazed! I hate that my own people are willing to risk the very things that define them! And most of all, I hate feeling like I have to make a deal with the devil to have any kind of hope at all! Because I'm just not sure which is worse—what the Dominion's done to Betazed, or what Tevren *might* do to it."

They stared into each other's eyes for a long moment, and Riker knew with certainty that her decision was made. "You're going," he whispered, and he found his throat constricting around the words as he said them.

"I don't really have a choice, do I?" Troi said bitterly. She gazed up at him, dark eyes flashing. "If it's this or nothing, I can't afford the luxury of worrying about what could go wrong. All I really know is that for the first time since the invasion, I have a chance to make a difference. That has to be better than doing nothing."

"I hope to God you're right, Deanna," Riker said quietly, "because no matter how this mission turns out for Betazed, or even the Federation, I'm most worried about how it'll turn out for you."

"Come."

It was later that day at Picard's invitation that Deanna stepped into the captain's ready room. "You wanted to see me, sir?"

Picard rose from behind his desk and waved her toward a sofa on the far wall. "Have a seat, Counselor."

She settled onto the sofa. The captain had had little to say during Vaughn's briefing, but she'd sensed his reservations about the commander's mission to Darona and the request of the Betazed resistance.

Picard moved to the replicator. "Cocoa, hot." He removed the fragrant cup and handed it to her. "Comfort food," he explained with a sympathetic expression that helped put her at ease.

She wrapped her fingers around the mug, grateful for its warmth. She'd felt chilled ever since Vaughn's first mention of Tevren and wondered if the resistance had any idea of the monster they planned to unleash.

The captain ordered tea for himself and joined her on the sofa. "You know why I've called you here."

"To discuss Commander Vaughn's mission."

Picard had never been a man to flaunt his emotions, but the tight smile he gave her now was filled with compassion. "Actually, I called you for another reason altogether."

Deanna sipped her cocoa and waited. The captain wasn't a man to be rushed. His actions were always planned, deliberate, and precise.

"There isn't a person on this ship you haven't helped in your capacity as ship's counselor," he finally began.

"That *is* my job, sir." His sudden change of subject left her puzzled.

"Myself included," Picard added. "Your steady presence has helped me through some of the most difficult moments of my life."

Deanna remembered well the many emotional traumas the captain had suffered, from assimilation by the Borg to Cardassian torture to the intense mind-meld he'd experienced with Ambassador Sarek. Any one of those experiences would have destroyed a lesser man.

"After our meeting this morning, I asked myself," Picard continued, "to whom does the ship's counselor talk when she has a problem? I decided to offer my services as a listener."

At the captain's sudden and unexpected kindness, tears misted Deanna's eyes. "It's different with the shoe on the other foot. I don't know where to begin."

"Tell me about this Tevren. His name isn't mentioned in our Starfleet database on Betazed. No one knew he existed until we received the resistance message."

"I'm not surprised. Most Betazoids have never heard of him—and for good reason."

Picard frowned. "If the information's classified—"

"It is, but since my own people have opted to divulge their best-kept secret, I see no harm in sharing it with you, sir. Especially since you'll be leading the attack on Sentok Nor." Deanna nodded, took a reinforcing sip of hot chocolate, and thought back to the day she first learned of Hent Tevren. "Seventeen years ago, during his first year of incarceration, I had just begun my advanced behavioral psychology internship at Darona's prison for the criminally insane. . . ."

When her shuttle landed at Jarkana spaceport on a bright summer morning, twenty-two-year-old Deanna was both excited and somewhat awed at the prospect of her new responsibilities on Darona. A uniformed attendant met her.

"Deanna Troi?" he asked.

She nodded, recognizing the prison insignia on his uniform sleeve.

"I'm Director Lanolan's personal aide. He's sent his private air car for you." Without another word, the stocky attendant had gathered her luggage beneath both arms and steered her toward the waiting vehicle.

He'd remained silent as they soared low over the landscape for her to see the view, but she hadn't minded the lack of conversation on the short trip to Jarkana, Darona's capital city. She'd been too busy taking in the fields of young grain and *cavat,* and many exotic plants she didn't recognize. In the distance, nestled among trees near meandering rivers, stood experimental farms and their outbuildings. Also lining the highway below were neatly fenced pastures where unusual specimens of farm animals from all over the sector grazed, and beyond them, to the west, the dark crags of the Jarkana Mountains rose in a ragged skyline against a rose-colored sky.

Deanna recalled holos she'd seen of prison locales of other cultures, harsh and unforgiving sites with climates of frigid cold or searing heat that did nothing to heal a sick or wounded soul. She was proud that her own people cared enough to rehabilitate even their worst offenders in an atmosphere of serenity and natural beauty.

Betazed itself was similarly parklike, lush and green over most of the habitable surface of the planet, but somehow she found the air on Darona different. With a start, she recognized the elusive feeling: freedom. For the first time in her life, she was completely on her own. She loved her mother dearly, but until today, all Deanna's trips and adventures had included Ambassador Lwaxana Troi, and her mother, like a force of nature, had a way of sweeping her daughter along in her plans with scant regard for Deanna's preferences. For the next four months, however, Deanna would be responsible to no one but Director Lanolan. Her weekends and holidays would be hers to spend as she wished. The prospect made her giddy with anticipation.

The air car hovered over the city, which by Betazoid standards wasn't a city at all but more a large village. Less than a hundred squat, square houses, built of adobe made from the indigenous red clay, lined the broad avenues. Extensive gardens surrounded each residence, and the scent of exotic flowers filled the air.

A few larger buildings made of sturdier industrial materials rose above the others in the center of the capital, and as she passed, Deanna read signs that identified them as government offices and research facilities. On the side of the city opposite the spaceport, the driver drifted to a halt in front of an imposing home whose red adobe walls had been whitewashed until they sparkled in the brightness of the sun.

The director, a tall, slender man with thick brown hair graying at the temples and a gentle expression, met her at the gate. "Welcome to your new home."

Deanna blinked at him in surprise. "New home? But the interns' dormitory—"

He waved aside her objection and ushered her into the foyer. "You'll use our guest house at the back of the garden for the length of your stay. You'll also be provided with someone to attend to your domestic needs."

"With all due respect, Director, I don't expect any special treatment."

He tucked her hand beneath his elbow and led her into the dining room where a simple but appetizing lunch had been spread. "As the daughter of Lwaxana Troi, daughter of the Fifth House, Holder of the Sacred Chalice of Rixx, and Heir to the Holy Rings of Betazed, you must be housed according to your station."

For a moment Deanna thought he was mocking her, but then sensed he was being sincere. When she started to protest, he stopped her with a wagging finger.

"Any special treatment, however, ends with your accommodations. Deanna Troi, who has excelled in her studies of psychology at both the University of Betazed and the Carven Institute, will find me a very hard taskmaster who shows no favoritism. You've exhibited great promise, and I expect you to live up to it. I'll schedule your assignments accordingly."

Deanna sensed a steel core beneath the man's amiable facade, a toughness she was certain his job as overseer of violent criminals often required. "Thank you, Director. I came to work and to learn."

"If you do as well as I'm expecting, I'm hopeful you

might find a permanent place on our staff when your internship is completed."

Deanna smiled, but made no commitment. She was keeping her options open, including the possibility of joining Starfleet, like her father.

Lanolan had no more to say on the subject of Deanna's internship, however, until after lunch, when Mistress Lanolan, his plump and pretty wife, served them nectar beneath the spreading branches of a *teskali* tree in the rear garden, then left them alone.

Lanolan took a quiet sip of his nectar, then set his goblet aside. "If you don't mind, I'd like to discuss your assignment."

Excitement coursed through her. She had studied and trained for this opportunity to put what she'd learned into practice. "You'll find me more than ready, sir."

"You'll work very hard here, Deanna, and you'll experience a great deal of frustration."

"Frustration?"

Lanolan spread his hands wide. "We're a prison facility, but not the average rehabilitation center. We have ample numbers of those on Betazed. As you know, we treat primarily the criminally insane."

"That challenge is one of the reasons I requested this assignment."

Lanolan steepled his long fingers and gazed at her over their tips. "We're able to cure many through psychopharmacology, a few through counseling, others through behavioral conditioning, many with a combination of all three approaches." He dropped his hands and shook his head, and his overpowering sadness flooded her senses. "But too many we are unable to help at all."

"The psychopaths, sir?"

Lanolan nodded. "Over four centuries of Betazoid research, combined with the best scholarship Earth and Vulcan have provided us on the subject, and we are still at a loss to correct this disorder." He paused, watching a small yellow bird land in a nearby bush. When he turned to Deanna again, he had assumed a teaching mode. "Give me your best definition of the psychopathic personality."

"There are several types, but the one you are most likely to encounter here is the aggressive type."

"And its characteristics?"

She felt she was back in school again, being grilled by the head of the psychology department at the university. "A complete disregard for right and wrong."

"You mean an incapacity to tell the difference?"

"No, sir. The psychopath knows the difference. It is simply of no consequence to him. He is centered on self-gratification, no matter how many laws or rules he must break to achieve it."

"But he suffers remorse?"

"None, sir. That is another of the psychopath's major characteristics. A lack of remorse as well as a refusal to assume responsibility. Whatever wrong he commits, someone or something else is always to blame. And this attitude is not a mere rationalization in the subject's mind. He truly believes himself blame free."

Satisfaction at her responses emanated from the director. "Tell me, Deanna, what causes psychopathic behavior?"

She suppressed a smile. He had thrown her a trick

question, but she was ready for it. "No one knows for certain. Despite, as you said, the long years of study of this particular personality disorder, scholars still disagree. Some believe the cause lies in the brain, either in a genetic predisposition or some kind of damage, or the failure of the central nervous system to develop adequately and at the proper rate."

Lanolan nodded. "And the opposing viewpoint?"

"Others believe the psychopath is created, molded by the experiences of early childhood."

"Negative experiences, such as abuse?"

"Yes, sir. But, oddly enough, spoiling a child, giving him too much attention or too many possessions, causing him to think too highly of himself in relationship to others, is also considered a possible cause."

"And you, Deanna, which side of these causal arguments do you come down on?"

This question was much more difficult, and she sensed much was riding on her answer. She thought for a moment.

"I believe it's possible that *all* are correct, Director. It depends on the individual and what forces of both nature and nurture have shaped him."

Lanolan nodded with satisfaction. "It's good to see you have a grasp of the fundamentals. You'll need to keep them at the forefront in order to handle your first assignment."

Eagerness bubbled inside her. "When do I start?"

"Tomorrow morning. We've received a new prisoner, a serial killer. I want you to do the background workup and initial evaluation on him. You will have several sessions with him and offer your diagnosis and recommendations for treatment."

Deanna frowned. "Is he Betazoid?"

The director nodded.

"Why haven't I heard of him? A serial killer is a rarity on Betazed. Why wasn't he in the news?"

"His name is Hent Tevren, and his name will never be known on our planet. After you've read his file, you'll understand why."

Before she had been allowed to read Tevren's file that first night in Lanolan's guest house in Jarkana, the director personally had unsealed and decrypted the information. What she had read had both sickened and terrified her.

The morning she arrived on Darona, Deanna had felt as if she could meet any challenge, that with her superior training and perseverance, no case was too daunting. The next day, trudging up the path behind the director's house toward the maximum security facility, she wasn't so sure.

Resembling a group of vacation villas more than a penitentiary, the prison sat on a low hill. To the east, it overlooked Jarkana. To the west, the mountains. A shield wall, invisible to the naked eye except as an occasional shimmer in the air, surrounded the compound, whose only access was through a barred entrance manned by guards. Director Lanolan was waiting at the gate, where Deanna presented her credentials. He escorted her through the arched portal into the gardens that lined the front walkway. In the heat of the summer morning sun, the fragrance of frangipani and *crystilia* lay heavy on the air.

"Those feathery red plants lining the walk are Diomedian scarlet moss," the director explained with enthusiasm as they made their way toward the administration building. "The delicate ground cover over there in the shade of the poinciana tree is *Draebidium calimus,* similar to Terran violets, and those unusual flowers to your right are *Zan periculi,* native to Lappa Four."

"A Ferengi world?" Deanna didn't have to be an empath to sense the director's fascination with what was obviously his pet project.

Lanolan nodded. "We've gathered specimens from all over the quadrant. Not only does our garden furnish a tranquil atmosphere for our inmates, but tending it provides them with fresh air and exercise. It's recreational therapy."

"Will Tevren be allowed to work in the garden?" she asked.

"Of course, if he wishes. The surrounding force field isolates him from other prisoners and blocks his escape. The psionic inhibitor implanted in his brain when he was convicted suppresses all his telepathic abilities. The man is harmless as long as the implant is functioning."

They reached the entrance to the administration building, and Lanolan motioned Deanna inside. "Tevren is waiting for you in counseling room two. Please report back to my office after you've completed your interview." His firm expression softened. "And don't worry, Deanna. He's a challenging patient, but I'm certain you can handle him."

"I'll do my best." Straightening her sand-colored tunic with its red-and-gold prison emblem on the sleeve and clasping her padd tightly for reassurance, Deanna marched down the hallway.

A guard at the entrance to the counseling room opened the door for her. "I'll be right here if you need me, Counselor."

With butterflies of apprehension dive-bombing in her stomach, Deanna stepped inside. Sunlight from floor-to-ceiling windows flooded the simply furnished room and shone through the force field that divided the space in half. On the other side of the shield, a short, nondescript man sat calmly facing Deanna, his hands folded on a table.

She had seen his holo in his file, but Tevren's was an eminently forgettable face, the kind that would never stand out in a crowd. Although he was only eight years her senior, his dark hair was already receding at his forehead and thinning at the crown. At first she found it hard to reconcile the milquetoast appearance of the man before her with that of a mass murderer.

Until she looked into his eyes.

The dark Betazoid irises glittered like chunks of black ice, and the pinched smile on his face seemed insincere.

Most disquieting of all, however, was the man's total lack of emotion. Unlike the effect created when a Betazoid shielded his thoughts and feelings from another—a phenomenon similar to what Terrans described as "white noise"—the psionic inhibitor implanted in Tevren's brain created an impression of emptiness within the man. Instead of the familiar reassurance of white noise, Deanna faced a forbidding yawning abyss, a black void that chilled her to the core.

Suppressing a shiver, she sat at the same table bisected by the force field and made herself meet Tevren's gaze.

"I'm Counselor Troi."

Tevren's smile broadened, although it never reached his eyes. "I wasn't aware that I'd be given special treatment. You're very pretty."

"My appearance is irrelevant. I'm here to help you."

"Really?" He blinked as if in amazement. "And how do you propose to do that?"

She mustered a smile. "I'd like to begin by asking you questions."

He leaned back in his chair, amusement flitting across his unremarkable face. "What kind of questions?"

"You do understand why you're here?"

His mouth widened in a sly grin. "They're afraid of me."

"They?"

"Everyone."

"And why is that?"

"Because I enjoy killing people."

Deanna suppressed her instinctive revulsion and forced herself to stay focused. "Tell me about yourself. Start with your childhood."

Tevren heaved a bored sigh. "Oh, must we play these psychobabble games?"

"Not at all," she replied evenly. "You can return to your cell anytime."

He appeared to consider her for a moment. "You're much prettier than those four walls. I suppose I'd rather stay here."

"You may stay if you cooperate with me." *Why doesn't he blink?* she wondered. His stare was distracting and unnerving. She breathed deeply in an attempt to loosen the knot of tension beneath her ribs. She had to be careful here. According to his file, Tevren was more than brilliant. His intelligence quotient was off the scale, and he seemed willing and able to play with her head—if she let him.

"Your childhood?" she persisted.

"It's all there in my file, which I'm certain you've already studied."

She pushed back her chair, stood, and headed for the door.

"Please wait," she heard him say.

Deanna turned and faced him with a sympathetic look. "I have better uses for my time than subjecting myself to your evasions."

She turned back toward the door.

"I was an only child," Tevren began. "My parents had almost given up on having children when I was born."

Deanna took another step toward the exit.

"They spoiled me terribly." Tevren's words came in a rush. "Everything I wanted, they gave me. They were trying to make up for—"

He stopped as if he'd said too much, and Deanna half turned around. "What were they trying to make up for?"

"Sit down and I'll tell you."

"Tell me and I'll sit down."

"I was born with telepathic ability."

Deanna worked to keep her expression blank. That significant piece of information hadn't been in Tevren's file, possibly because the only other people who knew it were his parents, who had been among his early victims. For the first time, she experienced a pang of sympathy for Tevren. The vast majority of Betazoid children developed their telepathic skills at puberty. Only a fraction of a percent were actually born with the ability, and without special guidance, these telepathic prodigies suffered incredibly debilitating psychological and social damage. Deanna had met and treated one, Tam Elbrun, when she was at the university. Tevren's premature telepathic skills were possibly a contributing factor to his personality disorder. *That might also explain why he, of all people, is my first case here. Lanolan must have known about Tevren's developmental aberration and my work with Tam.*

She resumed her seat at the table. "That must have been difficult for you."

"On the contrary." His tight little smile returned with an illusion of warmth, giving his unremarkable face a semblance of charm. "It put me at a tremendous advantage, always knowing what my parents and others were thinking. It made the adults around me much easier to manipulate."

Her sympathy evaporated, and her objectivity returned. "Would you say you had a happy childhood?"

He shrugged. "It was the only one I knew. What could I compare it to?"

"Did you have many friends?"

"Several children wanted to be my friends. I am able to exert a certain charm when I wish to, but no, I didn't have friends."

"Why not?"

"People bore me."

"Why?"

"Most are stupid."

"Stupid?"

"Compared to me. I have four university degrees. I could have earned more, but what was the point?"

"Four degrees, yet the only job you've held is as a government researcher. With your intellectual capacity, shouldn't you have advanced further in your career?"

"You're stupid, too, you know."

Troi refused to be baited. "I'm smart enough to realize you're insulting me because you don't want to answer my question."

This time his grin split his face, gracing his ordinary features with a certain attractiveness. "I like you, Counselor Troi."

"Then talk to me."

He pushed back from the table, retreated into his half of the room, and stood before a window. Sunlight streamed down on his upturned face, its bright light accentuating the pallor of his skin, the thinness of his hair. A pink scar glowed at the base of his skull where the inhibitor had been inserted. He continued to stare out the window as he spoke. "My position as a government researcher gave me the highest clearance to the official records of Betazoid history. I became privy to secrets only a handful of people on our world have ever known."

"And you liked this feeling of power?"

He pivoted quickly on his heel, rushed to the table, and leaned across it with his palms spread, his face within a millimeter of the force field. "It's more than a feeling, Counselor. The power is quite real."

Real enough that only the psionic implant in his brain protected her from it, she reminded herself. "Tell me about it."

He yawned, as if bored, and drew back from the force field. "It's all in my file."

"Fine." She called his bluff and rose to leave.

"But if you'd rather hear it in my own words . . ."

She bit back a sarcastic reply. The director was recording the interview. She wanted no record of her losing her control on the first day of her internship. She slid back into her chair and nodded. "Your own words."

Looking very pleased with himself, Tevren sat and leaned back in his chair. "Several hundred years ago, a small, secret society arose on Betazed. Members of this cult dedicated themselves to developing their telepathic skills in creative ways. I found this classified information fascinating and amused myself for a time by attempting to develop some of their simpler skills on my own."

"What kind of skills?"

"Harmless little amusements, such as amplifying and projecting intense emotions into the mind of another. The ability was useless, really, except for its potential to make others either extremely uncomfortable or to appear foolish in their reactions to the unwanted feelings." He frowned with distaste. "Besides, the physical and mental effort I had to expend to project the emotion wasn't worth the fun I received from the results."

"So, in essence, you became a telepathic practical joker," Deanna observed.

He nodded solemnly. "A situation far beneath my intellectual dignity. So I decided to accept a greater challenge."

Deanna waited, knowing and dreading what she was about to hear.

"The classified records of this secret cult," Tevren continued, "indicated that they had stumbled onto the ability to kill telepathically. That discovery, however, was their downfall. When several members availed themselves of the opportunity to kill with their minds, they were discovered by the authorities. When the authorities realized what the cult had uncovered—a lethal potential in every Betazoid but unknown to all but the members of this cult—the government moved in. They arrested the entire movement, imprisoned them for life, destroyed the instructions for their special skills, and sealed the records of their activities, even of their very existence. For the next four hundred years, only Betazoids with the highest security clearance knew such a group had existed."

"So you taught yourself to kill."

Tevren nodded, obviously pleased with his accomplishment. "It was relatively easy, really, once I reasoned it out and practiced a few times."

Like the majority of Betazoids, what Deanna found most disturbing about the man before her—about any criminal—was his lack of empathy. Because her people were so attuned to the thoughts and feelings of those around them, crime on her planet was rare. Internalizing the pain, fear, and emotional damage his actions would cause often stopped the would-be criminal in his tracks. Tevren obviously suffered no such restraints.

"Why did you kill?" She sincerely wanted to understand. "Was it revenge? Jealousy? Ambition?"

Tevren laughed, a dry husky sound like the rustling of dead leaves. "You psychologists are all alike, trying to see some great motivation behind every behavior. When I killed—except for my parents, whom I killed for practice—it was just for fun."

She tried not to show her horror. For the first time she truly understood why the authorities had locked Tevren away and buried his crimes. If word of his atrocities were to surface, if the knowledge he'd rediscovered were made public, the peace of Betazed might end forever.

She forced herself to ask the next question. The answer, of course, hadn't been in his file. And given what he'd just told her, she was certain it wasn't documented anywhere. But she hoped his answer would give her some insight into his psychopathology. "How did you kill these people, Tevren?"

He leaned forward again, until static from the force field sparked against the tip of his nose. He drew his lips back in a smile, his eyes glittering. "Remove this damned inhibitor from my brain, and I'll be happy to give you a personal demonstration."

Troi put aside the memory of the sadistic gleam in Tevren's eyes. "For four interminable months, I worked with Tevren for several hours each day," she told Picard.

The captain regarded her with compassion. "Were you able to help him?"

She shook her head. "He was no nearer rehabilitation the day I left Darona than he had been the day I arrived. If anything, Tevren became more entrenched in his depraved fascination with death. He took perverse pleasure in describing every vicious detail of each of his murders, the agonies of his savaged victims, the so-called cleverness of his brutality. Director Lanolan worked with him, too, with no better results than I had. We tried everything—recreational therapy, behavioral conditioning. Even antipsychotic drugs were a dismal failure."

Picard raised an eyebrow. "I take it Tevren didn't care for gardening."

Deanna nodded. "Since he could no longer kill people, he took great joy in mutilating the director's prize plants. He was punished by confinement to his quarters, but he actually seemed to prefer the isolation."

"And he never revealed how he killed with his mind?"

"I don't think he could, not as long as the inhibitor was functioning. He implied the skill had to be conveyed telepathically."

"I'm afraid I don't understand something, Counselor," Picard said with a frown. "You said Tevren claimed to have developed the ability after studying the records of a cult. Why couldn't the resistance do the same?"

"Because the records were historical, not technical. I think they gave him clues. From what I could piece together from his usual half answers, it took him three years just to reason out the process of utilizing his psionic talents invasively. If it were any easier for a Betazoid to learn it on her own, there would be more like Tevren. But with someone to teach it . . ."

"Deanna," the captain said, "the people of Betazed are among the most benign, enlightened, and peace-loving I've ever known. I know from studying their history that your people's telepathy and empathy were a force for civilizing your planet and creating one of the most unified and compassionate civilizations in the Federation. At the risk of playing devil's advocate, I find it hard to believe that the knowledge of the mere capacity for abusing those talents would threaten your culture."

Troi smiled faintly. "That's kind of you to say, Captain. And you're right. To some degree, my culture owes whatever good it's achieved to our ability to know one another telepathically. It's made us truly whole in a way few species ever become. But every culture, no matter how benign, struggles with its own capacity for evil. That struggle is hardest on a telepathic species, where the slightest thought of violence, destruction, even death, can potentially be made manifest. There's a reason the Vulcans struggled so long to master their passions, and still do. They know the capacity for evil can never truly be purged. Mastery is the best anyone can hope for."

"Hmm," Picard murmured. "Your point is well made, Counselor. What's your estimation of Tevren? Will he cooperate?"

Troi took a deep breath. "That's another variable in all this. It's been seventeen years. I honestly don't know how much he may have changed, if at all. It may be that after seventeen years of incarceration, he'll do anything to be free. Or it may be that he simply won't care anymore." Deanna set her cold cocoa aside. "He's truly a monster, sir. The man enjoyed wringing the last desperate breath from his victims. I read the autopsy reports. They all died slowly and savagely, their minds destroyed one tiny piece at a time. And this," Troi said, "is the person in whom the resistance feels compelled to place their hopes."

Picard turned to look thoughtfully out the curved window of his ready room. "'How dead we lie because we did not choose to live and shame the land from which we sprung.'"

Deanna nodded. "Death or shame. Betazed's choices exactly. Was that a quote from Shakespeare?"

Picard shook his head. "A. E. Housman, another human poet."

"One who also understood the nature of war."

"Ah, but did he really?" the captain asked.

"What do you mean?"

"Housman," Picard explained, "never met a Jem'-Hadar."

Chapter Four

JEM'HADAR EVERYWHERE.

On a rocky ledge above the Loneel Valley, Lwaxana Troi lay on her stomach and studied the deep forest below through powered binoculars. Concealed by a hooded cloak of striated grays and browns that matched the surrounding stones, she counted the soldiers of the scouting party crashing through the underbrush below.

Eighteen!

Not only had the number of patrols doubled, their size had doubled as well. If the increase continued at the current rate, the occupation force would soon swell to more than fifty thousand, not counting the damned Vorta bureaucrats who controlled the Jem'Hadar on behalf of the Founders. It was only a matter of time until the soldiers came for the resistance, who were hanging on by a thread in their mountain stronghold and praying help would arrive before the final massacre.

Enaren, where are you?

Her thought snapped petulantly into the darkness. Her cousin was no longer as agile as he'd been in his youth, and it didn't seem possible that he could slip un-detected through the enemy troops that ringed the mountain stronghold of the Betazed resistance. For all she knew, the Jem'Hadar had already killed him.

I'm here, Lwaxana, behind you, but don't move. Wait until the Jem'Hadar have passed.

She sighed with relief before her temper kicked in.

You've had me worried out of my mind! she scolded, then for interminable minutes remained motionless until the last of the soldiers disappeared into the thick trees of the coniferous forest. Leaping to her feet, she whirled to face Cort Enaren. *Did you get it?*

She needed no reply. The disappointment in his tired eyes and the defeated slant of his shoulders communi-cated his failure.

He shook his head.

Hurry, she ordered him. *They'll return soon. We have to take cover.*

With a grace and swiftness that belied her age, Lwaxana traversed the ledge and slid into a nearby crevasse. The opening, invisible unless one knew of its existence, was one of only two portals into the moun-tains where the Betazoids' resistance fighters and gov-ernment in exile had established their headquarters. The craggy peaks ringed the caldera of an ancient vol-cano and were honeycombed with tunnels and caves formed millions of years earlier by bubbles of volcanic gas as the lava cooled around it.

High concentrations of fistrium in the surrounding

rock and the depth of the underground caverns protected the colony of fifteen hundred from detection by Dominion sensors. Here the leaders of Betazed had established their temporary homes and would make their stand until the Jem'Hadar were driven from their planet.

Or die trying, Lwaxana thought. That grim possibility became more likely with each passing day. If the Jem'Hadar didn't kill them first, they might all succumb to disease without proper medical supplies.

Shaking off her gloomy introspection, she followed the narrow, winding path among the boulders, trailing behind Enaren and wondering how much more heartache the poor man must endure. His son and heir, Sark, had failed to return from his mission to contact Starfleet, and Enaren did not know whether Sark had been successful, or even if he'd survived. To make matters worse, two days ago Cort's infant grandson and namesake had contracted Rigelian fever, a horrible illness similar to the infamous bubonic plague on Earth.

Over a century ago, spacefaring Betazoids had brought the Rigelian fever home from one of their voyages. In the intervening years, to augment the antidote, ryetalyn, her homeworld physicians had developed a vaccine, but the prophylactic was too powerful for the physiology of any child younger than six. Thanks to the vaccine's effectiveness, however, the fever had all but disappeared from the planet. The illness survived only in insects infesting vermin of the inaccessible wilds, like the tunnel rats that inhabited the caves of the Loneel Mountains.

Yesterday, Damira, Enaren's daughter-in-law, had

noted the tiny fleabite on her son's thigh. Within hours, his temperature had spiked. The doctor had administered ryetalyn, but his supplies were limited, and more doses would be needed to insure the child's recovery— and to treat other children who might become infected. Enaren had volunteered to venture out of hiding to secure more of the precious medicine.

I can't believe a hospital so close to the wilderness had no ryetalyn, Lwaxana complained.

Enaren stopped and turned to her, his emotions pounding her mind like fists. Rage. Sadness. Overwhelming fear. *There's no hospital.*

But the village—

The Dominion warned that anyone involved in the resistance movement would be punished.

Lwaxana shook her head impatiently. *What does their warning have to do with the hospital?*

Enaren trembled with anger. *The Jem'Hadar caught a resistance cell meeting there. They took the members prisoner and burned the building to the ground—and the drugs with it—as a warning.*

His face ruddy with outrage and despair, he pivoted on his heel and continued toward the tunnel that led to the caverns, a vortex of emotions swirling in his wake. Lwaxana followed, fuming with anger. In all their long history, although they'd maintained a regulatory force, her people had seldom needed the military. With their telepathic abilities, they had cultivated more peaceful pursuits. The perpetuation of peace had led to Lwaxana's interest in diplomacy, to promoting the resolution of conflict through negotiation and understanding. But diplomacy was useless against the Dominion. While the

Vorta seemed well versed in giving the appearance of reasonability, all their courteous overtures of friendship and apologetic explanations for each outrage committed against the Betazoid people came down to a single message: *Cooperate or die.*

At first she'd been certain Starfleet would force the Dominion back, just as they'd once forced back the Romulans, the Klingons, the Borg. But as the early days of the occupation stretched into weeks, it became clear to Lwaxana that Betazed's hopes for salvation rested as much with itself as they did with Starfleet. The Federation was fighting a war for its very survival on too many fronts, against a foe that never let up. Horror had filled her when the resistance got word that the Twelfth Fleet had been destroyed, leaving the people of Betazed to face the Dominion alone.

She refused to give up hope, however. She would not have it said that a daughter of the Fifth House had failed in her duty to keep her world free for her children. Her daughter Deanna, at least, was safe, or as safe as one could be aboard a starship fighting the Dominion. If dear Jean-Luc couldn't protect the *Enterprise* and her daughter from the Jem'Hadar, then the gods help them all.

She worried most about Barin, her two-year-old son. She had to protect him not only from alien soldiers but from the deadly fever that threatened all the young children of their mountain stronghold. Even though the men had set traps to clear the tunnels of vermin that might carry disease, more outbreaks of the fever were expected. She hoped Chaxaza, another of her cousins, who tended Barin while Lwaxana stood watch outside, had checked the boy for fleabites.

The thought of her small, rugged toddler made her smile and quicken her steps. Deanna, although a mature woman in her own right, would always be her "little one," so Lwaxana had adopted the Tavnian diminutive Barin for her younger child. In his father's language, Barin was her "little one," too.

Descending deeper into the caverns, Lwaxana picked up the scents of habitation: smoke from cooking fires, spices from foods roasting for dinner, and the tang of herbs intended to cover the stench of too many unwashed bodies packed too tightly together. Because water had to be carried in backpacks from the wilderness rivers, bathing and laundering were luxuries most had learned to live without.

Physical proximity was not the worst hardship for the residents of the stronghold. In a telepathic society, complete privacy was practically an impossibility, but at least before the war, all had lived in houses or farms set spaciously apart to allow some psionic elbow room. Here, true privacy was even more rare than water now, and as a result, tempers often flared.

Especially that of Sorana Xerix, daughter of the Third House. Her protests reached Lwaxana even before she entered the cavernous common area where women gathered during the day.

My best robe, Sorana whined, *and it's ruined with soup stains.*

Be thankful the stains are food and not blood, Lwaxana shot back, drawing herself to her full height and fixing Sorana with a withering stare. *With so many of our people dead and dying, my dear, your complaints are becoming a royal pain in the ass.*

Sorana's blast of offended pride and righteous indignation washed over Enaren and Lwaxana at the entrance to the chamber, and its other occupants glanced up in expectation. Damira, her ailing baby clasped against her breast, cried out in anguish when she realized Enaren's failure to obtain more ryetalyn.

Don't despair, he reassured her. *I'll try another village tomorrow. The doctor has enough to keep the boy comfortable until then.*

Barin broke from Chaxaza and raced across the room toward his mother, his chubby legs pumping, his arms spread wide, his delicious giggle balm for her aching heart. She scooped him up in her arms and hugged him tight.

"No bug bites?" she asked.

He shook his head, brown eyes shining, and patted her cheeks with his plump hands. "Cha'za looked."

Sorana glared at Lwaxana across the room, but Lwaxana for once was in no mood for an extended confrontation. After another fierce hug, she handed Barin back to his caretaker. "Call the resistance leaders together in the meeting room," she instructed in a voice ringing with authority. "We have decisions to make."

She spoke aloud, recognizing that not all inhabitants of the stronghold possessed the same degree of telepathic abilities. Some projected and read thoughts with more ease than others. When matters of communal concern were discussed, Lwaxana insisted on the spoken word. "The better informed, the less likely people were to panic" had always been her maxim. Today she wasn't so sure. All the news pending before the council was bad.

At the chiming of the sacred bell that signaled a meeting, people streamed in from other common rooms and private alcoves, where a blanket or quilt hung across the opening afforded the only privacy available. Most of the tiny cubicles were furnished with only the barest of necessities, items the occupants had grabbed in haste and carried on their backs as they fled the Jem'Hadar.

In spite of efforts at shielding, a multitude of thoughts and emotions jammed the air in the great chamber that served as the council hall. From her place on the dais at the end of the room, Lwaxana watched the others arrive, sensing fear and despair in some, renewed hope and determination in others, and a guarded watchfulness in a few.

Their backgrounds were as varied as their emotions. Many of the leaders came from the cities, where they'd previously held high government office or venerable professorships at the universities.

Just as numerous were farmers and craftspeople and their families from Betazed's outlying villages. Diverse in profession, wealth, and knowledge, they shared one common goal—to drive the Jem'Hadar from Betazed soil, even if each of them must sacrifice her life to do it.

When the group had first fled the Dominion invasion and entered the stronghold, they had elected Enaren as their leader. Eleven other members of the ruling body, including Lwaxana, joined him on the dais, and he stood to address the other leaders and the crowd, which had assembled to observe the deliberations.

Enaren explained his failure to obtain more ryetalyn, and a shiver of fear for the children traveled through the group. "But I will try again tomorrow. Meanwhile, we must continue fumigating and setting traps for vermin."

He yielded the floor to Okalan, the council member who oversaw water and supplies. "The increased Jem'Hadar patrols make it almost impossible for us to reach the river. We must halve our water rations. We have pipes and cisterns in place, but the rainy season is still weeks away."

Grumbles filled the air, and Lwaxana noted with satisfaction that Sorana had the decency to look ashamed.

After Okalan took his seat, Lwaxana rose to present her report. The most skilled among them in diplomacy and negotiations, she had been assigned the task of planning strategy against the invaders. "If Sark Enaren delivered our message to Starfleet, help should arrive soon. The Federation knows that the longer they wait, the harder it'll be to oust the Dominion."

"And what if Starfleet doesn't come?" a *cavat* farmer from Condar village demanded.

"Sooner or later, they will," she said. "Betazed is part of the Federation. Our sons and daughters serve in Starfleet."

The farmer leaped to his feet and said aloud what the rest of them already knew. "We can't be idle waiting for Starfleet! There's a ketracel-white distillery near my farm. If we blow up the cursed thing, the Jem'Hadar will die."

With revulsion, Lwaxana pictured the tubes puncturing the green-gray skin and carrying the enzyme that kept the soldiers alive. "Your plan would be a good one, but for one other fact. Our operatives have witnessed ketracel-white being unloaded from freighters arriving from Sentok Nor, so there must be another distillery there. If so, the Jem'Hadar would continue to receive their sustenance, and the retaliation against our people for the destruction of the distillery would be savage."

Enaren shook his head sadly. "Matters cannot become more savage than they already are. The lists of dead and missing are growing by the hour. And our operatives on the outside have noted a disturbing trend."

"What kind of trend?" Lwaxana asked and felt the assembly hold their collective breath, bracing themselves for bad news.

"When the Dominion forces first arrived," Enaren said, "they took away thousands of our healthy and strong young people—"

"Slave labor for their damned space station," Okalan said with a scowl. "None of them returned. We must assume most were worked to death. And those who survived are still slaves on the station."

Enaren nodded. "For the past few weeks, however, the list of missing reveals that the Jem'Hadar are abducting the most talented of our telepaths."

Lwaxana stiffened at the news. "Why take only those with the greatest ability?"

Enaren shrugged. "Either the Jem'Hadar are killing talented telepaths in hopes of crippling our ability to communicate with one another—"

"Or," Lwaxana suggested, "the Dominion has become interested in their talents for some other reason."

Enaren set his lips in a grim line. He glanced first to

the council and then across the hundreds gathered in the chamber. "We have many of the most talented telepaths of Betazed here in this room. The Jem'Hadar will be looking for them. We must be even more vigilant than before."

"If we're lucky," Okalan said, "the enemy will assume we managed to escape the planet and call off the search."

"I don't think we can hope for that," Lwaxana said. "If the Jem'Hadar really are somehow targeting our strongest telepaths, they'll scour every village and burn every forest to find us."

"We can't just sit here and wait for them to come for us," the *cavat* farmer yelled. "We have to fight."

"We're doing all we can," Lwaxana snapped.

"Which hasn't been nearly enough," Enaren replied. "Our hope now is that our message got through, and that Tevren will be brought to us."

Uneasiness rippled through the room like a foul wind. None, Lwaxana knew, liked the idea. "If anyone has an alternate plan," she challenged, "the council is open to hear it."

The room was quiet until the silence was broken by Okalan, who was shaking his head as if in grief. "All our hopes in a madman," he muttered. "By the First House . . . what have we come to?"

Chapter Five

"VAUGHN TO TROI."

Deanna sighed and stopped in midstride down the corridor leading to the counselor's office, knowing Vaughn's call meant the next phase of unpleasantness was about to begin. She steeled herself and tapped her combadge. "Troi here."

"Please meet me in holodeck two in half an hour for combat drills." Vaughn phrased his words as a request, but the underlying hardness in his deep voice made it seem more like an order.

"Commander, is this necessary?" Troi asked. "I have a great deal of paperwork—"

"Table it," Vaughn said. *"We have little time until the mission, and a great deal of ground to cover beforehand. I want you ready."*

"Ready for what?"

"For anything."

Deanna hesitated. She had continued to sharpen her combat skills when she had the chance, but she suspected Vaughn wouldn't consider her abilities up to the needs of the mission. On the other hand, a physical workout would probably do her some good. No doubt Vaughn knew that.

She couldn't help recalling, however, that her least favorite courses at Starfleet Academy had been those in hand-to-hand combat, where close contact made tuning out her opponent's emotions impossible. In her subsequent Starfleet assignments, she'd had to kill on occasion, both in self-defense and to protect the lives of others, but those deaths haunted her. With her empathic abilities, she had *felt* her enemies' pain, had sensed their fear, and their spirits draining away until only soulless voids remained. Each time she'd been compelled to take a life, something of her had died with the victim.

"How long since your last refresher course in hand-to-hand combat?" Vaughn's voice demanded over her comm link.

"Too long," Deanna admitted. "And I should warn you, Commander, I've never had much of a killing instinct. Most Betazoids don't."

"But you have a survival instinct. That's a start. Thirty minutes, Commander. S.O.B.s only. Vaughn out."

Deanna sighed again and would have laughed at Vaughn's little joke if the situation weren't so deadly serious. In recent years, Starfleet had designed a uniform variant specifically for ground-based combat operations. Characterized by their padded black fabric—unbroken except for the division-specific color stripe that cut across the chest, shoulders, and back—the uniforms were supposed to be referred to as "surface operations blacks." Of course, it wasn't long before somebody shortened the name to S.O.B., a designation that was quickly extended to anyone who put on the uniform. Deanna had never expected to be involved in a mission that required her to don the garment, and wondered how much of the nickname was self-fulfilling.

After detouring back to her quarters and quickly replicating the uniform, she put it on and stood in front of the mirror for a few minutes, feeling ridiculous and trying not to think about how dark all of Starfleet's uniforms had become in the last few years. It was, she believed, symptomatic of a fundamental shift in the Federation's cultural psychology, a response to the growing number of threats in an increasingly hostile universe. Her days of wearing flowing azure dresses on the bridge were long gone.

Now Vaughn required her to wear *this*. She thought again about Betazed, about the effect she feared Tevren's knowledge might have upon it. And part of her wondered if Vaughn was now doing the same thing to her: turning her into a stranger that the Deanna Troi of ten years ago would have reviled.

Vaughn. When she had met him earlier that morning, Deanna had still been coping with the news of the defeat at Starbase 19, and so had spared little thought for the man himself. Now, as she thought back to this morning's meeting, she reviewed the unconscious impressions she'd been too preoccupied to consider at the time, and compared them to what she recalled of his infrequent visits to the Troi household decades ago.

Deanna's earliest memories of Vaughn went back to childhood, years before her empathic abilities had developed. He'd been a friend and colleague of her father's and, she recalled, a source of tension for her mother. Even back then he'd seemed old, and Deanna remembered wondering, in the way children sometimes do, what had carved such deep lines into the man's face, especially around his eyes. Those lines had cut even deeper in the years since.

To Will and probably to most humans, Deanna realized, Vaughn seemed curt, somewhat harsh, perhaps even a little condescending. But thanks to her empathic sense, she knew this was an incomplete picture. There was a kind of "mist" around Vaughn, indicating he'd had his guard up emotionally—a fairly standard technique for officers involved with advanced tactics and intelligence work, but only partially effective most of the time. The mist meant that she couldn't read him as clearly as, say, Captain Picard, but it couldn't keep certain intense emotional states from getting through. Even so, she found she'd only picked up two clear emotions from Vaughn during the morning meeting: a self-directed bitterness and, she now realized, a sincere concern for Deanna's well-being. Everything else was white noise.

Accustomed to forming a generally accurate profile of someone after only a first encounter, Troi was frustrated by her inability to see clearly past a veneer that Vaughn had obviously spent years fortifying, precisely in order to discourage what she was attempting. She wondered if her father had developed similar skills.

The thought completed a circuit in Deanna's mind,

and she suddenly recalled the last time she'd seen Vaughn, when she was only seven years old. He was there, in their home on Betazed, speaking quietly to her mother just before a grief-stricken Lwaxana had told young Deanna that Ian Andrew Troi was dead.

Deanna walked to her desk and swiveled the computer display so she could see it. "Computer," she said. "Show me the personnel file of Commander Elias Vaughn."

The computer screen on her desk showed a standard personnel record, complete with a recent visual. Vaughn had been born on Berengaria VII in 2275. *Exactly a century old,* she thought. It was an age by which most Starfleet humans were already retired. Academy class of '97. There was no information about his subsequent postings, and no specific current assignment other than the innocuously worded "consultant," which almost made Deanna laugh aloud.

Frowning, she said, "Computer, search for Elias Vaughn in the historical database."

The number of items listed was surprisingly paltry for a man who'd served in Starfleet for nearly eight decades, but he'd had a tumultuous career, to say the least: the civil war on Beta IV, the genocidal holocaust on Arvada III, the Tomed incident, and one or two others. The database didn't even list the Betreka Nebula, and Deanna knew that Vaughn and her father had served there together.

She suppressed a sigh of frustration. The facts were so sparse a spy would have a better background cover than the limited information available on the commander.

She really didn't want facts, however. She wanted more about his character. What made the man tick? Traveling from assignment to assignment with no permanent place to call home had to be the loneliest of lives. Did he need no one but himself? She couldn't help wondering about his emotional life, his self-control, his impulses and appetites. Who were his friends? His family? His record listed no wife, but a daughter who was a recent Academy graduate serving as an ensign on the *U.S.S. Sentinel.*

But everything else she sought was conspicuously missing.

So much for the official record, she thought. *Well, there's always the old-fashioned way.* She still had a good opportunity to learn something meaningful about the man whose command she'd accepted, and that opportunity awaited her in holodeck two.

"Beverly?" Deanna reached the holodeck entrance just as the doctor staggered out. Normally groomed immaculately, Beverly Crusher sagged against the corridor wall, sweat dripping off her forehead, her hair a ratty tangle. Like Deanna, she wore her surface ops blacks. She patted her face with a towel and fought to draw air into her lungs.

The doctor held up a hand to forestall Deanna's questions of concern. "I'm all right."

"When did Commander Vaughn recruit you for the mission?" Deanna asked.

"Right after he recruited Data," Beverly panted. She took a moment to regain her breath. "I haven't had a workout like that since running through the Celtris III scenarios with Jean-Luc and Worf."

Deanna scrutinized her friend with concern. The Federation wounded were pouring into the sector, and every doctor at Starbase 133 had been working round the clock. Not only did Beverly's face reveal exhaustion from her session with Vaughn, the lines around her eyes had deepened, and the circles beneath them had darkened since yesterday.

Deanna understood more than most that treating the injured brought its own tolls. Beverly would know firsthand the horrors, the sacrifices, the losses of friends and families and homes. And no matter how strong the physician's psyche, continuously dealing with bad news and dying patients wore down even the most resilient souls. Small wonder Beverly had accepted the assignment to Darona.

"He's waiting for you," the doctor said, straightening her shoulders.

"What do you think of him?"

Beverly shrugged. "He's not the first hundred-year-old I've met who could go up against holographic opponents, or even real ones. Most people don't give it much thought, but there are actually a lot more active centenarian humans in Starfleet than is generally known. One of the benefits of an ever-lengthening life span." She smiled wryly. "Just the same, I'm glad Vaughn's on our side."

"You almost sound optimistic," Deanna said. "I wish I could be."

Beverly put a hand on her friend's shoulder. "Deanna, Jean-Luc told me a little about the issues you're struggling with. I can really only try to imagine what you're going through right now. But let me ask you something. Do you have faith in your friends on the *Enterprise* to do everything we can to help win back Betazed?"

"Of course I do."

"Then you need to have that same faith in your people back home. Trust them to get through this without forgetting who they are."

"Easier said than done," Deanna said. "Tevren—"

"I know," Beverly said. "But I also know you. And if even half the Betazoids are anything like you or your mother, I think Betazed will endure whatever Tevren brings to it."

Deanna mustered a grateful smile and squeezed her friend's hand. "Thanks, Beverly." And with an encouraging nod, the doctor set off for her quarters, leaving Deanna staring at the holodeck doors.

Letting out a deep breath, she stepped forward. The doors parted at her approach. Inside, she saw to her surprise that the holodeck walls were bare but for the diode grid. No holographic environment. She'd expected a Darona simulation—a city street, maybe the prison interior, with a squad of holographic Jem'Hadar waiting to ambush her.

Instead, she saw only Vaughn standing in the middle of the room, the red stripe of his S.O.B. standing out against the otherwise black uniform. In contrast to Beverly, he hadn't broken a sweat. And his breathing appeared to be perfectly even.

"Try to kill me," he instructed.

"I beg your pardon?"

He beckoned her closer. "Make your best move."

She didn't advance but dropped into a widespread

stance, left foot forward, left fist up and ready for a jab. Keeping her weight on the balls of her feet, she bounced lightly, slowly circling, sizing up her opponent for weakness.

She couldn't find any.

She feinted, moving in and out, testing his reaction but keeping her distance. He didn't so much as blink.

"Come on, Deanna," he taunted softly. "Come get me. Take me down."

She ignored his jibe and watched his blue eyes for a hint of movement. Just because Vaughn had asked her to attack didn't mean he wouldn't do the same. And while her offensive strikes weren't particularly powerful, she'd practiced her defensive maneuvers more. She preferred him to attack her, so she could turn his superior strength against him.

Not that she thought she had a chance against a combat veteran like Vaughn, but she didn't want to embarrass herself completely either. He had more strength, more stamina, and decades more experience. She already knew how this exercise would end. The question was simply how long she lasted.

"I'm only an old man," he taunted again. "Nothing in comparison to the Jem'Hadar on Betazed." She circled lightly as Vaughn spoke. "Did you know that before battle the Jem'Hadar perform a ritual ceremony? 'I am dead,' they chant. 'As of this moment we are all dead. We go into battle to reclaim our lives. This we do gladly because we are Jem'Hadar. Victory is life.' "

He stared at her with a penetrating gaze and repeated the chilling incantation. " 'Victory is life.' Come get me, Deanna."

"Is that an order, sir?" She kept her guard up, her eyes alert.

"Very good." He nodded approval. "You can't be taunted into attacking. But then I never doubted your common sense." He shifted his stance slightly. Mentally, she sensed his mind quickening to a higher state of vigilance. If she hadn't been focused, she would have missed the tiny sign. Still she was barely prepared for the force and swiftness of his attack.

Vaughn lunged with the speed and grace of a Bajoran *hara* cat. In comparison, she deliberately slowed her reaction and feigned clumsiness, dropping to her buttocks and back on the mat, planting the soles of her feet into his stomach, catapulting him over her head, using the momentum of his attack against him.

In anticipation of a head-first dive, Vaughn lifted his arms over his head. His palms hit the mat, and he rotated smoothly forward. She rolled backward with his momentum and somersaulted until she straddled his chest. Summoning a *kiai,* a shout from deep within, she simultaneously aimed a knife-hand blow to his neck. He blocked her strike with an ease that suggested he'd envisioned her attack before she'd even thought of it.

"A stiff-wristed palm to the base of the nose should have been your choice of a killing blow," he said. "You have the strength to crunch the nose bones into the brain. Try again."

She started to stand, assuming he meant for them to begin on their feet. Instead, he pulled her back down with firm gentleness. At his touch, she sensed a mental weariness that told her he'd taught this exercise more times than he would have liked. "Hit me. Use the base of your palm."

"I won't—"

"Do as I say," he demanded.

Beneath his exterior sternness, she sensed his sympathy for her dislike of fighting. "I can't just—"

"You can. Hit me." He tapped his nose. "Here."

She knew she possessed enough power to drive the tiny bones into his brain. And she knew he would stop her before she succeeded. Still she hesitated.

Intellectually comprehending that her strike wouldn't succeed was one thing. Using all her force and skill to attempt to kill a Starfleet officer during a training exercise was another matter entirely.

Deanna tensed. "I can't."

"Show me the move in slow motion," he ordered.

She did as he asked, stiffening her hand and cocking her wrist at the required angle.

"That's fine. At least you know the drill."

She rolled off and sat on the deck, breathing heavily more from stress than from exercise. "Taking a life has never been easy for me."

Vaughn sat up next to her. "When the time comes, you'll react with the necessary amount of force," he assured her.

"How can you know that?" She hated the taking of life, and she wondered if she could perform adequately and efficiently to protect herself and her crewmates in dangerous situations. "I might hesitate at a critical moment."

"You won't."

"How can you say that with such assurance?" She

not only heard the meaning in his words, but *felt* his complete faith in her.

In the space of a few short minutes, Vaughn had proved that even though he was a hardened soldier, he was also someone who didn't use more force than required to do a job. Neither did he exhibit any joy in combat. Clearly he understood her dislike of killing. But the question, she knew, wasn't whether or not she could trust Vaughn. It was whether she could go through with her decision to join him on the mission.

She reached out empathically, sensed in him complex emotions, feelings that he reined in tightly, and she assessed his deep weariness, at odds with his tough and energetic exterior. Unable to pinpoint whether he was tired of special operations, the war, some other aspect of his life, or a combination of the three, she came to believe he had a good heart. Sparring with him suggested he wasn't the type to hurt anyone he didn't feel compelled to. He valued life. He wasn't a career soldier because he relished the thrill of battle; in fact, as far as she could tell, he truly hated it. He was doing a job he didn't want to do, simply because he believed in the objective.

"I know you won't fail when the time comes," he said finally, "because you have good genes."

Deanna frowned. "You mean from my father."

"Don't sell your mother short, either. Lwaxana is as formidable an individual as I've ever met. She and Ian—" He stopped and looked at her, then, smiling wistfully. "You probably don't remember the first time we met. You were just a baby."

"No," Deanna admitted. "But I do remember the last time we met."

Vaughn's smile faded, and he looked away. "I'm sorry, Deanna," he said quietly. "Your father was a good friend to me. He saved my life once, and I'd have given anything to do the same for him. I know that doesn't change the fact that I went home from that last mission, and he didn't."

Deanna didn't know what surprised her more, the fact that her father had saved Vaughn's life, or the revelation that Vaughn had been there when he died.

Seeming to guess her thoughts, Vaughn shook his head. "The details aren't important. What matters is that when things were at their worst, Ian Troi always did what needed doing. Your mother is the same way. And, I suspect, you are too. But believe me when I tell you that if there was anyone else I could turn to so I could spare you all this, I would."

Deanna felt ashamed then, knowing she would never wish the dilemma she was faced with on anyone else, but knowing also that to turn her back on it was never really an option. Where this path she was now on would take her, she didn't know. But her course, at least, was finally clear.

Deanna got to her feet, offering Vaughn her hand. "Show me more."

Vaughn looked up at her. A look of sorrow came briefly to his eyes, then quickly hardened into determination. After a moment, he took her hand and pulled himself up.

Tilting her head back, Deanna closed her eyes as the spray of hot water warmed her skin, soothed her aches, and relaxed her mind. After four grueling hours sparring with Vaughn—followed by two more hours of combat with holographic Jem'Hadar after Vaughn had excused himself for another meeting with the captain— Deanna had gone back to her quarters, stripped off her uniform, stepped into the shower stall, and simply let the heat and steam envelop her. The water, as hot as she could stand it, massaged her flesh in ways the sonic setting couldn't compare.

Deanna collected water into one cupped hand and then released it, letting it dribble through her fingers. Plans were proceeding apace now. After weeks of inactivity, the *Enterprise* had come alive as repair teams scurried throughout the ship, battle drills got under way, and new crewmembers rotated aboard from the starbase. One way or another, it seemed, the assault on Sentok Nor was going forward, though what would follow was still anyone's guess—just as it was still uncertain how her team was going to make it to the surface of Darona undetected.

Something stirred suddenly in her mind. As always, she sensed Will's presence at the door of her quarters before he signaled. "Come in, Will," she called.

Through the sound of the cascading water, she followed the trail of Will's emotions as he entered her quarters: his surprise at seeing the combat uniform tossed carelessly on the floor of her living area; his boyish thrill of realizing she was in the shower; his gentlemanly hesitation as he realized he'd come at an awkward time. "You want me to come back later?" he called.

Deanna said nothing, her eyes still closed against the water, soaking in Will's reassuring presence in her mind as she soaked up the heat.

Imzadi . . .

"Deanna? Did you say something?"

"Just a second, Will," she said finally, her eyes opening. She couldn't see past the steam.

"I can come back—"

"No, it's all right," she said, turning off the shower. "Hand me my robe, would you?"

Hesitation again. He was wondering if she was sending him a signal. And part of her, she realized, was wondering the same thing. Her history with Will was long and passionate on numerous levels, and always seemed just on the verge of reigniting, especially during times of personal crisis.

You really should know better, Deanna, she admonished herself. *Try to remember you're a counselor.*

She heard him fumbling for the robe near the entrance to the bathroom. "That's quite a head of steam you have going in there," he commented.

"Helped me to relax," she said, reaching through the steam. "You should try it sometime." She could see him now, a silhouette in the mist, which of course meant that he, in turn, could see her.

He handed her the robe. "It seems to be having the opposite effect on me," he admitted. "But I think you knew that."

She froze. *Of course,* she thought. Will wasn't empathic, but he also wasn't likely to forget that she was, and he knew perfectly well that she could read him like a book, emotionally.

Nudity wasn't an issue to most Betazoids. But realizing that Will had seen through her, Deanna suddenly felt naked. Exposed. She quickly wrapped her robe around herself. "I'm sorry, Will. That was . . . that was unfair of me. And stupid."

The fog was lifting. She could see his face now. He was smiling at her. Not mischievously, but affectionately. "Why? Because you feel that if we gave in to our impulses, it would be for the wrong reasons, and at the worst possible time?"

"Isn't that how you feel?"

"That's a rhetorical question, Deanna. You *know* how I feel."

"Then why do we do this to ourselves?"

"Honestly? Because I think when you get past our suppressed mutual lust, we actually care about each other too much to risk making this choice just because we're suddenly afraid it may be our last chance. But either way, it's not something either of us should feel sorry about."

Deanna smiled crookedly and looked up at him. "Are you after my job?"

"God, no. Who would want it?"

Will let out a satisfying *"Oof!"* as Deanna punched him in the stomach, after which she reached for a towel and wrapped it around her head as she walked past him into the living area. "So what does bring you to my quarters at this late hour, Commander?"

Will made a show of holding his abdomen as he staggered after her. "Some news that I thought might brighten your evening," he gasped dramatically, then sobered, grinning in that way he had that came more from his eyes than any other part of his face. "I just found out how Vaughn expects to get to Darona."

Chapter Six

GUL LEMEC ASCENDED the turboshaft of Sentok Nor, the Cardassian-engineered space station that glittered in the sky above Betazed. Unlike the majority of *Nor*-class stations, Sentok had not been designed as a facility for refining space-borne materials. The Dominion's war with the Federation had led to new uses for the massive assemblage of steel and composites. Instead of miners, Sentok Nor's habitat ring housed Cardassian soldiers and engineers, while its central core was outfitted as the system's primary Jem'Hadar breeding facility. The station's cargo holds stored war matériel and captive Betazoids brought up from the planet, as well as the lab complex for the experimental work that played such a big part in the Dominion's decision to target Betazed for annexation in the first place. And its graceful pylons—only three of which had been completed so far—

served as docking ports for Dominion and Cardassian warships.

If the decision had been his, Lemec would never have allied his world with the Dominion. He despised the vat-grown soldiers and their unctuous Vorta keepers. First and foremost, Lemec was a patriot, and he harbored a deep resentment of the alliance that had been bought with Cardassia's independence. Only the chance to be on the winning side in a war against the hated Federation offset being forced to share his command of the Betazed occupation with the Vorta Luaran and her Jem'Hadar.

And if cooperating with the soft-voiced, repellent Luaran strengthened his position as prefect of Betazed and Sentok Nor, then Lemec would swallow his distaste and appear conciliatory. At the present, Luaran was less an impediment to his success and eventual promotion than the ego-driven Dr. Crell Moset, the renowned Cardassian scientist who had set up shop aboard the station to direct the bio-research that the Dominion had made their top priority.

Unfortunately, Moset's insatiable requests for more subjects for his experiments prevented the Betazoids from accepting their fate and cooperating fully with their conquerors. The more civilians Moset required, the more rebellious and entrenched the resistance movement on the planet became. Lemec was counting on Luaran's help to stem Moset's excesses, at least until Lemec could ferret out the resistance leaders and stabilize control of the planet.

He forged his way through the day crew in the operations center to the commander's office and tried to keep his impatience under control. Much to his annoyance, the Vorta had called another meeting of the administrative staff.

He entered the office, and Luaran glided smoothly around the desk to greet him. With difficulty, the Cardassian smothered his frown of distaste. Her frail form and soft pale face offended his sense of aesthetics. Lemec, however, kept his opinions to himself. He would not allow his dislike of Luaran to show. He would hold his tongue and bide his time, hoping for her support in tempering Moset's demands.

Luaran offered the gul his favorite morning beverage of hot fish juice, and he accepted with a curt nod of thanks, then mumbled a greeting to Moset.

The exobiologist was on sabbatical from the University of Culat so that he could contribute to the war effort. Renowned for his brilliance in nonhumanoid exobiology, Moset, in addition to his classified experiments, oversaw the production of Jem'Hadar on the station. With a weathered visage and graying hair, Moset had entered Luaran's office humming as if he had no cares in the world. He was always humming, Lemec thought with irritation. Someday he was going to stuff a combat boot down the doctor's throat to shut him up and give a poor gul some peace. Apparently unaware of how much his habit annoyed others, Moset brushed a speck of lint from his laboratory coat and accepted a cup of hot fish juice.

"I need more Betazoid subjects," Moset demanded before the Vorta had a chance to state the purpose of her meeting.

The muscles in Luaran's face tensed slightly before

returning to their customary calm. "You have received an adequate number."

"Yes," Lemec agreed. "Use the ones already being stored in the docking ring."

"They don't have the appropriate genetic markers."

"Then send them back to the planet," Lemec insisted. "They're a drain on our resources."

"They will be of use later, once I've broken the genetic code." Moset glared at Lemec. "If you'd bring me half as many subjects as you've been executing, I'd have what I need."

Lemec was unperturbed by the accusation. He would not tolerate insurrection and sabotage.

"You're shooting Betazoids?" The disapproval in the Vorta's voice was muted but unmistakable. "Can't you find a better way to control them?"

"The ones on the planet were shot as an example against their resistance movement," Lemec said. "The ones executed on the station were attempting to destroy our production of ketracel-white. I think you'll agree that we must deter both."

"I remind you, Gul," Moset said, "that my research is the reason we are here at all. But I cannot do my job if you keep shooting prisoners I could use—"

"You won't have a job or a life if I don't keep this station safe." With the greatest effort, Lemec reined in his temper another notch. "In the past few days we've found ruptured EPS conduits, sabotaged replicator systems, and turbolifts that stop only between decks. Defective airlocks are a constant problem. I suspect the slave laborers did much of their sabotage during the building of the station, but only now is the full scope of the damage they inflicted becoming known. The new laborers are equally duplicitous. Their telepathic abilities inform them of what's happening in your laboratories, Moset, and they're rebelling against it."

"That's why I called you here today," Luaran told them. "We must rectify these problems."

"I need more Cardassian troops," Lemec answered. "Thanks to the good doctor's experiments, we can't even keep Jem'Hadar soldiers aboard the station. Those we breed here have to be ferried to the surface before they reach maturity. We should request reinforcements for the station from Cardassia Prime."

The Vorta folded her arms over her narrow chest and shook her head. "We have the full allocation. The others are needed elsewhere."

Lemec started to press the issue, but held his tongue at the determination in her expression. Moset, however, seemed not to know when to quit.

"Give me the rebellious Betazoids instead of executing them," he pleaded. "It's just senseless killing."

Lemec's derisive laugh escaped before he could squelch it. "I wouldn't think the man who experimented on living Bajorans and killed thousands in his so-called hospital would be so sensitive."

Moset frowned. "You're a fool, Lemec. My concern is for my work—not the welfare of my subjects." The doctor's lips quivered in outrage. "Minds far superior to yours respect my genius. The Legate's Crest of Valor for my work on the Fostossa virus is proof of that."

"You know where you can put your Legate's Crest," Lemec said with a snarl.

"Gentlemen." Luaran held up her hands, her violet

eyes glowering. "I expect you to do your jobs, which"—she smiled with irritating sweetness—"you cannot do if you are quarreling with one another."

Lemec nodded in reluctant acquiescence. "Luaran," he said, forcing his voice to sound calm and reasonable, "I cannot adequately govern both the planet and the station without more Cardassian soldiers. And commandeering additional Betazoids from the planet will only compound the station's—and the planet's—security problems."

"I implore you," Moset's voice swelled with passion. "I cannot continue my research until I have Betazoids with the appropriate genetic makeup. And," he added as if in afterthought, "the Dominion must have a steady supply of Jem'Hadar and ketracel-white to keep up the war effort. I need slave laborers to help with production."

Lemec bit his tongue. Moset didn't give a vole's ass about the Dominion war effort. All the damned doctor cared about was his cursed science. But the crafty Moset had taken the tack that Luaran would favor.

She nodded in calm agreement with Moset. "I have been given specific instructions by the Founders to do whatever is necessary to facilitate your project, Doctor. You have my personal assurance that more Betazoids will be rounded up."

Moset preened at his victory, and lorded over Lemec with a triumphant grin.

Luaran turned to Lemec with an apologetic smile. "As for you, Gul . . . Please don't shoot them."

Breathing deeply, Dal Cobrin fought against claustrophobia and tried to estimate how long he'd been in the capsule that enclosed him. The bright lights burned without ceasing in the Cardassian doctor's laboratory on the space station, so Dal had no method of calibrating time. It seemed like months since the Jem'Hadar had grabbed him and loaded him, along with dozens of other frightened Betazoids, onto the freighter headed for Sentok Nor. Once aboard the station, he'd been transported directly from the docking ring into the tiny container that held him now.

From what he'd managed to ascertain from his fellow Betazoids, they had all been similarly imprisoned, confined in these narrow tubes and further restrained by some kind of energy field. Their minds had been unimpaired, but Dal had long ago begun to wish for blessed unconsciousness. The knowledge that he and his friend Ellum were the last of the dozens who'd accompanied them to the station brought him no satisfaction, only the certainty that either he or Ellum would be the next victim of Dr. Crell Moset.

Dal no longer cherished any hope for survival. Moset's assistants had transferred one Betazoid after another from the pods to the laboratory tables. Dal had been painfully aware of the agonies they'd suffered there. None of them had ever returned to their pods.

Now he wished he'd volunteered to be the first chosen from his group. In the beginning they had died quickly, but Moset must have learned in the interim how to keep his subjects alive longer, although the result of his experiments was always the same—death.

Not all Moset's subjects had died, however. Dal was

aware of the presence of others scattered throughout the station, but most were in a deeper state of stasis than Dal's companions had been and were unable to communicate. Only his highly developed telepathy allowed him to sense the ones that were still alive.

Knowing his inescapable fate, lying paralyzed day after day, week after week, while his fellow Betazoids died under Moset's painful ministrations, had been its own kind of torture. Not only had Dal had to listen to the screams, he'd had to feel their terrible fear and acute pain. Dal felt as if Moset snuffed out his life over and over again.

His only hope of escape was a speedy death.

He attempted to focus his thoughts away from the gruesome activities of the lab, to console himself with memories of his childhood, a happy time free of worry and pain. He remembered his first glimpse of his wife Lorella during his days at the university. Their favorite meeting place had been the botanical garden, filled with fragrant flowering plants and exotic off-world greenery. Later, he'd enjoyed his assignment as a science teacher at his first post in the Northern School District.

He worried now over what had happened to Lorella and the children. Were they even still alive?

He and his family had survived the initial invasion and had immediately joined the resistance. The Jem'Hadar had captured him while he'd been on a reconnaissance mission. They'd stunned him and detained him in a holding cell until they'd gathered enough prisoners to ship to the station. At least, thank the gods, his wife and children had escaped his fate.

Moset and his assistants, however, had often discussed among themselves the fact that the resistance had been destroyed, so Dal doubted that any of his family still lived.

A weak mental whimper emanated from the mind of a woman who lay strapped to Moset's table, and Dal's nerve endings burned with empathy for her horrible pain. He hoped, if his family were dead, that they'd died quickly. Some things were worse than death.

He'd often wished he could emulate the selfless attitude of the Jem'Hadar. Along with Betazoids, these soldiers also served as subjects of Moset's deadly experiments. The Jem'Hadar had no fear. Their only thoughts were to serve the Founders, and apparently they had no qualms over dying for their cause, whether in battle or under Moset's knife.

As hard as he'd tried, Dal could find no purpose to Moset's experiments. He knew enough science to hazard many guesses, but none seemed reasonable. Of one thing, however, Dal was certain. Moset was insane, and that very insanity made it impossible to divine the doctor's intent.

Moset and his assistants entered the laboratory, signaling the beginning of another round of tests—and probably the beginning of Dal's last hours, as well. He faced the prospect stoically. Days ago, his fear had given way to resignation. Dying on one of those surgical tables would be his fate.

An assistant approached Dal's capsule and manipulated the controls. In a sparkle of light, Dal was transported to a laboratory table and strapped down firmly. His mind searched for Ellum and found him still in his pod. His poor friend. He would face one more cold day of life alone.

Moset ignored both Dal and the Jem'Hadar who had entered and lain calmly down on the adjacent table without coercion. The doctor frowned at the information on his padd, then performed a microcellular scan on both his subjects, a procedure Dal recognized that would give Moset readings of the cells' functions at the molecular level. Dal, however, had no idea what the scientist was searching for. He simply took a perverse satisfaction in the Cardassian's obvious irritation with the results.

"Place neurocortical monitors on both subjects," Moset ordered.

An assistant placed the devices on Dal's and the Jem'Hadar's foreheads. The monitors would record encephalographic data.

"Configure the Betazoid's monitor to alarm when critical psilosynine readings are detected in his brain," Moset added.

The paralyzing effects of the stasis field no longer held Dal, but full-body restraints prevented any movement. Stronger people than he had struggled against them and failed to break free. Dal didn't even try.

Instead, he attempted again to determine the nature of Moset's experiments. Dal was just a science teacher, not a doctor, but he knew that every Betazoid possessed psilosynine, a neurotransmitter chemical. Was Moset trying to engineer some kind of microorganism to attack cells with a specific DNA sequence? But if so, why? Killing the Betazoid population made no sense. The Dominion's mandate was to expand their empire, not destroy their enemies. Genocide was not their goal. Not usually, at any rate.

Dal caught sight of Moset's expression, and the scientist's single-minded determination frightened him. The width and scope of Moset's experiments reflected their importance to the Cardassian and Dominion alliance, but Dal couldn't figure out what Moset hoped to gain from performing cranial surgeries, extracting genetic material from healthy Betazoids, and implanting that material in Jem'Hadar.

Following his usual procedure, Moset and his team began with the Jem'Hadar. Using a gleaming archaic scalpel, the scientist peeled back the skin at the forehead. A high-powered saw cut through the cranial bone and exposed the underlying brain tissue. Through the entire procedure, the Jem'Hadar exhibited not one flicker of pain.

Then it was Dal's turn.

"Increase neural stimulation to the Betazoid," Moset directed. "Increase neurogenic radiation."

Pain blossomed through Dal's head. He grunted and would have writhed from the agony if the restraints had not held him.

Let this be over quickly, he prayed.

"Use a hypospray on the Jem'Hadar," Moset said.

"For pain?" the assistant asked.

Moset shook his head with impatience. "Use the paralyzing agent to keep him from moving."

The assistant rushed to comply.

"Drechtal beam," Moset said.

An assistant handed him the device, and Moset employed it. "I've severed the neural connections. Now, apply the bioregenerative field. I need maximum accelerated cell growth."

"Bioregenerative field applied."

Moset moved to Dal's side. "Increase the neural stimulation again for the Betazoid."

As if his mind were suddenly on fire, Dal convulsed at the pain.

Through a haze of agony, he heard Moset order the plasma infusion unit. The fluids and electrolytes it dispensed were one of Moset's measures intended to keep Dal alive as long as possible.

He tried to beg them to stop, but no words left his mouth, only a piercing primal scream.

Something stabbed the back of his neck, and even through his pain, Dal knew they were extracting matter directly from his brain.

"Apply the sonic separator and the trilaser connector," Moset ordered. "Quickly. Quickly."

"We're losing the Jem'Hadar."

Over his own suffering, the dying soldier's confusion and agony registered in Dal's mind.

"The Betazoid is dying," Moset's angry voice announced. "He's no use to me now."

Dal tensed as heat burned his brain. Then blessed blackness claimed him and ended his agony.

Chapter Seven

"ENERGIZE," RIKER ORDERED.

The first officer waited with Deanna Troi in Transporter Room Three for the remaining key officers of the mission to come aboard the *Enterprise*.

"Aye, sir." The technician initiated transport.

On the transporter pad, beamed energy solidified into the forms of two old friends: Chief Miles Edward O'Brien and Lieutenant Commander Worf.

"Welcome aboard, gentlemen." Riker greeted both arrivals with a broad grin.

"Commander," Worf said with a nod.

"I trust your journey went well, Mr. Worf?" Riker asked.

The Klingon nodded again. "Admiral Ross's order to divert to Starbase 133 came just after the successful completion of our mission to Bolarus. The *Defiant* and its crew are at your service." Never especially talkative unless duty demanded it, Worf seemed even more distant than usual.

Not surprising, given his recent loss, Riker thought.

O'Brien, by contrast, seemed as warm as ever, though it was immediately apparent that the war had aged the engineer, deepening the furrows on his forehead beneath his curly chestnut hair and adding fresh lines to bracket his mouth and merry eyes.

"Hello, sir. Counselor," he said. "Keiko sends her love."

Riker acknowledged the greeting from O'Brien's wife, but his eyes were drawn to Deanna and Worf. Ignoring the Klingon's inflexible military bearing, Deanna had stepped forward and warmly embraced her old shipmate and former lover.

The meeting was not their first since their fleeting romance had ended, but none of them had seen Worf since the death of his wife, Jadzia, another casualty of war, killed only two months ago.

Typically, Worf bore no outward sign of grief on his dark face, his expression as stiff as the ridges on his forehead, but it didn't take much empathy to feel the man's heartache. Will knew Deanna would want to comfort Worf, to help ease his loss, but she and Worf both had jobs to do. The war wouldn't allow time for any but the briefest acknowledgment of the tragic changes in their lives.

After a quick and awkward embrace, Worf stepped back from her. His dark eyes spoke volumes. "I grieve for the loss of your world, Deanna."

Deanna placed her hand over Worf's doubled hearts. "And I grieve for the loss of yours."

Seeing Worf and being reminded of his wife's death brought home to Riker that he could take nothing for granted. But brooding over the losses and upcoming danger would do none of them any good. Forcing his mind back to his duties, Riker motioned toward the door. "Forgive the rush, gentlemen," he said, "but we're expected at the mission briefing. If you'll kindly follow me . . ."

"This is insane," Riker blurted at Vaughn a short time later.

From his position at the opposite end of the conference table in the observation lounge, Captain Picard wasn't surprised by the outburst. He constantly relied on his first officer to speak his mind, though usually not so forcefully.

Vaughn also seemed unperturbed by Riker's objections. The mission leader stood beside a viewscreen on the far wall, amusement tugging at the corners of his mouth. "Don't hold back, Commander. Tell us what you really think."

Will shook his head and pointed to the Betazed system tactical graphic displayed on the viewscreen. "You can't expect the *Enterprise* and only three Saber-class light cruisers to go up against a dozen Cardassian and Dominion ships of the line. We'll never get anywhere near Sentok Nor."

Picard had shared the same concerns with Vaughn earlier, but the captain had also accepted that three light cruisers were the maximum Starfleet could spare. All other ships within range were either disabled or fighting along the extensive front, struggling to prevent Dominion forces from penetrating Federation space. Besides, Picard wasn't about to express his reservations in front of his crew. For the mission to succeed, they had to *believe* that it would, or they were beaten before they left the starbase.

Seeing Worf and O'Brien gathered once again around the table with Riker, La Forge, Data, Troi, and Crusher brought back a number of fond memories—pleasant times Picard now forced himself to set aside in order to face the current crisis.

"I would share your skepticism," Vaughn said, "except for the factors in our favor."

As if forcing himself to relax, Riker took a deep breath, but his expression dared Vaughn to prove him wrong. "I'm listening."

"First, Captain Picard will lead the task force against the Dominion fleet," Vaughn said, "and Starfleet has full confidence in his abilities. The starships *Tulwar, Katana,* and *Scimitar* will be under his command. Saber-class starships may be small, but therein lies their strength. They're fast and easily maneuverable.

"Second, we may not have to destroy the enemy fleet. We simply have to keep them occupied long enough for you and Mr. La Forge to to beam aboard Sentok Nor with a team, complete the job, and beam out."

"In a heated battle," Riker said, "even ten minutes can be a lifetime."

"Ten minutes may be all we'll need, Number One," Picard stated with a calm he didn't feel. The captain realized how much would be at stake when they engaged the enemy defenses. He had already discussed tactics with the captains of the light cruisers. Each was aware that her ship and crew might not return from this action, a possibility they had each accepted when they volunteered.

"Let's move on," Vaughn said, and indicated the sixth planet ringing Betazed's sun. "This is Darona. Because its population is small, the Dominion has garrisoned less than a thousand troops there, according to our intelligence. However, those troops are vital to the Dominion because of the planet's strategic location. It makes an excellent listening post to scan the shipping lanes and observe movements of ships and supplies."

"If the Dominion forces are using long-range scanning equipment," Data said, "beaming onto the planet undetected seems unlikely."

"You're right, Mr. Data. Which is precisely why Admiral Ross has assigned the *Defiant* to get the extraction team to Darona," Vaughn said with a nod to Worf. "She'll be operating under cloak."

Data's eyes narrowed, and Picard could almost hear the subprocessors humming in the android's brain.

"It is my understanding, sir," Data said, "that the Dominion possesses the capability to detect cloaked vessels. Will that not be a problem?"

Worf spoke up. "Perhaps not. On Deep Space 9, we have been looking for ways to improve the effectiveness of the *Defiant*'s cloaking device ever since we learned the Jem'Hadar possessed countermeasures. Chief?"

O'Brien picked up the ball and ran with it, speaking

directly to Picard. "It took a while, but I think we finally came up with a solution. It's based on the same principle Commander La Forge first devised to defend ourselves against the Borg back on the *Enterprise*-D. By randomly rotating the field harmonics of the *Defiant*'s cloak, we should be able to stay below the threshold of the Dominion's sensors. With luck, the Jem'Hadar will have no idea we're in the area."

"I take it you haven't had a chance to test your modified cloak yet?" Riker asked.

O'Brien shook his head apologetically, "No, sir. My assistant and I actually worked out the final kinks after we left DS9. But the real test will come only when we're facing a Jem'Hadar ship."

Picard looked at Vaughn. "Then, assuming you can make it to the surface successfully, Commander . . . what next?"

"According to Commander Troi, beaming directly into the prison facility isn't an option. We'll need to make contact with the warden, Director Lanolan, and secure his cooperation in releasing Tevren. We'll be wearing surface blacks for maximum protection, with native coats over them. And with the help of Dr. Crusher's skills, even Mr. Data will be able to pass for a Betazoid."

Picard turned to Troi. "You think Lanolan will cooperate?"

She glanced at him with dark eyes still haunted by the depth of her dilemma and the discomfort of her decision. "I can't imagine he'll like it, but I think he'll understand the necessity."

"While on Darona," Vaughn continued, "we'll be operating without combadges—a total communications blackout. We don't want the Jem'Hadar homing in on our transmissions. Once we have Tevren, Data will activate a subspace transponder that Commander La Forge will install today in his positronic systems. When Data gives the signal, the *Defiant* will lock on to that transmission and beam the team out."

"And by that time," Picard added, "Commander Riker's team should have destroyed Sentok Nor."

Vaughn nodded. "That's the idea. The *Defiant* will proceed to Betazed and deliver Tevren to the resistance."

"Piece of cake," Riker said with more than a trace of sarcasm.

"Let's hope so," Vaughn said evenly. "Any questions?"

"I have a comment," La Forge said. "Destroying Sentok Nor is fine in theory, but I'd be a lot more comfortable emptying our torpedo launchers into it than trying to blow it up from the inside the way you're proposing."

"Inadvisable," Vaughn said. "Even if our task force wasn't already contending with a dozen enemy craft, the station is still able to defend itself."

Picard turned to O'Brien. "Chief, what can we expect from Sentok Nor?"

"Massive armaments and heavy-duty shields at least, sir," O'Brien said, "if it's that similar to Deep Space 9. And we should expect upgrades from the original design. Commander Vaughn is probably right when he says that getting a team in will be easier than trying to destroy it from a distance."

Vaughn nodded. "There's also the fact that there's almost certainly some Betazoids on board. We have an obligation to try to get them off before we take out the station. Obviously it won't be easy, but that's why Mr. O'Brien is going with the boarding party."

O'Brien looked up. "Me, sir?"

But La Forge had already deduced Vaughn's meaning. "You're the Federation's leading authority on Cardassian space stations, Chief. If anybody would know how to blow that monstrosity up from the inside in the shortest time, it'd be you. Frankly, I wouldn't want to try this without you."

"With all due respect, sir, I spend most of my time trying to keep Deep Space 9 from falling to pieces," O'Brien reminded him, "not figuring out ways to blow it up. But I appreciate the sentiment."

Eighteen hours after the briefing, and after the fourth day of combat drills with Vaughn, Deanna prepared to join Elias, Worf, Beverly, and Data aboard the *Defiant*. Will had come to the transporter room to see her off, and even dismissed the transporter operator so he could spend a final moment alone with her.

"I know you don't want to hear this," he said, "but I'm gonna say it anyway. Be careful."

Deanna smiled. "You too. I'll see you soon." Suddenly she had her arms around him, and Will was hugging her back, his long arms wrapped tightly around her.

"You know what I'm feeling, don't you?" she heard him ask unnecessarily.

"Yes," she said. "Me too." After a moment, she said. "Promise me something, Will?"

"You name it."

"Promise you'll never let me go."

Will smiled. He knew what she meant, and that it had nothing to do with their embrace. "That depends," he said. "Does it work both ways?"

"Of course."

"Then, yes," Will said. "I promise."

Later in the *Defiant*'s mess hall, as the ship warped through space under cloak, Deanna sat in silence, keenly aware of her turbulent emotions and finding the ship strangely disquieting. She missed the familiar decks and faces of the *Enterprise*. Vaughn, amazingly, seemed comfortable regardless of his environment and adjusted as easily to new surroundings as Data. Worf, to his credit, had provided them with every comfort his ship had to offer—such as they were.

She allowed herself a wistful sigh. She had hoped to spend time with Worf, but his duties as captain had kept him too occupied for them to share even a few moments alone together. Through his fierce Klingon demeanor, she continued to feel his devastating grief over Jadzia, and Deanna's frustration at being unable to comfort her dear friend added to her agitation.

Shortly before their arrival at the edge of the Betazed system, she, Vaughn, Beverly, Data, and Worf had convened for a briefing in the mess hall.

In preparation for their assignment, the away team had donned their S.O.B.s, equipped themselves, and put on dark hooded coats that, Deanna assured them, were typical on the planet. With the exception of Deanna, the team wore dark cosmetic lenses that made even Data appear Betazoid at a glance, once Beverly had altered his skin's pigment to something comparable to Deanna's.

"We can't transport directly into the city of Jarkana without risking detection by Jem'Hadar sensors," Vaughn said.

Worf pointed to a map on his padd. "I suggest an insertion point here, a kilometer outside the city. You are less likely to attract attention, yet close enough to make your way into Jarkana easily on foot."

Transporting directly into the prison facility would have decreased the risk for the away team, but the presence of Jem'Hadar security forces in the city had eliminated that option. From her previous stay in Jarkana, Deanna recalled little cover on the roads leading into the city and worried about exposure, but Vaughn explained that remaining in plain sight was another way to hide. The away team simply had to blend in with the native population to keep from being noticed.

Vaughn turned to Deanna. "When's the most foot traffic on the main road?"

She considered what she remembered of the terrain and what she knew about the people. "When the farmers take their fresh produce into the city in the mornings. It's only a short distance from the open market in the center of the city to Director Lanolan's house, assuming he hasn't moved in the last seventeen years."

"Let's hope he hasn't," Vaughn said, and checked the chrono on his padd. "That means we're go for transport in less than thirty minutes."

"The *Defiant* will remain cloaked," Worf said, "until it is time to transport you onto the planet. We are out of the usual shipping lanes there, so we should remain undetected."

Data frowned. "Have you ascertained if your modifications to the cloaking device will be effectual?"

Worf shook his head. "There is no way to know until the cloak is exposed to Dominion sensors. However, the current best-case scenario shows that remodulating the cloaking field will overtax the system in a fairly short time."

"Overload?" Vaughn asked.

"That is one possibility," Worf acknowledged. "The other is an automatic shutdown, which would merely require reinitializing the cloaking device after a cooldown period. But the end result would be the same: exposure."

"Sounds like this may not be the breakthrough you were hoping for," Beverly said.

"It is not," Worf said, clearly trying to contain his frustration. "But we have no alternatives." After a moment, he said, "As agreed, once you beam down, the *Defiant* will go quiet and remain out of contact for at least twelve hours. If you run into difficulties on Darona and Commander Data activates his subspace signal before the designated rendezvous, it may take some time for the *Defiant* to get within transporter range."

"Understood," Vaughn said.

A voice from the bridge sounded over Worf's communicator, and the captain responded before turning to the away team. "The *Defiant* is approaching Darona. I am needed on the bridge. Report to the transporter bay. Die well."

On the viewscreen, the class-M planet Darona spun with deceptive serenity as Worf strode onto the bridge and settled into the center seat.

"Half impulse power, Mr. Nog," Worf ordered the Ferengi ensign at the conn before opening a comm channel to the transporter bay. "Away team, prepare for transport."

"Ready, Captain," Vaughn answered.

"On my mark, Ensign," Worf told Nog. "Two . . . one . . . decloak and energize!"

In the common room of the resistance stronghold, Lwaxana Troi considered her two-year-old son with an objective eye. Every day he showed more signs of having inherited his mother's indomitable disposition.

"Barin, please eat." She lifted a spoonful of chopped *sadi* fruit to his tightly compressed lips.

"No!"

Pushing a strand of hair off her forehead, she stifled her frustration. *No* had become Barin's favorite word, not an unusual development considering his age and stage of maturity. In a situation where food was scarce and strictly rationed, however, she couldn't grant the little tyrant the luxury of his tantrums. He needed all the nourishment he could get.

"Just one taste," she said reasonably. "You'll like it, I promise."

"No." He stamped his foot and turned his head to avoid the proffered spoon. "Don't want *sadi*. Want chocolate."

She could thank Deanna for the boy's preference. Her daughter had sent them an ample supply of the confection before the war started, and with careful rationing, Lwaxana had managed to dole out an occasional treat to Barin until only a few weeks ago.

"But this is chocolate," she improvised. "It's just yellow. And juicy. And tart."

Barin shook his head defiantly, unconvinced, but Lwaxana's attention had already been drawn to the approach of Enaren. She sensed his agitation even before she heard his footsteps pounding down the tunnelway. Within seconds, he thundered into the room.

"What's wrong?" she demanded.

"Two members of the scavenging team just returned. The Jem'Hadar have captured Okalan."

She dropped the spoon into the bowl of minced fruit and handed it to Chaxaza. "Where?"

"They grabbed him just as he was leaving the hospital at Condar village," Enaren said. "The others in his group were hiding and managed to slip away."

"What about the ryetalyn?"

Enaren shook his head. "Okalan had it when the Jem'Hadar captured him."

Lwaxana bit back a curse of frustration. The doctor had used the last of the ryetalyn to save Enaren's grandson, but afterward, three more children had come down with the fever. One hovered near death. Without medication, he'd die before sunrise. "Perhaps Okalan dropped it along the way in the hope we'd find it."

"We can search," Enaren said. "It was the last ryetalyn known to be within a hundred kilometers."

Lwaxana reached for her cloak on the bench behind her. "Let's go."

"Where do you think you're going?" Enaren asked in amazement.

Taking charge, Lwaxana drew herself to her full height and tinged her voice with the irrefutable tone of command. "The other members of his team will show us where Okalan was captured. Then we'll follow his trail and locate him."

Enaren gaped at her as if she'd lost her senses. "And if we find him? What good will that do?"

Lwaxana bristled at his lack of faith. "Okalan and I are two of the strongest telepaths in this cell. If I can communicate with him without his guards seeing me, he can tell me what happened to the ryetalyn."

Enaren shook his head. "It's a fool's errand."

Lwaxana's eyes flashed with fury. "Tell that to the parents of those sick children."

Enaren hesitated. "It's almost sunset. The beasts begin foraging at dark. And if we use our phasers, we'll draw the Jem'Hadar down on us."

"Then arm yourself and the others with blow guns," Lwaxana ordered. "And hurry."

With few modern weapons, the resistance had reverted to the blow guns and darts of their primitive ancestors to protect themselves from wild animals and even to kill tunnel rats. Most of the men and women had become proficient in the use of the small tube, fashioned from the hollowed stems of the *corzon* plant and armed with *tarna* thorns dipped in the deadly poison of the *zintaba* root. The toxin killed instantly.

After ordering Chaxaza to persuade Barin to eat and swiftly kissing her son, Lwaxana led the way into the tunnel that exited the caverns. Enaren followed. The other members of Okalan's team, the stocky young *cavat* farmer and a gigantic blacksmith, both from Condar, joined them as they left the stronghold.

What if the Jem'Hadar have transported Okalan? Enaren demanded. *We'll never find him.*

I know where he might be, the *cavat* farmer answered. *The ugly brutes have commandeered the community hall as a temporary headquarters in this province. My guess is they took him there.*

We have to hurry, Lwaxana insisted, *before they decide to move him somewhere else.*

The rest of her thoughts she shielded to herself. If the Jem'Hadar suspected Okalan was a member of a rebel group, they'd torture him for information. Both the Dominion and Cardassians were experts at painful interrogation, and although Okalan was strong and dedicated, she had no assurance he could withstand his captors' brutalizing tactics. If he broke, he might give away the location of their stronghold, and, gods forbid, the terrible secret of Hent Tevren.

With the *cavat* farmer in the lead, they raced along the narrow wilderness path worn by the beasts they hoped to avoid. Branches whipped Lwaxana's face until it stung with lacerations, and she stumbled over rocks and tendrils of vine, but she refused to slow her pace. Only once, when her cloak caught on a bush of *tarna* thorns, did she stop and force herself to unhook it carefully. The least scrap of fabric would alert an enemy patrol to their presence in the area. With her garment freed, she sprinted after the others, ignoring the stitch in her side and the painful compression of her lungs as she struggled for air. On one occasion she heard beasts crashing through the underbrush, but the sounds led away from them toward the river, not the village.

The tiny group maintained their draining pace for over an hour until the farmer stopped and held up his hand to signal a halt.

The village is just ahead, he announced.

Take us to where the forest comes closest to the community hall, Lwaxana instructed. *We can't risk being seen.*

I played in these woods as a child, the blacksmith said. *Follow me. I know the way.*

The glow of village lights was barely visible through the trees, and the only sounds the occasional barking of dogs and the rustle of a gentle wind through the overhanging branches. Lwaxana followed the men, at one point dropping to all fours to creep through the vines that blocked their way.

After several minutes of tedious travel, the blacksmith motioned them to stop. *The community hall is over there,* he said, pointing east through the trees.

I can't see it, Enaren grumbled.

If we move any closer, the blacksmith said, *anyone at the community hall can see us.*

Then I'll have to try from here. Lwaxana settled on a nearby tree stump, drew her cloak around her against the encroaching chill, and opened her mind. *Okalan, are you there?*

The answering blast of agony and fear almost knocked her to the ground. *Lwaxana, is that you?*

Yes, I'm here, in the woods near the village hall. Where are you?

The pain of his injuries cascaded through her, setting up sympathetic responses along her nerve endings. Her entire body vibrated from the shared agony. A glance at the men who accompanied her indicated they had not picked up Okalan's thoughts.

Okalan's nearby, she told them, *and in horrible pain.*

They have me in the hall, Okalan managed to send through his suffering.

The ryetalyn, she asked. *What happened to it?*

When they brought me here, there was a Cardassian officer, Gul Lemec. He took the ryetalyn and poured it into the dirt.

Lwaxana suffered a spasm of grief for the dying children at the stronghold, then turned her thoughts back to Okalan. *We'll try to get you out.*

It's no use. I'm half dead already. The gul suspects my involvement in the resistance. They've tortured me for information, but so far I've denied everything.

Lwaxana sensed not only Okalan's pain, but the weakening of his spirit. His torturers would keep him alive and in excruciating distress until he told them what they wanted to know.

We'll get you free— Lwaxana began.

No! Okalan's refusal was powerful, in spite of his injuries. *They've gouged out my eyes. My fingernails are gone. And they've passed more electrical current through me than I ever thought a body could endure. There's only one thing to do for me now, and for yourselves.*

Lwaxana refused to consider what he was suggesting. *Okalan, no.*

Dammit, listen to me. My interrogators just left. They'll give me time to recover to keep me alive. Then they'll begin again. Before they took my eyes, I saw an open window in this room. Every ten minutes, a Jem'Hadar sentry passes and checks on me. One is almost due. If you kill me as soon as he passes, you'll have ten minutes to escape before the next sentry sounds the alarm.

Tears sprang to Lwaxana's eyes. Okalan must have sensed her anguish.

Lwaxana . . . don't make me beg you.

Lwaxana turned to Enaren. He had sensed much from hearing her side of the conversation, but when she told him Okalan's request, the blood drained from his ruddy face. His lips trembled for a moment, then he squared his shoulders and met Lwaxana's gaze. *He's right. We have no choice.*

Steeling herself, Lwaxana held out her hand to the *cavat* farmer. *Give me your blow gun.*

Enaren pushed her hand aside and removed his own weapon. *Okalan's my oldest friend. I'll do it.*

Before Lwaxana could protest, Enaren slipped through the underbrush toward the clearing. In what seemed only seconds, Lwaxana felt Okalan's gratitude and relief that his old friend was ending his life, his pain, and any chance that he might break and betray those he loved.

Okalan welcomed death the way he'd lived, fearlessly, bravely, and with dignity. Wrenching sadness at the loss of a good man tore Lwaxana's heart. Okalan's thoughts slowed, emotions dimmed, then ceased for all eternity.

It's done. Enaren's grief at the loss of his friend and his rage at the Jem'Hadar were palpable.

Let's get back, Lwaxana ordered when Enaren reappeared, tears streaming down his aged cheeks. To herself she thought, *We have a vigil to hold for a dying child.*

Chapter Eight

AS THE TRANSPORTER EFFECT TOOK THEM, Deanna felt certain that the *Defiant* was shaking under weapons fire. But when she solidified on the planet's surface, she stood intact with the other members of her team in a field of *cavat* that towered high above their heads.

Before anyone could move, Vaughn spoke quietly. "Jem'Hadar patrol. Four of them on the road about one hundred meters ahead."

Deanna heard the heavy boots of the Jem'Hadar tromping closer on the adjacent road. At the ominous rumble, her muscles tensed and her mouth went dry. Above her, high thin clouds rippled across the scarlet sky, and the morning sun hung low and bright on the horizon. A hawk wheeled overhead, and close by, the melodic trill of a songbird provided an ironic counterpoint to the sinister tread of the approaching enemy patrol.

"Act natural," Vaughn ordered the away team in a soft voice.

"Respectfully, sir," Data said with a puzzled frown, "how does one act naturally in a *cavat* field?"

"First, don't call me *sir*," Vaughn responded quietly. "Then try picking *cavat*."

Deanna forced a smile and reached for the nearest ear of *cavat,* a Betazed staple comparable to Terran corn, and tried to ignore the trembling of her hands. Her previous encounters with Jem'Hadar had been at a distance in ship-to-ship fighting. She expected her first face-to-face meeting to be intimidating, to say the least.

Data shrugged, then gamely grabbed a ripened ear, wrenched it easily from the stalk, and glanced around. "We need a container."

Deanna unwound her wide scarf and held it in front of her. "Will this do?"

"You are very resourceful." Data dropped the *cavat* into the scarf and reached for another ear.

"When I was a little girl," Beverly said in a bright and animated tone with only a slight quaver of nervousness, "my grandmother had a huge garden. One of the high points of the year was the first ripened corn. Grandma Howard would start water boiling on the stove, and I would pick the corn and rush it straight inside to the waiting pot. That hot corn dripping with fresh butter was the sweetest thing I've ever tasted."

"As good as chocolate?" Deanna asked in disbelief.

"Uh-huh," Beverly said, "but in a different way."

"Good," Vaughn murmured, "keep up the chatter." Then louder he added, "We should take some *cavat* back to the city for lunch. As hungry as I am, I don't know if we can carry enough." Vaughn's deep, hearty laugh echoed through the field and sent the nearby songbird into flight, squawking in protest. The others—even Data, who had engaged his emotion chip in order to blend in more easily—joined in the laughter.

Maintaining a patter of meaningless small talk, the team quickly gathered two dozen ears and secured them in Deanna's makeshift sack. Data swung the heavy bundle easily onto his back.

"Let's head for the road," Vaughn ordered quietly. "We'll seem less suspicious if we show ourselves to the patrol. Deanna, if they stop us, you do the talking. You're more familiar with the planet than the rest of us. But everyone remain alert. If they give us trouble, we'll have to take them out."

Take them out?

The idea of hand-to-hand combat with the Jem'Hadar wiped Deanna's mind suddenly blank, and she could recall nothing Vaughn had taught her. She could only hope that he'd drilled her so thoroughly, she would react immediately and instinctively if the time came.

The group made their way along one of the furrows, their boots gouging the earth and filling the air with the pungent scent of rich loam. In the peaceful natural setting, Deanna would have found the interstellar war raging in the heavens around them hard to believe if she hadn't been a veteran of so many conflicts.

Searching the skies, she prayed she'd been wrong in suspecting the *Defiant* had come under attack. The Daronan atmosphere had revealed no evidence of a conflict—no massive explosions, no trails of smoking debris, but that meant nothing.

With Deanna in the lead, the away team stepped from the field onto the hard-surfaced road. None of them glanced toward the Jem'Hadar patrol fast approaching from the east. With luck, Deanna thought, her team could continue west toward Jarkana without drawing attention. A group of farmers, clustered around a wagon drawn by sturdy Daronan oxen, trudged ahead of her. If she and the rest of the team hurried, they could blend in with the crowd.

"Halt!" a harsh voice behind them ordered.

Deanna stopped and turned. Beverly paused on one side of her, Data and Vaughn on the other. Deanna caught sight of the commander and blinked in surprise. If she hadn't known better, she would have sworn Vaughn was a changeling. The tall officer had shrunk inside his coat, seemingly losing inches in height, his posture suddenly projecting only feeble harmlessness.

She had little time to appreciate Vaughn's metamorphosis before she found herself almost toe-to-toe with the Jem'Hadar leader. The members of his patrol, weapons drawn and aimed at the away team, waited a few feet away.

"What are you doing here?" the patrol leader demanded.

"Picking *cavat.*" At Deanna's first up-close confrontation with a Jem'Hadar, she was struck foremost by the immensity of the soldier, and next by the fierceness of his appearance. His cobbled skin, pierced with protruding bones like rows of teeth, reminded her of pebbles on a rocky beach. With his ashen complexion, gray uniform, and huge size, she figured fighting a real Jem'Hadar would seem the equivalent of attacking a small mountain.

His emotions and those of his group bombarded her, and the soldiers made no attempt to hide them. She sensed dedication to the Founders, contempt for their foes, and an eagerness for combat. She hoped she could defuse the last.

"The *cavat* in this field is harvested by machines," the Jem'Hadar leader said with suspicion. "You don't belong here. Present your ID chips."

Deanna's mind whirled. If she couldn't come up with a convincing explanation, her team would have to fight its way out. Vaughn might be able take down one of the soldiers, if he could reach one before being shot, and Data with his superhuman strength could probably handle two, but she wasn't convinced she and Beverly together could disable the fourth without their weapons.

Estimating how long she would need to retrieve the phaser concealed under her coat, Deanna pointed to Vaughn, who was staring at his feet. "See my senile father there?" She shifted her attention to Data. "And my brainless brother? If we had brought our IDs with us, they would have lost theirs. My sister," she nodded to Beverly, "and I do well just to keep up with these two simpletons, much less keep track of bureaucratic red tape. If you wish to follow us into the city, however, I'll retrieve our credentials from our home."

The patrol leader frowned but held his fire. Perhaps he saw no glory for the Founders in vaporizing two dullards and a couple of women, although Deanna sensed his willingness to kill them all where they stood.

"What's in the bundle?" He pointed to Data's back.

With the back of her hand, Deanna whacked Data in the ribs and swallowed a grunt of pain at the impact of her hand against his bioplast sheeting. "Hey, idiot. Show this soldier our *cavat*."

Falling easily into his simpleton role, Data set the bundle on the road and with irritating slowness, untied the scarf. With the knot free, *cavat* rolled in every direction.

"Now see what you've done," Deanna yelled and cuffed Data on his ear. "You've bruised it, and it won't be fit to eat."

Another of the Jem'Hadar approached and poked at the *cavat* with his rifle. Apparently convinced the vegetable was what it appeared to be, he moved back into his position with the patrol.

"Where do you live in the city?" the leader demanded.

"Near the prison," Deanna said. "My family and I work as domestics in Director Lanolan's home and on the grounds."

She held her breath, wondering if it would be her last or if their charade as a dysfunctional family had convinced the Jem'Hadar they were harmless.

"Next time you venture out," the Jem'Hadar said with a snarl, "have your ID chips, or we won't hesitate to shoot you."

"Yes, sir," Deanna said meekly. "Thank you, sir. May we go? We want to catch up with our friends." She motioned to the farmers who had moved quickly ahead on the Jarkana road.

The patrol leader waved them forward. With uncharacteristic clumsiness, Data rebundled the *cavat* and slung it on his back. Beverly offered Vaughn the support of her arm, and the away team started toward Jarkana as fast as Vaughn's limping old-man pace would allow. The Jem'Hadar patrol pivoted and headed in the opposite direction into the countryside.

"Nice work, Deanna," Vaughn said.

"Thanks. I'm sorry, Data, that I had to hit you."

"The blow was very convincing," Data said, "but it did not hurt me. I am certain, however, the same cannot be said for you."

Deanna gingerly massaged her bruised hand. "You give a whole new meaning to the term *thick-skinned.*"

Beverly flashed her a grin. "You're quite an actor."

Data nodded in agreement. "Once this war is ended, you must participate more often in our dramatic presentations. You would make a fine Kate in *The Taming of the Shrew.*"

Once this war is ended . . .

Deanna wondered how many of them would live to see that day—or if they would want to if the Jem'Hadar continued to hammer the Federation. She had just experienced a small but extremely unpleasant taste of what living under Dominion rule would be like.

Once the patrol had disappeared, Vaughn straightened and picked up his pace. Soon the away team caught up with the band of farmers headed for market and trailed in their wake. Even at a quick walk, Deanna had time to study the countryside. Much was as she remembered from seventeen years earlier, but here and there among Darona's rolling fields and efficient farms were blackened swaths of scorched earth where a crop had been burned or a building destroyed, ugly reminders of the Dominion occupation.

If Darona, with only a small garrison of Jem'Hadar, was this scarred, she thought with a sinking heart, what had fifty thousand Jem'Hadar done to Betazed?

Emotions from the group of farmers drifted back to her, with fear the most prevalent, especially in the younger children who had not yet developed the capacity to shield their feelings. Although a few adults laughed and joked among themselves, Deanna sensed their efforts at making the best of a terrifying situation.

Upon nearing the city, both vehicle and foot traffic slowed, and the away team found itself detained at the end of a long line.

"Traffic jam?" Beverly asked.

Data rose on tiptoe to see over the crowd ahead of him. "It is a checkpoint. A Vorta is supervising a group of soldiers searching those entering the city."

A sudden stillness descended on the crowd.

"No, please," a man's voice cried out. "It's my fault. Don't—"

Weapons fire flashed ahead of them. The crowd stifled a collective gasp, and the group's horror and revulsion enveloped Deanna like a choking cloud.

"What happened?" Beverly asked.

Deanna couldn't speak. She'd felt exactly what had transpired, and the horror of it threatened to overwhelm her.

Data, who had been studying the scene intently, reported, "They discovered a weapon on the farmer. The Jem'Hadar shot his entire family."

"Deanna?" Vaughn said quietly. "Are you all right?"

Deanna fought back tears and nodded. "Just give me a second." *Breathe. Get past it. Now isn't the time . . .*

"Are they searching everyone?" Vaughn asked Data.

Data nodded. "It appears so."

Vaughn turned back to Deanna. "Is there another way into the city?" Inside their coats, they each carried a phaser rifle. In addition, Data concealed a tricorder and Beverly her medical equipment.

Deanna swallowed and pointed to their left to a rough track winding uphill between tall bushes. "That footpath will take us to the director's house. It circles the city to the prison on the other side."

Vaughn nodded. "Then we'll use the footpath. Lead the way, Commander."

The team moved away from the crowd and started up the narrow track of hard-packed red clay that ran behind the extensive gardens of houses on the eastern edge of the city. They had traveled only a short distance when a familiar voice called out behind them.

"Halt!"

Deanna turned to see the Jem'Hadar patrol they had encountered earlier bearing down on them. Beside her, Vaughn shrank back into his old man guise. Beverly took Vaughn's arm as if holding him upright, and Data set the bundle of *cavat* at his feet. Outwardly, her friends appeared both calm and puzzled at the Jem'Hadar approach, but Deanna sensed their coiled readiness to strike in an instant.

"Why are you avoiding the checkpoint?" the patrol leader demanded.

"We're avoiding nothing," Deanna said. "This path

leads to Director Lanolan's house and our home. Besides, my father's mind is failing. The noises of the city frighten him, so we take this route instead of passing through all the hubbub and traffic."

The Jem'Hadar leader motioned them onward. "We'll follow you. When you reach the director's house, we'll determine if you are who you say."

"Who else would we be?" Data, resuming his simpleton role with ease, asked in a puzzled and childish tone.

"Shut up, you idiot!" Deanna snapped. "Just pick up the *cavat* and get moving. We're already late."

With an exaggerated sigh, Data grabbed the bundle. Deanna shoved him ahead of her on the path, and Beverly, aiding Vaughn's faltering steps, brought up the rear. The patrol followed, and Deanna could feel their eyes boring into her back, could read the suspicion in their thoughts. She hoped Lanolan or his wife would be at home to welcome them, or her team would end up battling the Jem'Hadar patrol.

She had forgotten how long, steep, and winding the footpath circling the city was, and their journey to Lanolan's home seemed to take an eternity. Playing on his feigned infirmity, Vaughn stumbled several times, but not long enough to slow their progress. None of them wished to push the Jem'Hadar's patience to the breaking point, because the narrow path offered no room for maneuvering if fighting broke out.

With relief, Deanna spotted the side track that split away from the main path and connected with the prison. She led the way down the steep slope toward the broad avenue and Lanolan's house. Beverly and

Vaughn tottered behind her, and Data placed himself at the rear of the group, a comforting shield between them and the Jem'Hadar.

A sweeping glance indicated the neighborhood and the prison on the hill behind the director's house remained undamaged by Darona's occupation force, but intact buildings didn't guarantee their occupants had survived. For the first time, Deanna wondered whether the Jem'Hadar had killed the inmates and if Tevren was still alive. Executing the Betazoid prisoners would have freed the maximum security facility for any prisoners of war the invaders wished to retain. Tevren's death would resolve her moral reservations about this mission, but without his help, what hope did the resistance have?

The Jem'Hadar remained hard on their heels when Deanna and her team turned onto the curving brick walk leading to Director Lanolan's front door. They climbed the broad stairs to the porch, and Deanna signaled their arrival at the entryway. The Jem'Hadar, weapons at the ready, waited at the foot of the steps.

The wide paneled door swung open, and an unfamiliar scrawny woman with a topknot of gray curls confronted them, her fists planted firmly on her skinny hips, her expression belligerent. Deanna could sense the housekeeper's fear. She saw the terror in the woman's eyes when she'd spotted their Jem'Hadar escort.

Before the woman could say anything that would blow their cover, Troi said, "Sorry we're late." And at the same time, she sent a quick thought into the woman's mind: *My name's Deanna Troi. Please, I need to see Director Lanolan.*

The woman still looked terrified, but defiant. "You must have the wrong house."

Before Deanna could utter a reply, the door slammed in her face, leaving the away team stranded on the porch with the Jem'Hadar blocking their retreat.

Chapter Nine

"BATTLE STATIONS."

Picard leaned forward in the center seat, his face set in concentration. The *Enterprise,* accompanied by the starships *Tulwar, Katana,* and *Scimitar,* sped through space toward the Betazed system at maximum warp to confront the superior Dominion force guarding Betazed and Sentok Nor.

"Picking up six Cardassian *Galor*-class cruisers and four Jem'Hadar attack ships," said Hernandez, the young ensign who had replaced Data at ops.

"Any sign of Dominion battle cruisers?" Picard asked.

"Two on long-range sensors, Captain."

"Damn," Picard muttered. He had hoped to pierce the station's defenses and leave the area before the battle cruisers arrived. The *Enterprise*'s mission, to drop shields in the middle of a battle in order to insert Riker's team and then retrieve them from the space station, would be difficult enough without having to contend with additional enemy ships.

"Slow to warp six," Picard ordered.

The sensors of the enemy fleet and Sentok Nor would pick up the Starfleet warp signatures, but he was counting on the Dominion not to expect the tiny contingent to drop out of warp right on top of the larger enemy force. The captain intended to preserve their element of surprise, but he also wanted to give navigation the best chance to leave warp in a superior tactical position.

"A ship is lifting off Betazed on course for Sentok Nor," Lieutenant Daniels at tactical announced.

"Identify," Picard ordered.

"It's a Cardassian freighter."

Picard relaxed. With minimum armament, one freighter would cause no problem.

"Our escorts?" Picard asked.

"In attack formation, sir."

The Saber-class vessels usually served as fast perimeter-defense ships in border regions. Presently guarding the *Enterprise*'s flanks, the light cruisers had already proved their worth in extensive action on several fronts. Their captains and crews would take full advantage of their agile vessels' maneuverability, which had repeatedly allowed them to hold their own against much larger opponents in hostile frontier regions.

The compact ships, with their crews of forty, saved weight and space through their internal nacelle configurations. The design feature made the vessels faster but also more vulnerable to full armor penetration and core breaches. Like a boxer who dances to avoid punches, the light cruisers had to keep moving to prevent a total knockout.

"Away team standing by to transport," Riker's voice reported from Transporter Room 2.

"Understood, Number One. Good luck." Picard turned to tactical. "Arm and target quantum torpedoes." He had waited until the last instant, not wanting the enemy to sense the *Enterprise* was powering up weapons until too late for them to react.

"Targeting," Daniels announced.

The captain tugged at his uniform, and the familiar gesture steadied him. "Helm?"

"Seven seconds to Betazed."

"Prepare to drop out of warp on my mark." Picard directed his order simultaneously to the Saber-class ships. "Two, one, mark."

The *Enterprise* entered normal space at full impulse. In the distance floated the massive hulk of Sentok Nor, its arching pylons and central cylinder dominating the sky over the planet. Two alert *Galor*-class attack cruisers raised shields. Seven others had yet to react.

"Fire quantum torpedoes."

"Torpedoes away, sir."

"Raise shields."

The Saber-class ships opened fire at the same time. Picard held his breath, praying their surprise tactic would work. On the viewscreen, streaks of light tracked the weapons to their targets.

At such proximity, the first barrage took only seconds to impact, and the lead Cardassian ship collapsed inward, wheeled into her sister ship, then exploded in an incendiary burst that lit the jet-black sky and destroyed the second ship along with it. A Jem'Hadar attack ship sustained hull damage but returned fire before the *Katana* finished her off.

The *Enterprise* shook from the impact of a Cardassian spiral wave disruptor.

"Shields at eighty percent."

"Damage?" Picard asked.

"A minor fire on Deck Three. We already have it under control. Sir, I'm picking up an energy spike from the *Katana*—"

Ahead to port on the viewscreen, Picard saw the *Katana*'s starboard nacelle explode, the blast ripping through the entire ship. *Forty good men and women lost in a heartbeat,* Picard thought sadly. But there wasn't time to mourn them.

"Ahead, three-quarter impulse."

Ensign Kell Perim, the Trill at conn, looked nervously at the viewscreen and the five Dominion ships between them and Sentok Nor, but she laid in the course without hesitation.

Picard reviewed his tactics. *Scimitar* and *Tulwar* would continue to draw enemy fire so the *Enterprise* could drop shields and transport Riker's team onto the station. The Dominion still had nine ships and the space station's armaments to oppose the smaller Federation force.

Protecting each other's flanks, the remaining four *Galor*-class cruisers closed in battle formation and bore down on the Federation ships. The enemy vessels advanced as a unit, the lead ship firing on the *Enterprise*.

The science console sparked as Daniels called out, "Shields down to fifty percent."

"Target their engines and weapons," Picard ordered.

At the tactical station, the lieutenant, trembling with adrenaline, his face tight with excitement, held his voice steady. "I have a weapons lock."

"Fire phasers!"

Phaser fire ripped into the closing enemy vessels and inflicted damage, but not enough to slow their approach. Picard left the oncoming enemy to his Saber-class escorts and turned his attention to the space station.

"Tactical, prepare phasers to target the station's shield generators."

"Pulse modulated to Chief O'Brien's specifications, sir."

"Concentrate phaser fire on Section 17 of the outer docking ring." The moment the words left his mouth, Picard wanted to recall them. Daniels knew the battle plan, and Picard wouldn't have repeated it with a more familiar officer—Worf, say—at the station. The last thing he wanted was to add to the nervous tension on the bridge.

"Fire!" Picard ordered.

Phaser beams lanced toward the station, only to be dispersed and absorbed by the shield envelope that glittered silver-green against the bombardment.

"We're coming into transporter range," Perim reported, sweat dripping down her face.

"Transporter room, stand by," Picard ordered. "Mr. Daniels, don't let up. I want those shields down."

The lieutenant at tactical shook his head. "Sir, the modulated pulse isn't penetrating the station's shields."

Picard tapped his combadge. "Number One, patch Mr. O'Brien into tactical. We have a problem."

Picard had planned a quick strike. Nothing fancy. No complicated battle plan—just quickly transporting the away team onto the station, then distracting the enemy long enough for Riker to do his job. A prolonged fire-fight with a superior force had never been part of the scheme.

From the transporter room, O'Brien gave orders to Daniels. *"Try remodulating the phase frequency like so . . ."*

Deep Space 9's chief of operations routed the data to the bridge's tactical station. Daniels recalibrated, his hands flying over his console.

"Fire," Picard ordered.

Again the station merely glimmered under the blasts. The shields held.

"It's not working," Daniels said, stating the obvious.

"Keep remodulating the frequency along its present curve," O'Brien said with calm confidence. *"Eventually you'll find the right one."*

Picard swore under his breath. The *Tulwar* and *Scimitar,* in spite of brilliantly executed evasive maneuvers, were taking heavy fire. The small cruisers couldn't hold off the Dominion forces much longer.

Again the *Enterprise* was strafed by Jem'Hadar phased polaron beams. The lights on the bridge dimmed, the auxiliary power kicked in.

"Damage on Decks Four, Eleven, and Twelve," Daniels said. "Shields down to twenty percent."

Picard realized they couldn't win this battle. With the station shields holding, the task force would have to withdraw, rethink their strategy for boarding Sentok Nor, and return to try again.

"Evasive maneuvers. Continue to target weapons arrays and fire at will. Keep us within transporter range." Picard hoped to buy time for the light cruisers to retreat with him. The helm responded sluggishly into a ninety-degree turn.

Immediately, collision alarms blared throughout the ship. Picard leaped to his feet and stared at the viewscreen.

Two Jem'Hadar battle cruisers appeared in their path, blocking their retreat.

Without bothering to announce himself, Gul Lemec stormed into Luaran's office on Sentok Nor. "The resistance is up to something."

The Vorta's mouth twitched in annoyance. "You're making too much of one prisoner's death."

Lemec spoke through gritted teeth. "I hadn't finished interrogating him." The gul slammed a primitive blow dart onto Luaran's desk. "This weapon killed him before he talked. I'm telling you, there's a conspiracy among the Betazoids. They're all supporting the resistance. We must crack down."

"Thus far, what you call cracking down has only produced more resistance," Luaran noted.

Lemec opened his mouth to protest, but a glinn marched through Luaran's open door. "We've gone to battle alert, sir."

"Status?" Lemec asked.

"Sensors have picked up four Federation warp signatures in this sector."

Alarms sounded. The gul followed the glinn from Luaran's office down to Level One, the command center of the station. In the sunken interface system which his men had nicknamed "the pit," Cardassians monitored every function on the station from engineering to ketracel-white processing, if the blasted Betazoid-assembled equipment was functioning as it should.

Lemec's gaze focused on the large display screen over the pit where the Federation warp signatures presented green trails of light. Dominion forces were yellow, outnumbering the enemy almost three to one, if he counted the approaching Jem'Hadar battle cruisers.

"Enemy ships are dropping out of warp," the glinn announced in surprise.

"Raise shields," Lemec ordered.

"Shields up, sir, but the station's weapons are still off-line."

The Vorta had followed them to the operations center and stared at the screen. "Are we in danger?"

Lemec shook his head. "With twelve ships, even without the defensive capabilities of Sentok Nor, we are the superior force. They have four lone ships."

"The Founders will not be pleased if our work is interrupted," the Vorta said, her voice trembling. The gul didn't respond, and she pressed him. "You don't anticipate a problem?"

"Nothing our forces can't handle."

The Federation ships blasted out of warp, opening fire at once. Within moments, two Cardassian cruisers and a Jem'Hadar attack ship were destroyed in a spectacular display of fire.

"The odds in our favor have suddenly decreased," the Vorta noted with irony.

"What's going on?" Dr. Moset asked as he strolled

into the operations center. "Why have our ships been destroyed?"

Civilians didn't belong in the middle of the war, and the gul would have been happy to send the doctor packing. Moset had been nothing but a first-class pain in the neckbones since he'd arrived on the station. Out of habit, Lemec held back his dislike. "I suppose you think I should have anticipated the Federation's desperate attack?"

"You should have anticipated my needs," Moset complained. "We have a freighter of Betazoids arriving. This interference is most inconvenient."

The gul's gaze zoomed in on Betazed and the unscheduled freighter approaching the station. "Order the freighter to turn back."

"Let the ship come." Luaran belayed his order. "According to the Founders' orders, Moset must have those prisoners."

Lemec shook his head. "That freighter doesn't have the embedded ID codes needed to enter the station during combat conditions."

"You're saying you've raised the shields?" Moset's voice ascended an octave. "That they can't dock?"

"Neither can the Federation." Lemec held his temper and settled for sarcasm. "If we lower the shields, Starfleet might decide to drop in for a visit."

Moset rolled his eyes at the ceiling. "You're obsessed with the Federation. I hardly think—"

"Federation forces just destroyed another Jem'Hadar attack ship," Luaran interrupted.

"Get those weapons back on-line," Lemec ordered. "Now!"

"No," Moset protested. "I won't have power diverted from my experiments."

"Your experiments are the reason our weapons are down," Lemec informed Moset. The Dominion and Cardassian forces still had an obvious advantage, so he took his attention from the screen to rebuke the doctor. "If you hadn't insisted that my engineers set up your equipment instead of completing the weapons repair and upgrade, we'd have the ability to defend ourselves."

"They are firing phasers at the outer docking ring," the glinn at tactical reported. "I've brought one phaser bank on-line. Shall I return fire?"

"No," Moset shouted and pointed to the screen and the slow-moving ship from Betazed. "If you fire, you might damage the freighter."

Lemec glowered at the doctor but enjoyed having the upper hand. Ever since they'd arrived at Sentok Nor, the civilian exobiologist had lorded his position over the gul. He'd used his influence with the Vorta and, as a result, weakened the station's defensive capabilities. Due to Moset's interference, the gul had problems on the station, and problems on the planet. Lemec grew thoughtful. He'd just returned from a visit to Betazed, where the natives had had the nerve to exterminate one of their own, right beneath his nose. Then the Federation dropped out of warp to do battle. A good leader had to ask if there was a connection between the incidents.

Unfortunately, Lemec didn't have enough information to draw a conclusion. He was in charge of tactics, however, and he would demonstrate the unimportance of Moset's wishes during a Federation attack. "That freighter is carrying Betazoids and a few Jem'Hadar. They're expendable. Target phasers."

"Phasers targeted," said his tactical officer.

"No. Please, don't shoot," Moset practically begged, and Lemec took pleasure in every squeal of protest. "A little phaser fire won't damage the station. I'm at a sensitive stage in my work and need those prisoners right away. I don't have time to wait for you to round up another group."

"Is there any way to accommodate the doctor?" the Vorta asked.

"Not without compromising the safety of this station," Lemec replied.

Moset's eyes flared with rage. Not bothering to hide his satisfaction, Lemec turned to tactical. "Fi—"

Moset shoved Lemec aside and launched himself over the console. Before Lemec could react, the doctor slapped the control panel. The station's shields dropped.

In moments, the two Jem'Hadar battle cruisers would fire phased polaron beams at the *Enterprise*'s weakened shields. From aft, two of the Cardassian cruisers recharged their spiral wave disruptors. With shields down to twenty percent, Captain Picard considered his limited maneuvering options, knowing his decision could mean the difference between escape and destruction.

"Captain, the station shields. They just came down."

Excellent. This might be his only chance to beam the away team onto the station, but with enemy vessels bearing down on them, there was only one way he could think of to make it work. However, taking advantage of the situation would risk his ship and his crew.

Picard didn't like to gamble with the lives of his people, but sometimes a shot at success was worth the risk—especially when the freedom of every Betazoid on the planet was at stake. He weighed the risks against the peril and made his decision.

The captain tapped his combadge. "Away team, stand by to transport. Tactical, prepare to lower shields."

"Sir?" Daniels wiped perspiration from his eyes with his sleeve.

"You heard me, Lieutenant. Stand by for my command and open a hailing frequency." The captain straightened his uniform and ignored the looks his bridge crew exchanged out of sight of the enemy. "This is Captain Jean-Luc Picard of the Federation *Starship Enterprise.* I'm afraid you have us at a disadvantage."

"Jem'Hadar are responding, sir."

"On screen," Picard ordered.

A thick-skulled Jem'Hadar First stared at Picard from the viewscreen. *"Prepare to die."*

"I'm prepared to surrender." Picard ignored the gasps from around him.

"We don't take prisoners." The Jem'Hadar raised his hand to cut off communications.

Picard spoke quickly. "This is the Federation flagship. Much of its technology is still highly classified. This would be the Dominion's first opportunity to examine a Sovereign-class vessel, as well as study its tactical databases. As a show of good faith, I'm dropping our shields."

Picard motioned to tactical. Daniels might not agree

with the risk his captain was taking, but discipline and training prevailed. Daniels lowered the *Enterprise*'s shields, leaving them completely vulnerable to attack. Picard continued with what he hoped seemed a careless disregard for his betrayal of the Federation. "Why don't you consult with your superior officer and get back to me about terms for our surrender?"

He was betting that the Jem'Hadar didn't have a Vorta on board. If the Dominion crew had to send a message and wait for further orders, Picard might buy enough time to transport the away team onto the station while his ship's shields were down.

Picard signaled Daniels to end transmission, and the viewscreen went blank. "Transporter room, energize!"

"Transport initiated, sir," came the reply. *"They're in."*

On Sentok Nor, Gul Lemec regained his footing in the operations center. He couldn't believe the cretin Moset had dared to lay a hand on a gul. Even worse, the fool had lowered the station's shields, putting all their lives at risk.

Raising his fist, Lemec fully intended to put a stop to the doctor's interference, but Luaran stepped in front of Moset. "Save your wrath for the enemy. There will be no fighting among ourselves."

"Just lots of dying if we don't raise our shields," Lemec shouted.

Luaran raised her eyes to the screen. "In a moment the freighter will have docked, and the station's shields can be raised again."

"Feel free to wait. In another moment we'll be blasted out of the sky." Enraged, Lemec rounded the console, fully intending to raise the station's screens and defy Luaran's wishes. With so many Cardassian lives at stake, Central Command would back his decision.

"Look." Luaran pointed to the viewscreen. "Our ships have the lead Federation starship trapped. We are about to finish her off. There's no need to waste the prisoners. Our enemy's shields are down."

Lemec's battle instincts rebelled against leaving the station's defensive shields lowered with an enemy so close—even a seemingly defeated enemy. He peered at the sensors, but spied nothing suspicious.

His communications officer glanced up with a confused look. "Sir, the Jem'Hadar say the Federation *Sovereign*-class starship is offering to surrender the ship and crew."

"Blast them out of space," Lemec ordered without hesitation.

"Absolutely not," Luaran countered. "Don't you recognize that ship? It's the *Enterprise*. Capturing her would be a huge coup for us and a demoralizing defeat for Starfleet."

"It's a trick."

"Really?" Luaran shook her head. "Do long-range sensors indicate a fleet of Federation ships ready to sweep down on us?"

"No, but—"

"Didn't you tell me our ships outnumbered them?"

"Yes, but—"

"Don't we have superior firepower?"

"Yes, but—"

"Tell them we accept—"

Alarms suddenly rang out.

"Status?" the gul asked.

"We're picking up a transporter signal."

"Shields up," he snapped.

Since his precious freighter had already docked, Moset didn't protest.

"It's too late, sir," the science officer explained. "They've already beamed aboard."

"Raise shields, Mr. Daniels, and fire at will," Picard barked. "Perim, evasive maneuvers!"

As the battle was joined again following the successful insertion of Riker's away team, Picard spared a moment to admire how well his crew had performed thus far. With the Federation forces stretched so thin, Picard had bargained with Starfleet to keep his senior officers by offering his lower-ranking crewmen to other ships. Now with most of his experienced officers on away missions, he'd been forced into battle primarily with wet-behind-the-ears ensigns and newly graduated Starfleet cadets. The situation aboard the *Scimitar* and *Tulwar* was no better. Under the leadership of experienced captains, personnel aboard the Saber-class ships were mostly rookies, too. In wartime, the neophytes would learn quickly or they wouldn't survive. The manner in which the inexperienced crew had conducted themselves up to now made hope surge within him. Under the most difficult of circumstances, they had obeyed orders, risking their lives without question.

Picard's initial gamble of surrendering to the Jem'Hadar had paid off, but greater challenges lay ahead.

Within the tactical inset on the viewscreen, Picard saw

that the *Scimitar* and *Tulwar* had broken formation and were each savagely strafing a Cardassian cruiser with concentrated bursts of phaser fire off the stern of the *Enterprise.*

Softening them up, Picard realized. If he acted quickly—

"Lock aft torpedo launchers," the captain snapped. "Full spread. Fire!"

As the Saber-class vessels veered away, pinpoints of red destruction fanned out from ports on the *Enterprise*'s stern, catching the overwhelmed Cardassian cruisers across the bows. One of the enemy ships erupted in a burst of light and debris. The other listed to starboard as small explosions ruptured the hull along its port side.

There was no time to savor the victory; the *Enterprise* shook again under enemy fire.

"Shields at fifteen percent, sir," Daniels called out. "Jem'Hadar ships are moving to intercept. Captain, I think they intend to ram us."

That won't do. Picard studied the tactical inset, then glanced at the chronometer. It was going to be close.

"Stay on course," Picard ordered. "Increase speed. Maximum impulse."

Perim glanced over her shoulder. "Sir, the Jem'Hadar ships—"

"Follow my orders, Ensign," Picard said calmly. "Full impulse."

"Aye, aye, sir." Picard could hear the tremor in Perim's voice, but was pleased to see her hands move quickly to execute his order. And as she did, the first of the Jem'Hadar warships swept toward them.

Chapter Ten

RIKER, LA FORGE, O'BRIEN, and a security detail of six beamed into an access tunnel of Sentok Nor's upper core near a panel that, the chief was certain, opened into the station's security office. Calling on the vast knowledge of Cardassian technology he'd gained on Deep Space 9, O'Brien had selected the insertion point. Like those of its sister station, Sentok Nor's eighteen-plus kilometers of access tunnels were effectively shielded not only from electromagnetic interference, but also, and more importantly for this mission, from active scanning beams.

"Unless Cardassian sensors have improved significantly," O'Brien said, "the station's security force will have a hell of a time finding us, especially if we keep moving."

"They know we're here," Riker said. "Sensors in ops will have picked up our transporter signals. We have to assume Cardassian and Jem'Hadar security teams are scouring every nook and cranny trying to locate us, so stay alert."

O'Brien craned his neck, taking his bearings. "Let's hope the resistance has drawn all the Jem'Hadar to the planet."

"Yeah," La Forge said with irony, "so that leaves only about fifty Cardassian engineers and who knows how many of their soldiers to slow us down."

"Our first objective is crucial," Riker reminded them. "Once we take control of the security office, we can shut down every system on the station—"

"Environmental, communications, engineering, and tactical," O'Brien said with a grin. "What more could a man want?"

Riker allowed his team a few moments to adjust to the warm, dry conditions with the slightly higher concentration of carbon dioxide in the atmosphere mixed for Cardassian comfort. In the cramped tunnel, where a cross-section measured a mere one-point-three meters by one-point-four meters, La Forge snapped on a light, and the toranium frames and duranium panels gleamed dully around them.

"Ready?" Riker asked O'Brien.

"Ready, sir." With efficiency and speed even in such tight quarters, O'Brien set up a portable force field generator to create an invisible wall blocking off an area eight meters in diameter and four meters high. The force field secured their portion of the tunnel and extended into the adjoining security office, preventing Cardassian reinforcements from pouring into the office and grabbing the away team as they exited one by one from the tunnel. Their Starfleet combadges contained receivers keyed to the force field generator, so they could move freely in or out of the field. Anyone else would be trapped either inside or outside the force field. Riker doubted, however, that they'd be lucky enough to find the security section unguarded.

"Commander," La Forge whispered, "the access panel into the security office is directly behind me." He wiggled into position in the cramped space, removed a device from his belt, then pressed it against the panel.

Riker motioned for half the security detail and O'Brien to retreat down the access tube and around a corner, just in case armed resistance awaited them on the other side.

La Forge slowly popped open the panel. Those around Riker held their breaths. An angry squad of Cardassians could be trapped inside the force field with them, waiting on the other side of that panel. Or Riker's group might find no one in the office at all. The team members would be most vulnerable during their exit from the tunnel, since the small opening forced them to enter the office one at a time.

His phaser set on stun, Riker took the point, diving and rolling through the panel's opening into the tiny office and surprising two armed Cardassians. The soldiers fired, but Riker kept moving, and the weapons blasted holes in the spot he'd just vacated, fortunately nowhere close to where the rest of his team waited.

Smoke from the burning metal stung Riker's nostrils. Adrenaline surged into his system and added power to his movements. His diving lunge knocked one of the thick-necked Cardassians off his feet and awkwardly tumbled him to the deck, giving Riker time to confront the second man. From the office floor, Riker side-kicked his foe's wrist, sweeping the Cardassian's phase disruptor rifle to the floor with a loud clatter.

The Cardassian sprang for the rifle.

Riker knocked it across the room. The Cardassian's hands came up empty, and he swore and turned his fury on Riker. The soldier charged, his large hands grasping for Riker's throat. Riker shifted and rammed an elbow into his opponent's jaw, heard it crunch as bones broke. The commander followed up with a damaging knee to the groin.

With a soft gurgle, the Cardassian collapsed, and his unconscious weight pinned Riker to the deck. Shoving the fallen man aside, Riker started to level his phaser at the other Cardassian, but his foe had regained his feet. He loomed over Riker, his weapon aimed, ready to fire.

"Don't move," La Forge ordered, his phaser pointed at the Cardassian's chest.

The Cardassian froze in surprise. Riker shoved to his feet, careful not to block La Forge's aim. "Thanks for the assist."

"I wasn't going to let you have all the fun," La Forge replied, never taking the focus of his ocular implants off the Cardassian. "Drop your weapon."

The Cardassian's finger flexed. La Forge reacted faster and fired his phaser. The second Cardassian hit the deck with a thud, and the engineer shook his head. "They never learn when to give up."

Riker wondered briefly how the *Enterprise* was far-ing. He had limitless faith in Captain Picard, but they'd transported away from a tactical nightmare—one Picard had deliberately taken the ship into so Riker's team could insert.

Then there was Deanna, who, along with two of his closest friends and one arrogant, inscrutable old man, might even now be fighting for her life trying to break a sociopath out of prison on an enemy-occupied planet—

Enough! Snap out of it, Will! Stay focused!

At Riker's signal, O'Brien and the rest of the team poured through the access panel. Riker ordered security to restrain and gag the wounded Cardassians and move them out of sight into one of the brig's holding cells.

O'Brien reached into his tool kit and took out a Starfleet tricorder and a Cardassian padd. The padd was specifically loaded, he'd claimed, with the root patterns of every decryption program the Cardassian military had in use until the Cardassians withdrew from Bajor. There was, of course, a very good chance a lot of them would no longer work. But a few still would. The trick was going to be finding the right one so they could hack in. O'Brien placed the padd on the desk, then set up an interface between the padd, the tricorder, and the security console.

Riker eyed the unlikely arrangement of devices warily. "I hope this works."

"So do I, Commander," O'Brien said without looking up.

Riker nodded toward the padd. "Who'd you say you got those codes from again?"

"Fellow I know on DS9," O'Brien said absently. "The guy who fixes my pants."

* * *

Standing before the door Director Lanolan's house-keeper had just slammed in their faces, Deanna Troi prepared to reach for her phaser. With their cover blown and the Jem'Hadar at their backs, the Daronan away team would have to fight their way to the prison.

"I'll take the leader," Vaughn whispered quickly. "On my signal . . ."

Before Vaughn could complete his instructions, the door swept open and Director Lanolan stepped onto the porch. "You must forgive Adana. The soldiers frightened her. Please, come in."

The director, tall and thin as Deanna remembered but with his dark hair now completely gray, stood aside for them to enter. Crusher assisted Vaughn, who continued his senile old man disguise, across the threshold. To maintain her character in the family charade, Deanna gave Data an impatient shove, then followed him inside.

We told the Jem'Hadar we're a family who work for you, Deanna advised Lanolan as she passed. *Please don't give us away.*

I'll do my best.

Once his visitors were inside, Lanolan descended the steps toward the patrol leader. Deanna and the others moved out of sight of the open door and, on Vaughn's signal, drew their phaser rifles.

"If Lanolan can't convince them we're his domestics," Vaughn whispered, "we attack first to gain the advantage. Understood?"

Deanna nodded with the others, but she feared for her mentor. The director stood directly in the line of fire between them and the Jem'Hadar.

"Is there a problem with my staff?" Lanolan's loud,

clear voice carried easily and echoed off the limestone floor of the foyer where the away team hovered in the shadows.

"They have been wandering the countryside without proper credentials," the patrol leader said.

"Idiots," the director said heatedly. "I've told them repeatedly, but they're not very bright, I'm afraid. Shall I send them for their ID chips now?"

The patrol leader hesitated, as if considering Lanolan's offer.

"Set phasers to maximum," Vaughn ordered in a soft but steely voice.

Deanna held her breath and checked her weapon, dreading the prospect of taking life but ready to carry out her orders.

"We've already wasted enough time," the Jem'Hadar said. "Be warned that if they're abroad again without ID chips, we'll kill them."

"Understood," Lanolan said in a conciliatory tone. "They are a trial to my patience as well, but with the war, domestics are hard to find, even poor ones."

Without another word, the Jem'Hadar patrol marched down the walkway and onto the road. A moment later, Lanolan stepped inside, closed the heavy outer door and locked it. He turned to Deanna, a thin sheen of perspiration glistening on his upper lip.

"That was close. Come." With three long strides, he crossed the foyer to what appeared simply another of the wooden panels that lined the walls, but with a flick of his hand along the top molding, the panel swung inward. "You'll be safe in here, in case the Jem'Hadar return."

Data stepped into the hidden passageway first, followed by Beverly, then Deanna. Vaughn brought up the rear with Lanolan, who closed and secured the panel from the inside before following them down a spiral staircase to an underground room. They entered through a utilitarian titanium-alloy door with an intricate locking system, but the room's interior, by contrast, was lavish in its furnishings. Comfortable chairs and sofas, lush tropical plants, and a state-of-the-art replicator provided the well-lighted area with a pleasing ambience. A cozy grouping of chairs around a table filled the corner nearest the food replicator.

"A bolt-hole," Lanolan announced, "one I built primarily for the safety of my wife in case any of our more dangerous prisoners escaped. Until today, I've never needed it, thank the gods."

He turned to Troi. "It's good to see you, Deanna, though I must admit, your visit has taken me quite by surprise. Please tell me you're here on behalf of the Federation, and that Betazed and Darona are about to be liberated."

Vaughn spoke up. "That's why we're here, sir. I'm Commander Elias Vaughn of Starfleet. This is Dr. Crusher, and Lieutenant Commander Data. We're part of a mission to help the Betazoid resistance drive the Dominion from your system. The situation is a bit complicated, but what it comes down to is that we need your help. Commander Troi can explain."

"My help?" Lanolan frowned. "I don't understand. What can I do? Wait, forgive me. Can I offer you refreshment? Are you hungry?"

Vaughn shook his head. "We haven't time to eat, but we'll take water if you have it."

Lanolan went to the replicator and quickly handed out bulbs of chilled Daronan spring water, which Data alone politely declined. Deanna's first sip of the distinctive sweet liquid brought memories of her months of internship tumbling back, triggering nostalgia for a simpler, gentler time when the universe had been a safer place.

Once his guests had been served and seated, Lanolan took a chair and turned to Deanna. "Now, will you tell me what this visit is about?"

Deanna nodded. As swiftly as possible, she recounted the Starfleet defeat in its attempt to drive the Dominion forces from the Betazed system, the formation of the Betazoid resistance, the building of Sentok Nor, and the plans to destroy it. She saved until last the resistance request for Tevren and their intention to apply his unique telepathic talent in their fight against the Dominion.

"You can't be serious." Lanolan's face glowed an unnatural white against the beige of his prison director's uniform, and he shuddered visibly with misgiving. His disbelief and reluctance rolled over Deanna in waves. In all her time on Darona, she had never seen the garrulous director at such a loss for words.

Vaughn looked down at him. "The request for Tevren's help comes straight from the leaders of the Betazoid resistance, Director. We're not insensitive to the ethical quandary the plan presents—"

"Ethical quandary?" Lanolan exploded. "Respectfully, Commander, have you any idea at all how dan-

gerous the individual you propose to take with you is? Or what would happen if he were unleashed?" He turned his glare on Troi. "Or what this 'talent' as you euphemistically call it would do if it were loosed among our people? How can you be party to this? You of all people! You've seen what he's capable of!"

"Yes, I've seen it," Deanna said quietly, meeting his eyes. "You know what else I've seen? Casualty lists. Names of dead Starfleet officers that seem to go on forever. I've seen the wreckage of spacecraft that once held hundreds, sometimes thousands of lives. And among the survivors of such carnage, I've seen men and women, wounded not just in body but in mind. And on this very day, Director, I felt a family of Betazoids— a father, a mother, and their children—as they were shot dead by Jem'Hadar while trying to enter Jarkana.

"The Federation isn't winning this war, sir," she went on, her words gathering strength as she spoke. "And Starfleet fears that by the time it can muster a force capable of ousting the Jem'Hadar from Betazed, the Dominion will have used our world to launch attacks upon others. But if this nightmare continues, it will not, it will *not* be because we didn't do everything in our power to end it. So please don't ask me how I can go along with this until you've seen what *I've* seen."

Deanna sensed her mentor's turmoil, even though he struggled to keep his emotions shielded. No matter how hard he tried, however, he couldn't hide his supreme loathing at the prospect of loosing Tevren on the civilized world.

Vaughn spoke quietly. "With your cooperation, Director, we may be able to do this quickly and with a minimum of bloodshed. We certainly don't want any innocents to be hurt in the process. But make no mistake, we'll take Tevren whether you help us or not."

Lanolan covered his face with his hands. "Please give me a moment. I need to think."

Taking pity on her old friend, Deanna crossed to the replicator and ordered his favorite drink, one whose consumption Madame Lanolan had always rationed severely: Saurian brandy.

She handed the glass to the director, who chugged it down as if it were vile medicine. He returned the snifter with a quivering hand. Again she sensed his emotions were closed and blocked, but she better than anyone else in the room could understand his anguish.

"You would truly storm the prison?" Lanolan asked Vaughn in disbelief.

No one could mistake the determination in the commander's eyes. "We'll do what we have to."

"But my guards are unarmed," Lanolan said. "The only means the Jem'Hadar left us to contain our prisoners is the force fields."

Deanna knelt beside Lanolan's chair and placed her hand on his arm. "Please, help us. We don't want to hurt anyone."

The old man slumped in his chair. "You've obviously had time to think through the ramifications of this insane scheme. As for me, I can see only tragedy in what you propose."

"The tragedy if we don't go through with it is far worse. Director," Deanna prodded gently. "We're running out of time."

He lifted his head and met her gaze. "I'll take you to him, but I'll also hold you responsible for what he unleashes."

Deanna shivered at the director's declaration and at the violent emotions clashing inside the man in spite of his attempts to hide them.

With a weary shove, Lanolan regained his feet and crossed the room. From a compartment by the replicator, he removed an older model of a Federation phaser and concealed it in his smock. "If we run into Jem'Hadar on the way to the prison, you'll need all the firepower you can get."

"Then let's move out," Vaughn said.

The trek through Lanolan's back gardens and up the hill to the prison took only minutes. At the director's instructions, the guards at the gate dropped the force field for the group to pass into the prison grounds. Deanna stared around her in disbelief. The exotic gardens she remembered from her internship were choked with weeds and dying from neglect.

The director read her thoughts and shook his head sadly. "Outdoor activity had to be discontinued once the occupation started," he explained. "Since we're no longer permitted weapons, we can't risk arming our prisoners with gardening tools."

He led the away team through the administrative section and down a long corridor to the maximum security facility. Guards stationed along the way lowered force fields for them to pass. Finally they stood before Tevren's cell, a room with the fourth wall an energy shield that blocked it from the corridor but allowed full view of the cell's interior.

Tevren stood in the middle of the room, his hands clasped in front of him, a half-smile playing on his thin lips. In a shapeless prison coverall whose yellow tint made his skin sallow, he looked shrunken and harmless, like a scholarly tutor or an overworked bookkeeper who rarely saw daylight. Deanna was struck anew at how someone so sadistic could appear so benign and unthreatening. His dark eyes, the dreadful void Deanna recalled so well, locked on her.

"Counselor Troi," he said softly. "You're as lovely as ever. To what do I owe this honor?" Except for his thinning hair and the deep lines around his eyes and lips, Tevren had changed little.

"We're getting you out of here," Deanna said.

"How delightful. It's been some time since I've seen the sun. May I ask why?"

Deanna looked at Vaughn, who shook his head. Deanna turned back to Tevren. "I'll explain later. For now, I need you to trust me."

Tevren's attention was on Vaughn and the others. "I'm guessing you're with Starfleet," he said with some amusement. "Now, why would Starfleet be interested in me?"

Vaughn's eyes narrowed. "Don't flatter yourself."

Tevren chuckled, delighted. His eyes went back to Troi. "You look haggard, Deanna, and it's more than just the years, I suspect. War going badly, is it? Things unpleasant back home? Coming here when the place is infested with Jem'Hadar is quite a feat. Some might even call it an act of desperation."

"Tevren, we don't have time—"

"*Make* time," Tevren suggested. "This is all quite a

fuss over someone no one ever wanted to see again. Unless, of course, I have something you want? That's it, isn't it?" And with that, his eyes gleamed. "They need me back home. They want to know what I know."

"That's right," Vaughn said.

Tevren's eyes refocused over Deanna's shoulder. "And you, Director, you agreed to this?"

Lanolan said nothing.

Tevren turned back to Vaughn. "What if I say no?"

"Then stay here and rot." Vaughn turned and started back up the corridor. The others followed on his heels.

"Wait!"

At Tevren's sharp call, his visitors stopped and returned.

"We don't have time for games, Tevren," Vaughn stated simply. "Are you coming or not?"

"I'm coming," Tevren said without hesitation.

"Director," Deanna said, never taking her eyes off Tevren. "Please lower the force field."

Lanolan did as bid and the field winked off. Tevren stepped forward to join them. At the same time, Deanna picked up a sense of terrible purpose emanating from Lanolan. When she glanced at the director, he had turned his phaser on Tevren.

"I'm sorry, Deanna," her mentor said. "I can't let you do this. I'll kill him myself first."

Before anyone could speak, Lanolan fired.

Chapter Eleven

"GOTCHA," O'BRIEN MUTTERED.

Crouching low behind the main console in the security office on Sentok Nor, the chief realized his efforts had borne fruit. Sifting through the decryption algorithms given him by Garak, the Cardassian exile living aboard DS9, he'd succeeded in hacking into the station mainframe undetected and now had access to a number of key systems, including autodestruct.

La Forge and his group had left to go below, their task to help override all three main processing computers located between Levels 14 and 21, deep within the station's mid-core assembly. Commander Riker had then left with the remaining members of the security detail when his tricorder showed a concentration of Betazoid bio-signatures emanating from the docking ring, leaving O'Brien alone but relatively safe in the security office, with instructions to initiate the autodestruct as soon as he was able.

After years of studying the thinking that had gone into the design and construction of Deep Space 9, and working constantly to reconcile the rampant incompatabilities between Cardassian and Federation technology, the irony of exploiting Deep Space 9's very weaknesses in order to use them against Sentok Nor wasn't lost on O'Brien. In fact, he was already making mental notes to correct the vulnerabilities when he returned home, to prevent anyone else from ever succeeding at what he was attempting.

He'd love to see the looks on his enemies' faces after he activated the station's autodestruct system. They'd quickly realize their manual backup had been destroyed, so they couldn't turn off the countdown.

Another part of O'Brien, however, couldn't help regretting that all this technology and the massive structure that reminded him so much of home had to be destroyed. If Federation forces hadn't already been pushed to the limit, Sentok Nor would have been a treasure worth keeping. Unfortunately, without sufficient military backup to overwhelm the Dominion forces in the system, destroying Sentok Nor outright was the only way to chase them off, and thereby weaken the Dominion's ability to hold the system.

He frowned at an unusually high power drain flowing to the cargo bays. Some of it was even being pulled from defense, and it was going straight toward the area Commander Riker had gone to investigate. What were they doing to pull that kind of power? Building weapons? Creating more Jem'Hadar?

"La Forge to O'Brien."

O'Brien tapped his combadge, which had been altered to constantly change frequencies so the Cardassians couldn't pinpoint their locations. "Go ahead."

"We're on site." La Forge and his team had reached the computer core. *"The mainframe's physical access port is destroyed. There's no way to manually stop the self-destruct countdown once we start it."*

"Stand by." O'Brien made several minor adjustments and corrected for fluctuations. "Ready now."

"Initiate autodestruct," La Forge ordered.

La Forge and his team simultaneously disengaged all three computers that operated every system in the station. O'Brien entered the autodestruct sequence the Cardassians already had in place.

"O'Brien, report," Commander Riker ordered over the combadge.

"Autodestruct sequence initiated, Commander," O'Brien announced. "The thermal energy released by overloading the fusion reactors will be comparable to seven hundred eighty standard photon torpedoes."

"Can you stop it?"

At the anxiety in the commander's voice, a wave of apprehension burned through O'Brien like acid. The last time he'd experienced that feeling was when he'd evacuated Deep Space 9 before the Cardassians invaded. The Federation had eventually retaken the station, but he had never forgotten how difficult leaving had been. Commander Riker's question made him wonder if he'd make it back to his home in the Bajoran system. He'd sabotaged Sentok Nor's computers so effectively the Dominion couldn't stop the explosion.

And neither could O'Brien.

"Not all the power in the universe can shut this baby down now, Commander. I suggest we contact the *Enterprise* and beam out of here."

"How long until detonation?"

"Fifteen minutes, forty-eight seconds."

"We can't leave yet."

O'Brien's mouth went dry. "Why not?"

"Meet me in cargo bay three and I'll show you."

In the corridor of the Daronan prison, everything happened at once.

Director Lanolan raised his phaser to fire. Tevren, aware that he was Lanolan's target, cried out. Suddenly Vaughn lunged between the director and the prisoner, shielding Tevren with his own body.

Immediately and instinctively, Deanna employed the training Vaughn had so recently drilled into her. With a powerful body block, she shoved the director off his feet and, at the same time, knocked his arm upward, ruining his aim as his phaser fired. When he struggled against her and attempted to fire again, she coldcocked him with a closed fist and confiscated his weapon.

Shaken and winded more from surprise than physical exertion, Deanna assessed the situation. Lanolan lay barely conscious at her feet. She regretted having struck her old friend and mentor, but he'd given her no choice. Tevren huddled in the far corner of his cell, apparently fearing someone else would try to kill him. Data and Beverly knelt on the corridor floor beside Vaughn, who lay ominously still with a smoking hole in his coat—one that went straight through to the other side. Dismayed, Deanna saw that Vaughn's right shoulder had been hit by phaser fire when he lunged to protect Tevren. Without her quick reaction diverting Lanolan's aim, Vaughn might have been killed.

Beverly pulled open Vaughn's coat to get a better look at the wound, then retrieved her medical kit from the folds of her own coat.

Scowling against the pain, Vaughn looked up at Troi. "Nice work, Commander. I knew you'd come through when the chips were down."

"Quiet," Beverly snapped.

Data shifted slightly, allowing Deanna to view for the first time the full extent of Vaughn's injury. All the skin and part of the muscle had been burned from the commander's right shoulder and upper arm by the phaser burst. She found herself wondering how much worse it might have been without the beam-resistant S.O.B. uniform.

"You're in way too much pain," the doctor told him after checking her tricorder. "I'll have to sedate you."

Vaughn raised his good arm and blocked her hypospray. "Wait." He turned to Deanna. "I'm turning command over to you."

Deanna stared. "You can't be serious. Data's the logical—"

"You know the prison and the planet," Vaughn said through his teeth, cutting her off. "And you're the best judge of how to handle Tevren. Leave me. I'll only slow you down. Now get out of here."

He dropped his hand, and then Beverly administered the hypo. The doctor, her face grim, looked to Deanna.

"His wounds are life-threatening. The phaser blast cauterized the wound, so he's in no danger of blood loss, but the beam was set on the highest setting. The damage to his central nervous system is considerable—there's no way I can treat it with a field medkit. He'll die if we leave him."

"I have no intention of leaving him," Deanna said. "He risked his life to save Tevren—no, to save Betazed. I won't abandon him to the Jem'Hadar."

"I can carry him," Data offered, "without impeding our progress."

"What about me?" Tevren had moved out of his corner into the hallway, but his hands shook from his close call with death. "You're still taking me with you, aren't you?"

"Oh, you're coming all right." Deanna threw off her coat and unstrapped her phaser rifle, taking off the safety and focusing her anger on the monster whose life Vaughn had saved. "And if you make one peep or slow us down a fraction of a second, I promise you, I'll succeed where Lanolan failed."

While Beverly applied a field dressing to Vaughn's shoulder, Deanna ordered Data to place the director on Tevren's bunk. "Search his pockets. He always carries a key that controls the corridor force fields."

After he and Beverly had shed their coats, Data retrieved the key, moved into the corridor, and activated the force field, trapping Lanolan in Tevren's cell. He handed the key to Deanna and hoisted the now-sedated Vaughn over his shoulder. Beverly gathered her medical equipment, slung the kit across her back, then readied her own rifle.

Sprinting down the corridor in front of her team, Deanna deactivated the first force field, waved the group out of the maximum security lockup, then reset the shield.

"What are you doing?" Tevren asked nervously.

"One dangerous prisoner is all I'm prepared to loose on Darona today," Deanna told him.

The group raced down the corridor toward the administration building, but when they stopped at the next force field, a prison guard on the other side caught sight of them. Worse, he recognized Tevren. Without hesitation, the man hit a panel on the nearest wall, and alarm klaxons blared throughout the facility.

Deanna hesitated. The guards were Betazoids, not the enemy, and just doing their very necessary and dangerous jobs, and she hated having to fight them. She didn't have time, however, for lengthy explanations or philosophical arguments. However much she might regret her actions, she knew what had to be done.

She dropped the force field and turned to Data and Beverly. "Set phasers on stun. Take down every guard you see. We have to get out of here before the alarm attracts the Jem'Hadar. Tevren, stay close to me unless you want to go hand-to-hand with one of the guards."

With a shiver, Tevren moved closer, and Deanna suppressed her disgust. For all his murders, the man was a coward.

Beverly raised her phaser and stunned the guard who had sounded the alarm. Two more burst from a nearby doorway, and Data, securing Vaughn with his right hand, retrieved the rifle from behind his back with the left and fired. Both guards dropped.

Once her team had entered the corridor leading to the administration building, Deanna reset the force field. "One more barrier, then the main gate, and we'll be out of this place."

The away team approached the force field that blocked the pathway connecting the administration building to the gate. Behind the shimmer of the energy shield, five Betazoid guards armed with pikes, knives, and clubs jammed the passageway. The lead guard lowered the force field, and his group charged.

Tevren shrieked and scurried back the way they'd come, only to find his escape obstructed by a force field. Beverly, Data, and Deanna simultaneously discharged their phasers, and three guards fell. Two, however, kept coming. Data took out one with another shot, but the last guard attacked Deanna with a flying leap and shoved her to the ground.

His momentum sent them both rolling, with his hands squeezing her throat. Deanna boxed his ears. The guard screamed with pain and loosened his grip. She followed with a knee that glanced harmlessly off his thigh. He wrapped his hands in her hair, but before he could tighten his grip, she slammed her forehead into the bridge of his nose and knocked him unconscious.

Breathless, she staggered to her feet. Over the last four days she'd practiced these moves with Vaughn, but they had always been just that—practice. This time the struggle had been life and death. She'd sensed the killing instinct in the guard's attack, and her newly-honed skills and instincts had saved her.

"Sorry," Beverly said, "but he was too close to you for me to risk a shot."

Deanna swiped the electronic key through the force field release. "Head for the front gate, and hurry. Those alarms are still screaming. They're bound to get the Jem'Hadar's attention."

"Shall I attempt to shut them down?" Data asked.

"No time." Deanna glanced around, located Tevren, shoved him ahead of her, and took off at a dead run. Beside her, carrying Vaughn, Data increased his speed with ease. Deanna raced through the director's prison garden. Tevren pumped his short legs like pistons in an effort to keep up with her.

Deanna halted before the main gate. Apparently its guards had been among the attackers in the administration building, because no one was on watch at the entry portal.

"What's that?" Beverly pointed down the hill to a gray blur on the road that ran in front of Lanolan's house.

"Jem'Hadar," Data said. "An entire patrol."

Deanna inserted the electronic key into the slot by the gate, but the force field that blocked their exit from the prison didn't waver.

"Let me try," Data suggested.

Deanna handed him the key. He shifted the still-unconscious Vaughn to a more comfortable position across his shoulders, and with lightning-quick movements of his agile fingers attempted to drop the field.

Nothing happened.

Data tried again, then shook his head. "The force field mechanism on the main gate must have a fail-safe. We require either an additional key or a specialized code to release the shield."

"They've upgraded since I was here," Deanna said.

"Then only one key was needed at this gate." She glanced down the hill where the Jem'Hadar were drawing closer. She hadn't wanted the command Vaughn had thrust upon her, but the responsibility for her crewmates and their mission was now hers.

Piece of cake, she imagined Will saying with his gift for understatement and an ironic grin. *All that stands in your way is a maximum-security force field and a fast-approaching patrol of Jem'Hadar.*

In the operations center on Sentok Nor, Gul Lemec snarled at his science officer. "Raise the shields before more of them transport over."

"There's a malfunction, sir," his officer replied. "We're working on correcting it."

"Damned shoddy Betazoid work." The gul glared at Luaran. "I told you the *Enterprise*'s offer to surrender was a ruse."

Moset peered over the console, his dark eyes beaming with pleasure at the sight of the freighter. The doctor's precious research might yet be his downfall, one Lemec could take advantage of by sending a report to Central Command. Such treasonous behavior as lowering the shields during battle conditions and allowing the enemy aboard Sentok Nor could not be permitted to go unpunished.

Lemec dispatched his troops to search for the intruders. One look at the sensors indicated the enemy would be difficult to find, especially if they'd hidden in the access tunnels where sensors didn't function well. "If Moset hadn't dropped our shields, we wouldn't have enemies among us now."

Moset viewed the outer ring, his face smug. "If I hadn't dropped the shields, I wouldn't be able to carry on my experiments. The Betazoids on that freighter were culled from the general population specifically to suit my requirements."

Lemec ignored the doctor's comments, his thoughts on more critical matters. He didn't have enough staff to guard the entire station. He would have to choose in advance which sections to protect. Where would the intruders strike? Sentok's Nor's command center? The fusion core? Environmental? Weapons?

If he knew their motives, predicting their actions would be easier. Were they here to spy and take back intelligence to the Federation? Or were they here to rescue the prisoners? Either way they couldn't be permitted to leave—not after viewing the sensitive experiments in Moset's laboratory. Especially not after the invaders discovered how shorthanded the Cardassians were.

Moset's damned experiments again! If it weren't for the doctor, Lemec would have had all the Jem'Hadar he needed to control and safeguard the station.

Lemec paced, pondering how best to proceed and considering his dilemma from several angles. He couldn't defend every nook and cranny of the enormous space station. "Send a squad to protect the fusion core. Station another here to prevent the intruders from taking over the operations center."

The battle still raged outside the station, but Lemec had full confidence in the ability of the Jem'Hadar and Central Command ships to repel the feeble Federation force. His first concern was the station.

The lights flickered, and emergency lighting flashed on.

"Sir?" His science officer stared at his console, his brow drawn tight with frustration.

Now what have the damned Betazoids sabotaged? "What's wrong?" Lemec kept his voice even.

"My station is down, sir."

"Start a systems-wide diagnostic," Lemec ordered.

"Sorry, sir. Almost every system is either overridden or off-line. Computer cores and ODN networks, electroplasma, communications, life support, and power— except for gravity and emergency lighting."

"No backups? That's unthinkable," Luaran insisted. "You Cardassians overbuild and do so in triplicate. What about the labs in the docking ring?"

"Still online. Their independent backups haven't been affected."

Luaren looked at the dark viewscreen and turned pale. Not even she could deny that every instrument in the operations center had gone dead. The unusual quiet was as somber as a funeral dirge.

Lemec frowned. "Why haven't emergency backup systems kicked in?"

"I don't know, sir," his chief engineer answered. "Something's wrong."

"As if I need a medal for plasma physics to know that," the gul rebuked him. "Tell me something I don't know."

His engineer pointed to a blinking red light, his eyes dark with horror. "Someone's activated the station's autodestruct system."

At the announcement, Moset's lower jaw dropped.

Luaran gasped. "How did the intruders obtain the self-destruct codes?"

"What difference does it make now?" Lemec pointed to two of his men. "Override the self-destruct manually. Go!"

They sprinted out of the operations center, but Lemec didn't hold much hope for their success. The intruders could have destroyed the manual system as well.

Lemec was already planning his escape. His private ship would take him to Betazed. Although he hated to lose the station, blowing her up was almost worth it to be rid of Moset. Freed of the doctor's constant interference that disrupted the peace on the surface, Lemec would soon have Betazed—and the annoying resistance—under total control. As for the destruction of the station and the experiments, the fault lay clearly with Moset for dropping the shields and allowing the intruders access.

"How long until the station blows?" Lemec asked.

"Without instruments, I can't give an exact time," the engineer said.

"Your best guess?" Lemec asked.

"Ten to twenty minutes."

Moset suddenly threw his hands into the air. "My research. We have to recover the data from my lab—"

Lemec smiled in satisfaction. "Considering the laboratory with your data is on the docking ring and the turbolifts are down, you won't make it."

"Sir, the turbolifts are the only system besides backup lighting that seems to be functioning."

"This is not a simple sabotage," Luaran said. "Whoever has done this knows Cardassian systems." She looked at Lemec. "It's possible that one of your own people is giving intelligence to the Federation."

Lemec bristled at the accusation. "It is also possible that the resistance is aiding Starfleet," he said in a tight voice.

The science officer asked, "Should I give the order to evacuate?"

Luaran nodded grimly. "Although with communications down, I doubt most will hear it. I will help Moset gather his research. We will reconvene on Betazed."

Lemec nodded, grateful that the Vorta had not made him responsible for Moset's research. If her precious Founders thought it was so important, she could damn well be the one to try to get it off the station.

As the gul scrambled toward the turbolift, he hoped that the fool of a doctor and the irritating Vorta were still in the lab gathering his oh-so-precious data when Sentok Nor went up in flames.

Chapter Twelve

DEANNA EYED THE FORCE FIELD across the prison gate that effectively prevented her team from escaping with Tevren. "Main control of the gate is in the administration building."

"I can return there and cut the power," Data suggested.

"Go," Deanna said, "but don't cut the power. I don't want to leave the entire prison unshielded. See if you can get the computer to release the gate. Room O-41."

Data shifted Vaughn off his shoulder and onto the smooth tile of the entryway, then raced in a blur of speed back to the administration building. Deanna paced, waiting for the shield to drop. While Beverly kept an eye on Vaughn, Deanna watched for the approach of the Jem'Hadar squad.

"You have Lanolan's weapon," Tevren said, noting the hand phaser on Deanna's hip. "Give it to me. I can help."

"Shut up," she snapped back.

Refusing to consider that Data might be unsuccessful, Deanna peered down the prison road. Although the approaching Jem'Hadar were obscured by a curve, she expected them to burst into view at any moment.

"The force field's down," Tevren shouted.

"I said shut up," Deanna repeated. "We're waiting for Data."

"You two go," Beverly said. "I'll stay with Vaughn until Data gets back."

"Won't do us any good. Data's the one with the transponder. None of us is going anywhere without him."

Suddenly Data could be seen sprinting back toward them at inhuman speed. The android replaced Vaughn across his shoulders and followed as Deanna led them through the gate. The group raced around the facility at a dead run. They had almost reached a path that led into the mountains when a blast from a Jem'Hadar rifle shattered a tree branch above Deanna's head.

"Take cover!" She waved her team behind a large outcropping just off the path. Data slid Vaughn to the ground behind the stone, then took his place beside Deanna. Beverly, phaser poised to fire, crouched at Deanna's other side.

"Can you tell how many?" Deanna asked Data.

He cocked his head and listened to the muffled steps of the oncoming soldiers. "Twenty-seven."

Tevren's soft voice was in her ear. "You can't kill them all yourselves. Give me a weapon. I can help."

"Forget it," Deanna said.

"If I die here," Tevren said, "this is all for nothing, isn't that right?"

Ignoring him, Deanna turned to Data. "Even from a secure position, three of us can't hold off twenty-seven Jem'Hadar. See that point in the path?" She pointed below to the way her team had come.

"Where it broadens?" Data asked.

Deanna nodded. "The Jem'Hadar will probably attack several abreast and give us multiple targets instead of a single-file line." She hefted Lanolan's phaser in her hand. "Set this to overload, figure the time to explosion, and toss it into the middle of the patrol."

Data didn't hesitate. With rapid movements, he adjusted the phaser to overload, and its ominous whine filled the air around them. The advancing Jem'Hadar, however, were still too far away to hear the telltale shriek of Lanolan's old phaser about to blow.

Watching Data's expression of concentration, Deanna could almost discern the humming of his positronic brain over the phaser's warning whine as he calculated the time until explosion.

Suddenly the android lobbed the weapon toward the approaching patrol.

Deanna jerked Tevren down behind the boulder, Beverly ducked beside her, and Data shielded the commander.

The phaser struck the path in the midst of the Jem'Hadar. Before any could cry out a warning, the resulting blast rocked the hillside, scattering soldiers, shattering boulders, and splintering fragments of Jarkana pines in every direction.

Debris rained on Deanna and her group, but before

the deluge stopped, she ordered her team to their feet. "Take out any survivors."

The carnage on the path below sickened her. Jem'Hadar emotions were strange, unlike those of most humanoid species she'd encountered, and much more focused. She shuddered from the emanations coming from the injured and dying.

Data quickly shot three of the enemy who had apparently brought up the rear and had been too far away to be affected by the explosion. Another Jem'Hadar on the fringe of the group pushed to his knees and attempted to fire, but Beverly's phaser struck him down.

Deanna waited, listening for movement, opening her mind to sense the presence of others still alive on the path. She heard nothing, felt no one.

"Let's move," she ordered. "Data, activate the transponder now. Let's hope the *Defiant* can lock on to us before something worse happens." She jerked her head toward the fallen Jem'Hadar. "There are plenty more where those came from."

Data slung the wounded commander over his shoulders once more and followed Deanna up the steep mountain path. Tevren followed Data, and Beverly brought up the rear, phaser ready for either Jem'Hadar behind or any unexpected moves from their prisoner.

The steep path was blocked occasionally by rock slides that the group had to scale. The exertion caused Data no trouble, and Beverly and Deanna, career Starfleet officers, took the ascent in stride. The out-of-shape Tevren, however, stumbled and gasped for air like a fish out of water.

"I need to . . . rest," he demanded.

"We can't stop now," Deanna said.

"Counselor," Data said. "I have sent the subspace signal, but I am receiving no acknowledgment pulse."

"Noted. Keep sending."

Deanna didn't need to voice her concern. Data and Beverly both knew what a lack of response meant. Either the *Defiant* had been destroyed by an enemy vessel, or Worf's ship was elsewhere, out of range.

"Keep moving," she ordered her team.

O'Brien, La Forge, and the security detail jogged quickly down a dark hallway and encountered no sign of Jem'Hadar or Cardassians. Without normal systems engaged, the hallway remained uncannily quiet. The group hurried onto a turbolift, weapons raised, ready to fight off deshrouding Jem'Hadar.

"Cargo bay three," O'Brien ordered.

At his voice command, the turbolift whisked them smoothly sideways. O'Brien kept his back to a wall, and the others did the same. Although the lift appeared empty, one could never be too sure with Jem'Hadar. He didn't want any of the shrouded soldiers suddenly appearing behind him out of this carbon-dioxide rich air in a surprise attack.

"Odd we haven't seen even one Jem'Hadar," he muttered to no one in particular.

La Forge nodded. "If you don't count the thousands we discovered incubating in the hatchery mid-core."

"If they're breeding them on the station," a security man said, "you'd think we'd have run across a few, at least."

O'Brien had worked solely in the security office, but

La Forge had made his way to the computer cores and back. Unless he'd had uncannily good luck, he should have spotted Jem'Hadar. Rather than making O'Brien feel better, the lack of enemy soldiers raised the hair on the back of his neck. There *had* to be Jem'Hadar on the station. So the only explanation was that they were shrouded, ready to attack.

La Forge exchanged a long look with O'Brien, who tightened his fingers around his phaser. Inside the turbolift the chief felt like a sitting duck.

"Can we halt the turbolift, sir?" O'Brien asked La Forge. "I think everyone should get out."

La Forge's expression was puzzled, but he nodded in agreement. Aware O'Brien had stopped short of their final destination, he said, "Commander Riker ordered us to come right away."

"With all due respect, I'd rather take a minute or two longer than walk into an ambush," O'Brien argued. "We can enter a tunnel from here and arrive undetected. We'll have to cut through cargo bay two, but our movements will be less predictable."

"Lead the way," La Forge said.

Having lived for years on her sister station, O'Brien was more familiar than the regular *Enterprise* crew with Sentok Nor's layout. He led the group through the darkened corridor to an access panel and prepared to fend off an attack at any moment. But they saw no one.

The lack of Jem'Hadar was raising the tension by the moment.

O'Brien opened the panel into an access tunnel that reeked of stale air. The team crawled inside. O'Brien wiped sweat from his brow. The Cardassians kept the station too hot for human comfort. With the computer systems down and environmental off-line, the station should be cooling, but he had yet to notice a temperature drop. His engineer's instincts suspected trouble, some factor he had overlooked, some fail-safe he wasn't aware of. He thought longingly of Keiko and his children and wondered if he'd ever hold Molly or Kirayoshi in his arms again.

"How far?" La Forge asked.

"Just around the next bend is an access panel into bay two. We'll take a short cut to Commander Riker and bay three."

A minute later, O'Brien popped open a hatch into cargo bay two. An acrid, medicinal smell flowed into the tunnel from the bay and almost made him gag, but he forced himself to enter the cargo area. Recollecting Commander Riker's experience when he'd surprised two Cardassians in the security office, O'Brien rolled onto the cargo bay deck, weapon in hand.

Instead of angry soldiers, O'Brien found a dark, uninhabited area with an eerie aura that raised goosebumps on his arms. First he'd been too warm. Now the super-chilled air raised his hackles. Either the space station was cooling faster than he'd thought possible, or this section had its own power supply. He recalled a lot of main power that had been shunted to this section and wondered what was going on.

The floor of the cargo bay was stacked with thousands of objects with only small pathways among them, but in the murky light, O'Brien couldn't tell what the Dominion had stockpiled.

La Forge poked his head through the access tube and frowned. "What's going on in here?"

"I have no idea." O'Brien approached one of the neatly stacked piles, flicked on his light, then recoiled in surprise and disgust. "They're Jem'Hadar bodies."

La Forge, phaser raised, came up beside him. He didn't have a light—his ocular implants precluded the need for one. The soldier's face was misshapen and grotesque, his limbs contorted as if he'd died fighting his own muscles. La Forge looked at the next soldier. O'Brien shone the light to see that this second body was equally twisted. Every corpse they checked appeared to have suffered the same fate. "Looks like they died from some kind of seizure."

O'Brien's stomach heaved, and he was glad he hadn't eaten in several hours. In the gloom he could make out thousands of bodies stacked in endless, neat rows.

O'Brien shuddered at the grisly scene in the giant morgue. "This is why we haven't run across any Jem'Hadar since we arrived. They were all dead *before* we got here."

"Sirs," one of the security detail called, "you better look at this."

O'Brien and La Forge stepped over to inspect another body. The dead Jem'Hadar had an incision around his head that left the brain in plain sight.

"Look at that—it's like they were operating directly on their brains," La Forge said.

"He's not the only corpse cut open," one of the security team noted. "There're stacks of them over here."

La Forge ran his tricorder over the body and

recorded the readings. "We should get out of here. Commander Riker's waiting."

The group moved between the dead bodies in silence, their lights illuminating rows upon rows of dead. O'Brien was glad these Jem'Hadar weren't alive to fight, but the sight of so much death depressed him.

In his peripheral vision, O'Brien caught sight of a flash of white skin, something that didn't belong among the gray-complexioned clones. He stopped and backed up.

"What is it?" La Forge asked.

"I thought I saw . . . there." O'Brien pointed his light at a humanoid corpse. Thousands of the surrounding corpses were also humanoid. Dread in his gut, he approached one. This body didn't have the pebbled ashen skin and contorted features of the Jem'Hadar, but a head incision exposing the brain had been done just the same. "She was Betazoid. This section must all be Betazoid."

"Maybe the Betazoids brought up a virus that killed them and the Jem'Hadar," La Forge suggested.

"Dr. Bashir could tell us what's going on," O'Brien muttered. "I wish he was here."

"I wish I wasn't," one of the security team complained. "There're more Betazoids over there."

O'Brien's combadge beeped.

"We have ten minutes and eighteen seconds until detonation." Commander Riker's voice sounded grim. *"I need you all in cargo bay three. Now."*

Chapter Thirteen

WILL RIKER HAD JUST ORDERED the rest of his away team to hurry to cargo bay three when he heard multiple footsteps approaching the bay doors. Inexact tricorder readings failed to identify friend or foe, so he ordered his security detail to duck into the shadows behind a group of containers.

Phaser drawn, Riker held his breath. A Vorta and several Cardassians hustled into the cargo bay. Riker signaled his team to remain hidden and peered over the top of a container, ready to fire, but only if detected. No reason to pinpoint their location for the enemy.

Cardassian security would have been combing Sentok Nor for Riker's away team ever since they'd transported onto the space station, but this group was moving too quickly for a search mission. Obviously, with the station's self-destruct mechanism on its countdown, they had important business in the cargo bay.

Otherwise, the Vorta and Cardassians would have abandoned the station by now.

Riker debated following them, but he desperately needed to discuss with O'Brien and La Forge what he'd found. While he waited for his fellow officers, he sent his security detail to follow the Vorta and her entourage.

"Don't let them see you," he whispered. "Find out what they're up to."

Within seconds after the Vorta's group had disappeared through a doorway, O'Brien, La Forge and the rest of their team entered the cargo bay. When they joined Riker, their gazes took in the strange pods of machinery filling the room around them. The containers were the size of torpedoes and sat like coffins upon catafalques.

"Each of these pods contains a Betazoid," Riker told them, "and there're thousands of them."

"Any Jem'Hadar in them?" O'Brien asked.

Riker frowned. "Not that I've seen. Why?"

O'Brien inspected the pods more closely and left the explanation to La Forge.

"Cargo bay two's a morgue filled with Betazoid and Jem'Hadar corpses," La Forge said. "Thousands of them, too."

"You sure they were dead?" Riker asked.

La Forge shivered. "We didn't check them all, but most of them showed signs of extremely invasive brain surgery."

O'Brien rejoined Riker and La Forge. With a sweeping gesture, he indicated the pods. "These people are all alive and in medical stasis. The station's power drain was due to these pods. Emergency generators won't keep them alive much longer."

Odd, Riker thought, how these prisoners were so important to the Dominion that they'd used backup generators in these cargo bays. What was so special about these Betazoids, and what had their captors done to them? Riker didn't know and had no time to find out. The entire station would self-destruct within eight minutes.

"We have to get them out of here," O'Brien said with a shudder.

Riker understood the chill going through the engineer. He felt the same way. Something very odd, very sinister was going on with these prisoners. Clearly the Dominion had had more than just territory in mind when they conquered Betazed. But whatever was going on, he couldn't leave thousands of helpless, innocent people to die when the station blew.

"Can we revive them?" Riker asked.

O'Brien shook his head. "I'm an engineer, not a doctor."

La Forge agreed. "Commander, we could kill them if we wake them up and they don't have proper medical—"

"If we do nothing, they'll die, too," Riker argued.

O'Brien squatted next to a container. Unlike Riker's earlier examination when he'd cleared the condensed moisture from the glass casing of the pod to peer inside, O'Brien inspected the wiring. "Maybe the *Enterprise* could transport a doctor over?"

"Even with a doctor to revive them," La Forge said, "there's no time to transport thousands before the self-destruct kicks in."

Riker couldn't stomach the idea of abandoning the very people they'd come to save. "There's got to be a way. We need a fast solution."

O'Brien cursed in surprise.

"What?" Riker asked.

O'Brien stood so fast he bumped his head on the edge of one of the pods. His voice rose with excitement as he rubbed the sore spot. "These stasis tubes aren't just keeping them alive. Each one doubles as a miniature transporter chamber!"

La Forge inspected the equipment and nodded in agreement. "The idea makes a sadistic kind of sense. If these are experimental subjects, why waste time and effort forcing a struggling victim into a stasis tube when they could beam them in directly?"

"Can we use their pods to beam them to the *Enterprise?*" Riker asked.

"Yes, but there's a problem, sir," O'Brien answered. "These transporters are very short-range, apparently not designed to reach too far beyond the docking pylons. The *Enterprise* would have to come within one kilometer of this cargo bay."

"At least we know the shields are still down," La Forge added. "But the timing's going to be critical."

Riker hesitated, weighing his decision. Considering whether to jeopardize the *Enterprise* to save thousands of Betazoids whose prospect of survival remained unknown had him wasting precious seconds. Crusher's medical team might never revive these people. And even if they did awaken, had they suffered such permanent damage that death might be preferable?

Even if the *Tulwar* and *Scimitar* could hold off the

remnants of the Dominion fleet, the transport would have to be almost instantaneous, or the *Enterprise* could be destroyed in the explosion along with Sentok Nor.

"Sir," one of the security detail he'd sent to follow the Vorta dashed into the room. "I heard the Vorta and Cardassians talking. Several squads of Cardassian soldiers are on their way here."

It's now or never, Picard thought.

The captain sat tensely in his command seat as the *Enterprise* continued at full impulse on a collision course with the Jem'Hadar warship. He was still playing his metaphorical cards close to his chest, waiting for his ace in the hole to drop out of warp.

Exactly on schedule, the *Defiant* decloaked directly behind the Jem'Hadar in the *Enterprise*'s path. A double salvo of quantum torpedoes and pulse phasers tore into the Jem'Hadar battle cruiser's starboard warp nacelle, setting off an explosion that sent the remains of the disintegrating vessel out of the *Enterprise*'s path and plummeting toward Betazed.

"The other Jem'Hadar cruiser is coming about," Daniels reported. *"Scimitar* and *Tulwar* are moving to intercept. "Sir, the *Defiant* is hailing us," Daniels said.

"On screen," Picard said.

Worf's dark expression had rarely looked so good to Picard.

"Good to see you, Mr. Worf." Picard gestured to the Dominion ships. "I appreciate the timely arrival. The attack ships are all yours."

Worf nodded. *"Thank you, Captain. I have several scores to settle with the Dominion."*

Picard turned to Perim. "Bring us about, Ensign. Pursuit course. Let's finish this. Mr. Daniels . . . at your discretion."

As the *Tulwar* and *Scimitar* converged on the remaining Jem'Hadar battle cruiser from port and starboard and opened fire, the *Enterprise* closed the distance on its tail and launched torpedoes. The combined assault proved too much even for the powerful Dominion ship. It spun away out of control, exploding as it went.

Picard then concentrated the *Enterprise*'s firepower on the remaining Cardassian ships.

"We've taken out the weapons array of one," Daniels announced, "and the shields of the other are badly weakened."

A spiral disruptor beam buffeted the *Enterprise,* and a fire erupted at the ops station. The engineer picked himself off the floor as the computer contained the fire.

"Shields gone, Captain. Hull breach on deck six."

"Seal it off," Picard ordered and turned his attention back to the Cardassian ships. "Hard about. Give us some maneuvering room."

Behind them, the *Defiant* delivered a killing salvo to one of the Jem'Hadar attack ships. Its hull caved in, flames licked the heavens, and the entire ship disintegrated like a massive fireworks display.

That left only two Cardassian warships and a single Jem'Hadar attack cruiser to defend Sentok Nor.

"Receiving a transmission from the *Defiant,* sir."

"Let's hear it," Picard ordered.

Worf's deep voice filled the bridge. *"I regret we can-*

not remain to finish off these Dominion vermin, Captain. As you know, we are expected elsewhere."

"Thank you again, Mr. Worf. And good luck." Picard tapped his combadge. "Picard to Riker. Status report."

"Chief O'Brien's plan worked like a charm, sir. Self-destruct is set to occur in less than seven minutes. But there's a snag, and no time to explain. You need to bring Enterprise *within one kilometer of Sentok Nor in the next five minutes."*

"Commander, we can't use the pods to transport these Betazoids to the *Enterprise*," La Forge informed Riker in the cargo bay of Sentok Nor.

"Why not?" Riker asked with a worried frown. In the few minutes left before the station's self-destruction, the *Enterprise* transporters alone couldn't beam out the thousands of imprisoned Betazoids. The pods' self-contained transport systems were the only way to move everyone safely to the starship before the station blew.

"The master controls aren't here," La Forge reported.

"Where are they?" Riker asked.

On his knees, O'Brien followed conduits from the pods into metal boxes flush with the decking. Using his light, he traced a line along the decking to the nearest wall and located where the wires exited from the floor and entered a junction box.

"We're running out of time," Riker warned.

"I'm working as fast as I can, sir." O'Brien moved his light over additional equipment to examine the systems. "This bay has its own generators for the pods, so we have the power we need for transport. There's obviously a dedicated computer networking them, but unless we can find it—"

"Sir," the security guard who had followed the Vorta earlier interrupted. "There's a huge computer system in the laboratory."

"Show us," Riker ordered. "Move out."

He hoped asking Picard to bring the *Enterprise* so close to a space station about to self-destruct didn't prove a futile gesture. However much Riker hated the thought of leaving the Betazoid prisoners to die, he had to be realistic. Given enough time, La Forge and O'Brien could undoubtedly pry the necessary secrets from the alien technology. Unfortunately, time was what they *didn't* have.

"We have less than five minutes," he warned his team. "Make 'em count."

The away team rushed out of one side of cargo bay three toward the laboratory just as a Cardassian squad burst through the doors on the opposite end of the bay. The thunder of the soldiers' heavy boots on the metal deck masked the sounds of the away team's escape. They drew no enemy fire, but Riker knew they'd barely eluded their pursuers and their presence wouldn't go unnoticed much longer.

The security guard motioned Riker to the left. "This way, sir."

Riker and the others followed the guard through a short passageway into a massive laboratory. The loud hum of the room's machinery covered the noise of the away team's advance. After the earlier dimness of the cargo bay, Riker squinted in the laboratory's bright lights. Gleaming metal counters lined with trays of sharp surgical instruments and rows of clear containers filled with tissue samples suspended in fluids suggested the laboratory's sinister purpose. Jem'Hadar and Betazoid bodies sprawled on gurneys, some with the tops of their skulls removed, others in various stages of dissection. Other Betazoids lay in pods like those in the cargo bay, and by the condensation of their breath on the transparent covers, Riker could tell the occupants were very much alive.

The commander pointed to two security officers and kept his voice to a whisper. "Guard our rear. Don't give our position away unless absolutely necessary. We need to buy La Forge and O'Brien time to find the main control to transport these pods."

"Understood, sir." The men moved away.

Riker turned and caught sight of the Vorta and a Cardassian scientist in an office whose translucent wall overlooked the vast laboratory. They appeared to be arguing. The Cardassian gestured wildly with his arms, and the Vorta kept shrugging and pointing toward the open hatch of an emergency escape pod. Clearly the Vorta intended to leave before the station self-destructed, but the Cardassian was refusing. What was so important that he would risk his life by remaining behind?

La Forge and O'Brien had rushed immediately to the computer system that filled the far wall. Large storage cabinets partially obscured them from view, but the engineers would be spotted if the Vorta and Cardassian left the office and walked in their direction.

Riker posted two men to guard the engineers and

took two others with him. He edged forward, hiding behind the large equipment cabinets, straining to overhear the argument in the office in hopes of learning the purpose of the bizarre experimentation on the Betazoids and Jem'Hadar. Peering around a corner, he caught sight of the Cardassian hopping up and down and clutching a padd to his chest. The Vorta moved toward the escape pod hatch, arguing over her shoulder, but clearly unwilling to abandon the Cardassian.

Riker still couldn't make out their words. Motioning his security detail to remain behind, he dropped to his stomach and crawled closer, trying not to think about the biomatter smeared on the deck. He quickly came within earshot of the heated conversation and could view the occupants of the office clearly from his position on the floor.

The Vorta's hands twitched with obvious agitation. "Dr. Moset, we must evacuate. Now."

"Not without my research!" the Cardassian shouted.

The Vorta shook her head. "There's no time to download all the files. You must start over somewhere else, Moset. Time is running out."

Unexpectedly, O'Brien tapped Riker on the shoulder, and the commander flinched but didn't make a sound.

"Did she say Moset?" O'Brien whispered.

Riker nodded.

"Sir, I remember from my briefings during the Cardassian War that Moset was stationed on Bajor. He's credited with finding a cure for the Fostossa virus, but among Bajorans he's almost as hated as Gul Dukat.

The Bajorans claim he performed unethical experiments on healthy subjects. They consider him a monster."

Riker pondered the implications of O'Brien's news. Scientists didn't usually experiment on the front lines. What was Moset researching among the Betazoids that was so damned important?

"Any luck with the computer?" Riker asked.

O'Brien shook his head. "The lab's computer is coded differently from the others on the station. We can't break into it in the four—make that three minutes we have left. We need the access code."

Time and Riker's options were running out. If Moset was unwilling to abandon his work on the doomed space station, the Cardassian scientist's experiments had to be something Starfleet needed to know about.

Riker didn't stop to think further. "Cover me."

He rose to his feet and aimed his phaser at the arguing pair who had yet to notice him. Taking advantage of their distraction, he moved closer. When the Vorta spotted him, her violet eyes widened with obvious distress.

"Don't move," Riker ordered.

Moset froze. The Vorta shoved the Cardassian in front of her and dashed for the escape pod.

Riker fired his phaser, but missed. The Vorta rolled through the open hatch and slammed it shut behind her. Riker let her go. Moset, the commander's primary objective, was trapped, weaponless and clearly terrified.

Behind him, Riker heard the pounding of Cardassian reinforcements on the doors of the lab his team had closed and locked behind them. He tapped his combadge and spoke to his team. "Fall back. Close ranks around me."

"Three minutes," O'Brien reminded him.

Riker kept his phaser trained on Moset. "You have ten seconds to give my engineer your computer access code—"

"I won't *give* you anything," Moset sneered.

"—or I'll leave you and your precious research to blow up with the station—and your *patients."*

Moset licked his bottom lip. His gaze took in the blinking lights that indicated the Vorta had already launched her escape pod.

O'Brien advanced on Moset and grabbed the scientist's padd. The Cardassian squealed in protest while O'Brien scanned it briefly, then shot Riker a can't-make-heads-or-tails-of-it look.

Riker thought of the Betazoids he was leaving behind to certain death and prodded the Cardassian. "You can stay here and die with your patients, or you can give us computer access and become a Federation prisoner." Riker shrugged as if the Cardassian's decision meant little to him. "Which is it going to be?"

Moset's internal struggle was obvious. He glanced anxiously from his padd clutched in O'Brien's meaty fist to his chronometer, ticking down the self-destruct sequence. "Very well, I'll cooperate."

Riker contained his sigh of relief and followed Moset from the office to the computer in the adjoining room. The away team moved with him.

Moset approached his computer console and uttered his access code.

"Two minutes to detonation," La Forge said.

O'Brien punched commands into the computer console.

"I suppose you want the other Betazoids, too," Moset said with a resigned sigh.

Riker snapped his head up in surprise. "What other Betazoids?"

"The ones in the freighter at Docking Pylon One." Moset shook his head in regret. "Those would have been my best subjects yet."

"How many?" Riker demanded.

Moset shrugged. "No more than a few dozen."

Riker tapped his combadge. "Riker to Picard."

"We're ready for you, Number One," Picard's steady voice came through from the *Enterprise*'s bridge loud and clear.

Riker spoke quickly. "Have the *Enterprise* scan for Betazoid life signs in the Cardassian freighter at Docking Pylon One and beam them aboard. They may need medical treatment."

"Understood," Picard replied.

"And prepare to receive several thousand Betazoids coming from the cargo bays. They definitely need medical teams. We'll transport them to the shuttlebay from here," Riker added, hoping O'Brien and La Forge could make the unfamiliar system work.

"Dropping shields," Picard told him. *"Initiating transport."*

Before Picard had finished speaking, Cardassian soldiers broke through the locked doors of the laboratory and started firing. Riker grabbed Moset and ducked behind the equipment cabinets.

"Energizing," La Forge announced, and the Betazoids in the lab disappeared from their pods in a sparkling transfer of matter to energy. "We got the ones from cargo bay three, too."

Riker wrapped one arm around Moset, knowing the transporter would pick them up as one mass.

The Cardassian soldiers advanced, and the fire from their weapons streaked through the lab like lightning and ricocheted dangerously close. The away team had no place to retreat.

O'Brien checked his chronometer. "Fifty sec—"

The engineer's voice and matter dissolved into bubbles of dancing light. Riker felt the familiar tingle. The captain had pulled them out just in time to prevent their being overrun by the advancing Cardassians.

Instead of finding himself in the *Enterprise*'s transporter room, Riker discovered his team had materialized on the bridge. The commander immediately handed the scientist over to his team's security detail. "Lock him in the brig."

"Aye, sir."

The team left the bridge with Moset, La Forge rushed to his station, and O'Brien joined him. Riker's quick glance at the viewscreen revealed the *Tulwar* and *Scimitar* darting through space, firing at the weapons arrays of two *Galor*-class attack cruisers holding positions in close proximity to Sentok Nor where they had followed the *Enterprise* in. A Jem'Hadar attack ship nearby listed at a sharp angle, plasma streaming from its engines. With the station's communications down, Riker realized with satisfaction, the enemy captains had received no warning that Sentok Nor's self-destruct sequence had been activated.

"Fifteen seconds to self-destruct."

"Signal the *Tulwar* and *Scimitar* to clear the area now!" Picard ordered. "Helm, go to full impulse. Get us out of here."

A surge of speed at one-quarter the velocity of light, and the remains of the Starfleet task force to Betazed was away.

"Put Sentok Nor on screen," Picard ordered.

Riker watched, expecting the station to explode in sections. When the end came, however, due to Cardassian efficiency, the deuterium blast took out every section at the same time. The energy produced was so massive, the explosion so complete, Riker detected no pieces, no debris. Just an orb of flame that expanded outward, destroying the remaining Jem'Hadar attack ship and consuming the Cardassian cruisers.

Within seconds, the light collapsed in upon itself. Where once had floated a massive Cardassian station, only star-dappled Betazed space, free from conquering invaders, remained.

Chapter Fourteen

THE SUN WAS SINKING behind the Jarkana mountains when Deanna announced that they had reached the rendezvous point, a ledge overlooking the valley where she had often picnicked during her internship. A slight indentation in the cliff wall provided shelter from the elements if they had to spend the night waiting for Worf.

Tevren collapsed facedown on the ledge, winded and exhausted. "This makes prison seem like a palace."

Data gently laid Vaughn in the shelter of the small cave, and Beverly dug out her medical kit. After examining the commander with her tricorder, she looked to Deanna with worry in her eyes. "We need to get him to a proper facility."

"Data?" Deanna asked.

The android shook his head. "Still no response to my signal. You and Dr. Crusher should get some rest. I will take the watch."

He settled at the opening to the small cave, phaser at hand, pulled out his tricorder, and swept the valley below. Urgently, he said, "Counselor, we have a problem."

Deanna left Vaughn's side and knelt beside Data. "Only one?"

"Several, actually," Data said, "But our most immediate is that nearly one hundred Jem'Hadar troops are advancing on our position from three directions. Our only avenue of escape is to continue climbing the mountain."

Beverly had joined them. "If we move Vaughn again, he'll die."

"How long before the Jem'Hadar reach us?" Deanna asked.

"Traveling at a quick march," Data said, "not less than fifteen minutes. Unless there are shrouded soldiers closer of whom we are unaware."

Tevren pushed to his feet. "You have only one chance to defeat that many troops."

Deanna stared at him, her stomach queasy with the knowledge of what he was about to suggest.

"Have Dr. Crusher remove this damned inhibitor from my brain," Tevren said with a pleasant smile, "and I'll take care of them for you."

Data continued to scan the countryside. "Once the Jem'Hadar reach the mountain paths, the steep terrain should slow their pace."

Deanna furrowed her brow. "I can't think of a strategy to improve the odds between a hundred enemy troops and the three of us. Suggestions, Data?"

"Ascending the mountain might buy us time," he

replied. "However, if we take Commander Vaughn, he will die from his wounds. If we leave him, the Jem'Hadar will capture or kill him."

"Any response to your transponder signal?"

"None."

In the growing darkness, the counselor paced the rocky ledge, their rendezvous point with the *Defiant,* a ship that might no longer exist. Her personal survival was the least of her worries. Her orders were to deliver Tevren to the resistance, and, in addition, whatever decision she made would determine whether Elias lived or died. The more she deliberated, the more her options narrowed to the one she least wanted to consider.

She left Data and Tevren on the ledge and entered the small cave where Beverly knelt, watching over Vaughn. "How is he?"

"I can keep him comfortable," Beverly said softly, her voice heavy with frustration, "but I can't keep him alive much longer without a medical facility."

"Tevren's psionic inhibitor." The words were gall in Deanna's mouth. "How long would you need in order to remove it?"

Beverly had studied the device in preparation for this mission. "A few seconds."

Deanna nodded grimly. The time factor, at least, would work in their favor.

The doctor sat back on her heels and stared at Deanna. "Is that your plan, for me to remove the inhibitor so Tevren can kill the Jem'Hadar?"

"If you can think of a better one, I'd be eternally grateful."

Beverly shook her head, then frowned. "But what if he kills us, too?"

With a grimace, Deanna stiffened her spine. "We'll be no less dead than if the Jem'Hadar get us."

Beverly's gaze met hers, and her friend nodded in tacit agreement. She reached for her medical kit and began rummaging through its contents. "Send him to me. I'd better get started."

Deanna returned to the ledge where Data stood calmly with his tricorder. His composure was a balm to Deanna's frazzled nerves.

"The first wave will be upon us in approximately ten minutes," Data announced.

Tevren stepped from the shadows of the rocks. His psionic inhibitor prevented her from reading his emotions, but she could sense his eagerness in the tension of his muscles and the anticipatory flick of his tongue across his thin lips. "You're going to let me do it, aren't you?"

Deanna's eyes bore into him. "A hundred Jem'Hadar are approaching out there. How many can you prevent from reaching our position?"

Pride glowed on his sallow features. "All of them."

"And us?" Deanna asked.

"How could you even think such a thing?" Tevren appeared offended. "I consider you my friends."

From a man who had taken great delight in torturing and murdering his own parents, Deanna found his assurances unconvincing. "How close do they have to be for you to have an effect on them?"

"They're close enough already," Tevren said.

"Go to Dr. Crusher. She'll remove your inhibitor.

Data, roll these large boulders in front of the cave opening. We'll need them as a protective barrier in case any Jem'Hadar get too close."

Data handed her the tricorder, and she monitored the advance of the Jem'Hadar while the android fortified their position. Suddenly a mixture of joy and hate washed over her, so powerful it almost dropped her to her knees. Beverly had disconnected Tevren's inhibitor, and emotions emanated from him in a strength she'd never felt in another Betazoid.

Footsteps sounded on the path beneath her, and she clambered behind the boulders and raised her rifle. Tevren had moved as close to the opening of the cave as he could without exposing himself to enemy fire. He cast her a gleeful smile, then closed his eyes.

Within seconds, screams of agony ripped the mountainside below them. Not the sharp, abrupt cries of lives cut suddenly short, but the prolonged, suffering wails of beings in torment. For a species known for its high tolerance of pain, their anguish was testimony to Tevren's killing skill and lack of mercy. He was extinguishing them slowly, hideously. The emotions of a hundred Jem'Hadar—anger, confusion, and excruciating pain—pummeled Deanna, assaulting her with the savageness of their deaths. Tevren's pleasure in killing, his elation at the Jem'Hadar's injuries, his intoxication with his own power mixed with the anguish of the dying. Sickened, she longed to slide to her knees and wretch, to cover her ears to block the horrifying screams, but she forced herself to stand watch, ready to fire on any Jem'Hadar who survived Tevren's sadistic assault.

The killing went on until she thought she could endure no more, and she feared her own mind would be ripped asunder by the onslaught of such intense emotions. Just as she reached the limits of her tolerance, quiet descended around her, and she sensed only Tevren's jubilation at the success of his massacre.

She tossed the tricorder to Data. "Anyone left out there?"

"I will have to step outside to make a broader sweep," Data said, "but present readings indicate no one within twenty meters."

"I'll go with him," Tevren said, "in case a squad of Jem'Hadar deshroud."

"Keep an eye on him," Deanna ordered Data. "And continue signaling Worf."

Data nodded and stepped outside the cave with Tevren. Deanna was happy to see the killer go. His self-congratulatory smile sickened her. Even if his homicidal skills had saved them, his savage delight in the deaths of their enemies offended every moral and ethical fiber of her being.

She glanced at Beverly, who knelt beside Vaughn, monitoring his vital signs. The usually unflappable doctor appeared badly shaken.

"None of them died quickly, did they?" Beverly asked.

Deanna shook her head. "Tevren saved our lives, but I'm less certain now than ever that taking him to Betazed is the right thing."

Beverly blinked in surprise. "You don't intend to disobey your orders?"

Deanna shook her head. "I'll take him there, if Worf

ever shows up to get us out of here. But I'll present strong objections to the resistance. I don't believe they're fully aware of what they've asked for."

Beverly frowned at the readings on her medical tricorder. "I hope Worf comes soon."

Deanna nodded. She worried for Worf, and she wondered how Captain Picard and the *Enterprise* were faring against the Dominion fleet guarding Betazed. By now, Will and Miles and Geordi had boarded Sentok Nor, and she prayed they would survive their mission. She'd lost too many friends already, and her shipmates on the *Enterprise* were more than friends. They were family. She couldn't bear the thought of losing any of them.

Weariness seeped through her, and she shook it off. She couldn't give in to fatigue.

"I'll see if Data received an answer to his signal."

Deanna stepped outside the cave into eerie quiet. No wind rustled the leaves, but the resinous scent of Jarkana pines filled her nostrils. Where minutes before the screams of dying soldiers had saturated the night air, not even a small animal stirred. Nor was there any sign of android or Betazoid.

Data and Tevren had disappeared.

The long-forgotten sounds of laughter and celebration rolled through the tunnels of the resistance stronghold, but for Lwaxana Troi, they came too late. She had not been among those who rushed to the cliff tops to watch the warships battling in the night sky above Betazed.

Chaxaza came running to Lwaxana's sleeping niche, her young face alight with excitement. "They've come,

Lwaxana! The Federation has sent help. We received word from our contacts at the Ridani spaceport. Sentok Nor is destroyed."

With the first surge of hope in days, Lwaxana looked up from her listless son, who lay cradled in her arms. "Any contact from Starfleet?"

Chaxaza's glance fell on the ill youngster, and her enthusiasm wilted. "None. But it may come soon."

Lwaxana pushed the boy's tousled curls back from his tiny forehead and absorbed the dry heat of his fever through the palm of her hand. "Barin is almost out of time."

Biting back tears, Chaxaza spun on her heel and rushed away.

With a weariness that made her feel older than her years, Lwaxana placed Barin on his small cot and wiped his limbs with a damp cloth in a futile effort to reduce his fever.

"Water," he choked through a parched throat.

Lwaxana reached for her cup and held the last drops of her water ration to his lips. He drank greedily, emptying the vessel. "More."

Tears filled her eyes. "There is no more, my darling Barin. Not until the men return from the river tomorrow morning."

The boy was too ill to protest further. He had contracted the Rigelian fever the previous day, and the disease had progressed rapidly. Without ryetalyn, he had no chance of recovery, and with the increase of Jem'Hadar patrols in every village within a hundred kilometers, no one had been able to obtain more of the medicine.

Three other children of the resistance cell had died after the night Enaren had been forced to take Okalan's life, but since then, the doctor had discovered an antidote. Processing a serum from a relative with a matching blood type, he had transfused antibodies from the vaccinated adults into the ailing children. The serum did not cure the fever, but it prevented the disease from killing its victims. Since the introduction of the serum, not a single child had perished.

Until now.

When Barin was stricken, Lwaxana had begged the doctor to use her blood to produce a serum of antibodies for her son.

"Your son is only half Betazoid," the physician had replied with deep sadness in his tired eyes. "An infusion of serum created under these conditions from pure Betazoid blood might kill him outright."

"But the fever will surely kill him if we do nothing!"

"We must wait—"

"For what? A miracle?"

"There is always the possibility the next scouting party might return with ryetalyn."

Lwaxana had shaken her head in despair. "We might as well wish the Jem'Hadar off-planet. Both possibilities are equally remote."

The doctor had laid his hand on her shoulder. "You will know when the time comes. Call me. If there is no hope, then the serum will do no harm."

His words echoed in her memory. She felt the fever rising in Barin's rugged little body, draining the life from him, and sensed the time to alert the doctor had come.

Shoving wearily to her feet, she stumbled to the opening of her sleeping niche and drew back the curtain. "Chaxaza?"

Her cousin hurried toward her from the common room, her face drawn with fear. "Barin?"

Lwaxana shook her head. "He is still with us. But the doctor must come quickly. Please, find him."

She dropped the curtain and returned to her son. As a leader of her people, she was required to be strong, to represent hope, to keep up their spirits. But as a mother, she had already lost one child. Her darling Kestra had drowned when she was a beautiful little girl of seven, and her death had devastated Lwaxana so terribly, she had repressed the memory for over thirty years. As a result, Deanna had been a grown woman before she'd learned she'd had an older sister.

Losing Kestra had almost killed Lwaxana. Compounding that blow had been the deaths of Ian Troi and Timicin, the two loves of her life. Now she faced the death of her only son, the beloved child of her older years. She knelt and buried her face in his cot, letting her tears flow.

Footsteps sounded in the tunnel, and the fabric covering the sleeping niche was brushed aside. With tear-stained cheeks, Lwaxana glanced up, expecting to see the doctor.

Instead, she discovered Sorana Xerix, but the woman lacked her usual haughty expression. Worry lined her forehead and bracketed her mouth, and her eyes were moist with unshed tears. "I brought you this."

In stunned surprise, Lwaxana accepted the bowl Sorana handed her. "But this is your entire day's water ration."

"I regret it's all I have to give."

With a cry of gratitude, Lwaxana wet her almost dry cloth and sponged her toddler's searing flesh. Then she tilted Barin's head for a long drink.

"The doctor is gathering his medical kit," Sorana said. "He'll be here soon."

She turned to leave, then hesitated in the opening. "It's not good to be alone at such a time. If you wish, I'll stay with you."

"Please." Lwaxana gestured toward the niche's only chair.

With a nod, Sorana took the seat, her presence surprisingly comforting.

"We've had our differences," Lwaxana admitted. "Why are you here now?"

"Because we also have shared tragedy," Sorana said. "Like you, I lost a child when I was much younger, but one does not forget the pain."

Lwaxana gazed at Barin, lying too quiescent on his tiny cot. "I've lost one child," she said fiercely. "I refuse to give up another."

Chapter Fifteen

"DATA?" DEANNA CALLED in a loud whisper.

Her voice echoed eerily off the rocky ledge, but she received no reply. Without combadges, which had been deemed too risky, she had no way of contacting Data and no idea why he had left without informing her of his departure. She wondered if he had picked up movement of more Jem'Hadar troops and gone out with Tevren to meet them, until her foot struck something on the ledge.

Bending down, she retrieved the object: Tevren's psionic inhibitor in the sterile pack where Beverly had placed it after removal. Deanna's blood ran cold at the sight of the inhibitor implant, apparently ground beneath someone's heel into the red stone until only fragments remained.

With terrible foreboding, she scanned the forest nearest the rendezvous point, fearful Tevren had somehow disabled Data and abandoned him. She saw two sets of footprints on the path leading up the mountain, one made by Data's boots, the other the distinctive tread of soft, prison-issue shoes.

Their departure made no sense. Even with his emotion chip, Data was unlikely to be susceptible to Tevren's psychological manipulations, especially in so short a time, so how had such a powerless little man overcome Data? And if Tevren hadn't somehow gained control of the android, why hadn't they returned yet? Could the Jem'Hadar be closer than they'd thought?

She had to find them both quickly. Data possessed their only means of signaling Worf, but more than that, he was her friend, and she ached at the possibility that he might be hurt or even killed while trying to help her homeworld. Besides, she was responsible for Tevren, and the last thing she wanted was his running amok among the unsuspecting citizens of Darona. Bad enough that they had to endure the Jem'Hadar occupation without adding a serial killer to their problems.

When Deanna stepped inside the cave, Beverly glanced up from her patient, her expression hopeful. "Did Data receive a response?"

Deanna shook her head and handed the doctor the remains of the inhibitor. "Data and Tevren have disappeared."

Beverly's eyes widened at the sight of the ruined inhibitor. "Dammit," she whispered. "We have no way to control him now."

"Finding him is my first worry. In the meantime, until I return, step onto the ledge at irregular intervals and fire your phaser into the air. If Worf returns, he'll scan this location and will recognize the Starfleet weapon signature. The sooner you can get Vaughn aboard the *Defiant,* the better."

"And the Jem'Hadar?" Beverly asked.

"We'll hope the *Defiant* homes in on your phaser fire before they do." Deanna checked the setting on her phaser rifle and released the safety.

"Be careful," Beverly said with a bittersweet smile.

"You, too."

Deanna hurried up the mountain path above the cave. Tevren was quick to tire, and she hoped to catch up with him before he could travel far. But she doubted she could take him by surprise. When Beverly had removed his inhibitor, Deanna had been astounded by the magnitude of his telepathic powers. Tevren would sense her coming a mile away. Her only hope was a face-to-face confrontation to coax him into keeping his original bargain—if she had a chance to speak before he struck her dead.

Climbing at a steady pace, Deanna had covered almost fifty meters when she sensed Tevren's presence ahead. His predominant emotion, anxiety, took her by surprise. Insecurity was the last impression she had expected.

She followed the path out of the forest and onto a broad escarpment. From the corner of her eye, she saw a slight movement on the far end of the ridge. Instantly she brought her rifle up, and through its sights she saw Data facing her across the darkness, with Tevren directly behind him, holding Data's rifle to the android's head.

"Don't come any closer," Tevren warned. "If you fire, I'll kill him."

Data made no sound or movement.

"Data," Deanna called, "are you all right?"

"He can't answer you," Tevren called, his voice almost snatched away by the wind.

Never once moving her rifle, Deanna inched her way forward, sensing Tevren's uncharacteristic anxiety with every step. "What have you done to him?"

"Another little trick I developed," Tevren boasted. "Only this one I managed to keep secret. Telekinesis. It wasn't easy, but I was able to force him to help me up here, and now I'm suppressing the central processor of his positronic net."

"Why?" Deanna asked. "You stopped the Jem'Hadar. I thought you were on our side."

Maybe if she kept Tevren talking, she could ascertain the source of his anxiety. If she could alleviate whatever was panicking the man, she would try to talk him into surrendering and returning Data's self-control.

"I heard you mention his transponder," Tevren said, breathing heavily. "Without him, your ship can't take me off this planet. I don't want to go to Betazed. They'll just use me, and then lock me up again."

Deanna said nothing. She couldn't bring herself to deny that his reincarceration was exactly what she intended to argue with the resistance. "Maybe if you cooperate, voluntarily, and help the resistance, they'll reconsider your disposition. You could become a hero."

Tevren laughed with a coldness even sharper than the night wind, but it was ragged. *Something's definitely wrong with him.* "And what use would I have for that, Deanna? *Stay back!*"

Deanna stopped. She'd come within ten meters of them, her weapon still raised, still searching for a shot.

But Tevren was barely visible in the darkness, hiding behind Data. She could see the silhouette of his head, but even at the stun setting a head shot could kill, and she wasn't prepared to go that far with him yet. Not unless she really had no other choice. She would take him to Betazed, tell the resistance what she'd witnessed of his killing spree, and leave the ultimate decision with them. But she was determined first to get every member of her away team off Darona alive.

"What do you hope to accomplish?" she demanded. "Even if you could elude the Jem'Hadar in this wilderness indefinitely—something I strongly doubt—how will you survive up here alone? What kind of life do you expect to have that would be better than returning home?"

"I'm not going back," he shouted. "If you try to force me, I'll kill Data, and you. Or you'll be forced to kill me, and what would that mean for the homeworld?"

Strange. Why would Tevren need to threaten her? Why hadn't he simply killed her as he'd killed the Jem'Hadar? *Maybe he can't,* she thought. *Maybe holding Data is taking all his concentration, and he can't employ more than one psionic technique at a time. And if he releases Data to kill me, Data will knock him out before he can pull the trigger.*

Deanna's patience was wearing thin. Vaughn was dying, the Jem'Hadar had certainly already sent out fresh troops to capture them, and she was freezing to death in the frigid wind that blew endlessly across the ridge. *So what's the solution? I can't afford to wait him out.*

"At least let Data go."

"And allow him to overpower me with his superior strength? Give it up, Deanna. It's not going to happen. Just leave. Now. Or I swear, *one of us is going to die.*"

That's when she saw the answer.

"Maybe not," Deanna said, and fired.

In the fraction of a second it took her finger to pull the trigger, Deanna's aim shifted slightly, until her sights were square over the right side of Data's chest.

The beam cut straight through Data, and into Tevren.

Tevren's grip on Data's phaser rifle slipped, and both of them, android and killer, fell to the ground and lay still.

Captain Picard strode through the *Enterprise*'s shuttlebay and into semi-organized chaos. The ship's evacuation limit had come close to being reached. His crew, however, had done an admirable job of making the thousands of men, women, and children freed from Sentok Nor as comfortable as possible. The Betazoids had been given pallets and blankets in short order, and the ship's medical teams moved quietly among their ravaged guests, dispensing kind words and encouragement with hot meals and medical treatment.

With so many people confined in a limited area, the huge bay seemed remarkably quiet. Although the children remained subdued, several cried for their missing parents. Many of the Betazoid adults paced and waved their arms in vigorous but silent debate. Some sat in groups, their lips moving only to chew their food. Others hugged themselves and rocked. Most slept.

Their telepathic abilities didn't cause Picard any misgivings. He'd been around Deanna Troi long enough to comprehend that her people considered probing anyone's mind without permission the height of impropriety.

Commander Riker approached and spoke quietly. "We're having a few difficulties, sir. They've selected a leader who wants to speak with you. Many Betazoids are demanding that we return them immediately to Betazed."

"Don't they understand the planet is still occupied by Jem'Hadar troops?" Picard asked.

"We understand," a gray-haired Betazoid woman said sadly, "perhaps better than you do, Captain." The woman made an effort to smile at the little boy she held in one arm, but the circles under her eyes and the tired slump of her shoulders revealed her weariness. She injected the child's arm with a hyprospray, then handed the boy to an assistant, straightened her back, and nodded to Picard. "I'm Dr. Nerissa·Povron. I was on the freighter and hadn't been transferred to the station yet, or I would be in as bad a condition as the rest of those in this bay."

"I'm Captain Jean-Luc Picard, and you are all most welcome on my ship."

"Captain, on behalf of my people, I want to thank you for rescuing us."

"No thanks are necessary. We're all on the same side, Dr. Povron. I wish my crew could do more to help."

The doctor led him and Riker through a cleared path between the rows of injured. "Most of our people have family on Betazed. They are anxious to return, but there is something more important we should discuss first."

Povron drew Picard and Riker toward a section of the injured who lay on pallets on the shuttlebay decking. Even to Picard's medically untrained eye, many appeared too sick or injured to recover, their lack of coloring just one factor indicating the severity of their injuries. Some were so emaciated their skin hung on their bones as if the Cardassians had starved them. A few were missing eyes. Those who appeared whole stared at the ceiling with blank, lifeless expressions and took no notice of their surroundings. Others had mumerous scars on their shaved heads, indicating they'd experienced more than one barbaric surgical procedure.

"The most serious cases are in your sickbay," Povron told him.

Picard's stomach tightened at the suffering these people had endured, aware that many lives had been destroyed and many would never recover. "Is there anything else you require?" Picard asked.

"Caskets for the dead." She pointed to bodies covered with blankets in the far corner. "I'm afraid many others won't last the night."

"I'll see what I can do," Picard told her.

She indicated those with scars on their heads. "These people are some of our most powerful telepaths."

"Why did the Dominion torture them?" Riker asked.

Povron hesitated. "I don't think they were tortured so much as experimented on. I've discovered signs of genetic manipulation. The surgeries they endured were performed on the area of the central cortex where telepathic activity resides."

"A Cardassian exobiologist named Crell Moset was

in charge of the experiments," Picard told her. "His earlier work was in virology. Are you certain his current interest is telepathy?"

"It's obvious," Povron said, "because all experimental surgeries were done on the telepathic cortex. And the last of us who came up on the freighter, myself included, were specifically chosen for our telepathic strength."

Picard tried not to stare at the hideous scars on the forehead of the closest Betazoid. "Do you think Moset was searching for a method to destroy telepathic abilities?"

Povron shook her head. "I am told there were thousands of dead Jem'Hadar on Sentok Nor who suffered similar cranial surgeries. I think what we are facing is the probability that Moset was harvesting Betazoid brain matter in an attempt to genetically engineer telepaths."

Telepathic Jem'Hadar. Picard repressed a shudder and exchanged a worried glance with his first officer. Already as formidable a foe as any the Federation had faced, Jem'Hadar with telepathic powers would be practically invincible. No wonder the Dominion had spared no expense and worked so rapidly to build Sentok Nor.

But the key question was the one that had yet to be voiced.

"Could Moset have succeeded?" Picard asked.

Chapter Sixteen

ON THE WINDSWEPT RIDGE of the Jarkana Mountains, Deanna struggled against the biting wind to reach Tevren. The killer lay flat on his back, a small, charred dot in his clothing just below his right clavicle. He was still breathing. Deanna felt no emanations from his mind. Unconscious.

Only when she felt certain Tevren wasn't about to reawaken did she turn to her friend. Data lay stiff and inoperative, and the front of his uniform smoked where her phaser had burned through the fabric and scorched the bioplast sheeting of his chest. She hurriedly reached behind his neck, released a flap on his scalp to expose the tripolymer skull within, and found the contact that would reboot his positronic systems.

Data's eyes blinked open, and he bolted to a sitting position. "What happened?"

"I shot you," Deanna explained. "Sorry."

"No apologies are needed, Counselor. I am certain you had a very good reason."

Deanna pointed behind him, and Data looked at Tevren, sprawled unconscious across the rocks. Deanna explained how and why Tevren had manipulated him.

"I will run a self-diagnostic to check for damage." Data's eyes shifted back and forth laterally as the android checked his systems. "Aside from a hole point-four centimeters in diameter in three of my upper pectoral struts, and a sear along one of my backup sub-processing units, all systems are in working order. Shall I reactivate the subspace transponder?"

Deanna nodded. "We need to get Tevren down to Beverly and sedated before he comes to. Otherwise, we're back where we started."

"Do not worry, Counselor. Some years ago, I mastered the Vulcan nerve pinch. If I feel him stir, I will render him unconscious myself."

Data shifted the stunned Betazoid over his shoulders with ease, and Deanna started down the mountain with Data and his ominous load close behind. If Tevren awoke before they could get him to Beverly, there was no telling what he might do to them. That threat caused Deanna to increase her speed, and she stumbled and slid several times in her haste. Data remained sure-footed and fast. At one point he reached out and grabbed her elbow to prevent her from tumbling head over heels down the steep path.

Data carried Tevren into the shallow cave and laid him next to Commander Vaughn, whose face had grown more pale in the short time Deanna had been gone. Data stepped back outside to stand guard and broadcast his signal.

"You need to sedate Tevren, quickly," Deanna said to Beverly, "and keep him under until we get to Betazed."

The doctor examined his wound first and verified that it wasn't life-threatening, then reached for a hypo. "What happened?"

"I had to shoot him."

"He didn't try to hurt you?"

"He seemed more anxious than angry," Deanna explained. "He didn't seem well when I found him, but he was threatening Data with a phaser."

With a puzzled frown, the doctor set aside the hypospray, picked up her medical tricorder, and ran a quick scan of the Betazoid. "I can't sedate him. The drugs would kill him."

"But if he wakes up—"

Beverly sat back on her heels and stared up at Deanna. "He's dying. He needs a sickbay as much as Vaughn."

"Dying?" Deanna said in disbelief. "But the wound—"

"It wasn't the phaser," Beverly explained. "All those years of having that psionic inhibitor in his brain have made him dependent upon it. The sudden renewed activity of his telepathic cortex, after years of inactivity, is killing him. I'm showing intense neural shock. His legs are already paralyzed. Even if he regains consciousness, he'll be in no shape to cause anyone harm."

"But he *can't* die," Deanna insisted.

Data hurried inside. "Counselor, I just received a

pulse in answer to my latest signal. The *Defiant* is here."

Within minutes, the away team was transported aboard the small ship. Crewmembers stepped forward to carry Commander Vaughn and Tevren to the medical bay, and Beverly followed. Deanna and Data went to the bridge to meet with Worf.

"I regret the delay," Worf said. "I came as quickly as I could after assisting the *Enterprise.*"

"I'm glad you're all right," Deanna said. "I was worried that the Jem'Hadar might have—"

"The Dominion has taken too much from me already," Worf said with his characteristic snarl. "Today I repaid a few debts."

"And the *Enterprise?*" Data asked.

"Captain Picard had the situation well under control when I left him," Worf said. "Commander Riker's away team was still on Sentok Nor, and the *Tulwar* and *Scimitar* were harrying the enemy."

Deanna noted Worf's omission. "The *Katana?*"

"Lost with all hands. They died valiantly as warriors."

Deanna quelled her grief. Forty lives had been lost on the *Katana* and Commander Vaughn was near death, but she realized the toll would rise geometrically before Betazed was liberated.

If Betazed was liberated. There were still fifty thousand Jem'Hadar on the planet, and if Beverly couldn't save Tevren, there might be fifty million before long.

"But you will be pleased to know," Worf went on,

"that long-range sensors are showing that their mission was successful. Sentok Nor has been destroyed."

"At least *something's* gone right today," Deanna muttered, then realized she'd spoken aloud. "Worf, I'm sorry. That's wonderful news. How long before we reach Betazed?"

Worf turned to the young Ferengi at conn. "ETA, Ensign Nog?"

"Forty minutes, sir."

"Steady as she goes."

"Deanna," Beverly's voice sounded over Troi's combadge *"I need you in the medical bay."*

Fearful of what news awaited her, Deanna hurried from the bridge. When she entered the medical bay, however, her spirits lifted. Vaughn, his right shoulder bandaged and his arm in a sling, was sitting up on one of the beds. His face lit up in greeting when Deanna entered the room.

"Your color has improved, Commander," Deanna said. "How are you feeling?"

"Much better, thanks to Dr. Crusher. I should be back to normal in a day or so. And, as I understand it, thanks to you and Mr. Data as well."

Deanna ignored the offer of gratitude. "I'll turn command of the mission back to you, then."

He shook his head. "Not yet, I'm afraid. Doctor's orders. Did I thank you for saving my life?"

She nodded. "But I should be thanking you. You were ready to die for Tevren."

"Not for Tevren," Vaughn corrected. "For Betazed. There's a difference. And I only did what any Betazoid would have done. Let's just hope it wasn't in vain."

On the other biobed nearby, Beverly completed her examination of Tevren and joined Deanna and Vaughn. "I'm afraid I have some bad news," the doctor said softly. "The unique technology of Tevren's psionic inhibitor isn't in the *Defiant*'s databases. And given the classified nature of Tevren's incarceration, I doubt very much it's in the *Enterprise*'s, either."

"Then we'll find the specs on Betazed," Deanna said.

Beverly touched her arm. "I don't think Tevren's going to survive this trip, Deanna. His deterioration is continuing, and I can't stop it. There's nothing more I can do for him."

Deanna couldn't believe it. "There's got to be something—"

"There isn't. I'm sorry. I don't know exactly how much longer he's going to last, but it isn't long. And he's asked to speak with you."

Deanna nodded. She could feel Tevren's extreme anxiety as she approached his bed. He turned his head toward her, his dark eyes no longer the same horrible void, but filled with the fear that emanated from his mind.

"Am I dying?" he demanded in his dry voice that reminded Deanna of the rustle of dead leaves.

"Yes," Deanna said softly. "Your body is reacting adversely to the removal of your psionic inhibitor."

"Poor little Deanna," Tevren said with more than a hint of sarcasm.

"Why poor me?"

"You're so deliciously conflicted. I've felt it ever since you broke me out of Lanolan's box. If I survive, you have to bring me home, and the prospect of other

Betazoids knowing what I know terrifies you." Tevren was obviously finding it increasingly difficult to speak. The words started to come out in ragged breaths, but he refused to stop. "Now I'm dying, and somewhere deep inside, in a place you won't admit exists, you're glad. Because it means you did everything you could for Betazed, and now you think fate has seen fit to absolve you of the responsibility."

Deanna said nothing and turned to go, but Tevren's bony fingers caught her wrist and pulled her back, forcing her to look at him. "Can't handle facing yourself, Counselor?"

Deanna glared at him in undisguised hate, but chose her words carefully. "Whether that's true or not is a moot point. For better or worse, you *are* going to die before we make it home, and the choice really is out of my hands now."

"Is it?" Tevren whispered.

Before she could react, he invaded her mind, pushing aside all barriers and forcing himself into her psyche. The events of his life cascaded through her in an instant, including every torturous deed and brutal murder he had ever committed. With horrifying clarity, she witnessed how he had killed his victims and, even worse, experienced the euphoria, the arousal he'd felt from soaking up the psychological terror and physical agony of his victims.

Recoiling in horror, she wrenched herself from his grasp, but it was too late. She knew everything Tevren had wanted her to know, and the thought of it made him smile.

"Go to hell, Deanna."

Alarms sounded on the biofunction monitors above his bed, and Beverly came running. Working desperately, she activated the neural stimulators on Tevren's temples and injected him with a massive dose of epinephrine. After several frantic minutes of treatment, the doctor reached up and switched off the monitors.

"He's gone," Beverly said. "I'm sorry. There was nothing else I could do."

Deanna turned away from Tevren's body and crashed against an instrument cart, toppling it as she fell against the wall. Her mind reeled from Tevren's intrusion and the awful truth of his dying malediction.

"Deanna!" Beverly cried, rushing to help her. The doctor eased her into a chair as Vaughn ran over, both of them saying her name over and over, demanding to know if she was all right.

All she could think about was the horrific burden Tevren had forced upon her, the knowledge that was now hers to share or withhold, the responsibility she thought she'd been freed from.

Filled with self-loathing and an anguish she thought would consume her, Deanna fled to her quarters, bitterly aware that Tevren had won.

With deliberate calm, Picard marched toward the *Enterprise* brig. O'Brien had already shown him the contents of Dr. Moset's padd, but it contained only indecipherable numerical data, and neither the captain nor O'Brien had been able to determine from those cryptic notes whether Moset had succeeded in creating telepathic Jem'Hadar. He had ordered the chief and La

Forge to work on it while he resolved to take a more direct approach.

In the corridor outside the brig, Picard paused and straightened his uniform. Recognizing the maneuver as a stall before an unpleasant task, he took a moment to draw a deep breath. The prospect of confronting the doctor who had killed so many Bajorans and Betazoids repulsed him. Assuming the guise of a friend and colleague sickened the captain even more, but the sham might be his only chance of getting Moset to talk.

The captain strode into the brig and, hoping their absence would create a more congenial atmosphere, dismissed the guards.

In the far right cell, Moset huddled on a bunk behind a force field, his head resting on the wall, his knees drawn to his chest. The moment he spied the captain, the Cardassian jerked to his feet. "Come to gloat?"

"On the contrary." Picard forced a warm and congratulatory tone. "I'm here to pay my respects to the man who won the Legate's Crest of Valor and made medical history for his work on the Fostossa virus."

Moset eyed him with suspicion. "How do you know about my work?"

"You're famous throughout the quadrant." Picard settled into a chair on the opposite side of the force field and tried to appear relaxed. "As a fellow scientist—"

"You're a Starfleet captain."

"True, but archaeology is my first love, and while my standing in the scientific community is insignificant compared to yours, I'm hoping you'll humor me."

The wariness hadn't left the Cardassian's eyes. "How?"

"This damnable war has kept me from my true passion, my science. I miss stimulating conversations with colleagues, especially those with superior intellects, like yours."

Moset preened slightly at the praise, and Picard stifled a smile. Perhaps the exobiologist's enormous ego would work in the captain's favor after all.

"Someday," Picard continued, "this war will be over. Then everyone will remember that scientists, not soldiers, make the most important contributions to society."

"The war keeps interrupting my work," Moset grumbled. "I needed more time . . ."

His eyes burned with passion, and Picard noted with satisfaction that, with each stroke to Moset's ego, the doctor acted less hostile.

"Your work is much bigger than the war," Picard said, struggling not to gag on his words. "And from what little I've been able to learn, it was quite compelling. Unfortunately, because my orders were to destroy the station, you may not receive the credit you deserve for your research aboard Sentok Nor."

"I have no doubt the Federation will execute me," Moset said glumly.

Picard didn't bother explaining that the Federation didn't kill prisoners. Instead, he used Moset's misinformation to his advantage. "Perhaps I might be of some assistance."

Moset's expression brightened. "You're offering to help?"

"If you explain your work to me, in lay terms, of course, I might convince my superiors that your scientific knowledge is more important than the petty political differences between our peoples."

"You'd do that?"

"I cannot promise I would succeed. However, I can assure you that you will not be executed and that you will get full credit for your work."

Credit enough to rot in hell, Picard thought darkly.

He kept his face impassive, knowing the notoriety Moset craved would keep the man behind a force field for the rest of his life. Recalling the dying Betazoids in the cargo bay, their suffering a direct result of the Cardassian's experiments, Picard felt no guilt for misleading the man.

"I was so close." Moset paced the brig, seemingly unsuspicious of Picard's interest. "First, I isolated the gene that allows Betazoids to develop telepathy. Then I designed a way to transfer the gene into mature Jem'Hadar."

"So you succeeded?"

"The Founders provided such a poor product to work with," Moset said with a disgusted shake of his head.

"The Jem'Hadar?" Picard recalled Riker's report of the thousands of Jem'Hadar that had not survived Moset's experiments.

Moset nodded. "In spite of the inferiority of these vat-grown soldiers, I made them telepathic."

Picard's blood turned cold, but he refused to reveal the horror that chilled him. Faced with a telepathic fighting force, the Federation might never win the war.

"My procedure worked," Moset crowed, then his exhilaration faded. "But the Jem'Hadar died."

"They all died?" Picard prodded in a sympathetic tone.

Moset was shaking his head at the frustrating memory. "Every damned one of them. Almost immediately."

"As a fellow scientist," Picard said, "I can certainly understand your frustration." The captain kept his voice even, consoling. "Perhaps you could explain to me *why* they died?"

And Moset told him.

Chapter Seventeen

IN TRANSPORTER ROOM TWO of the *Enterprise,* Deanna struggled to keep her emotions under control. A few moments earlier, she had bidden Worf and Miles O'Brien good-bye, and their parting, although guardedly cheerful on the surface, had been underlaid with sadness. With war raging across the quadrant, Deanna didn't know if she would ever see either of them again. They were sorely needed back on Deep Space 9 and in the front lines.

In addition to the sorrow of parting with friends, the counselor struggled with apprehension over her upcoming visit to the resistance. Although she hadn't heard from Lwaxana since the invasion of Betazed, she had always assumed her mother and little brother had managed to survive. Once Deanna reached the surface of the planet, she would learn the truth of her family's fate. Tapping her forehead lightly with her fingertips in the reassuring meditation technique, she concentrated on positive thoughts to ease her inner turmoil.

The transporter room doors opened, and Commander Vaughn strode in, fully recovered from his wound, followed by Will. The color had returned to the older officer's face, as had the quickness to his stride, but she still sensed an underlying ennui whose cause she'd never been able to identify. Most likely he was tired of the war. Everyone was sick to death of it.

"We're beaming down with you," Will said without preamble. "Things are getting bad on the surface. According to the *Enterprise* sensors, the Jem'Hadar have been busy since Sentok Nor was destroyed. They're rounding up civilians indiscriminately and having a good number of them shot, probably hoping either to break the resistance, or find it. As far as we can tell, they've done neither, but the civilian death toll is rising fast. We don't have much time."

Deanna nodded. "Then let's go."

"I'm still worried that the Jem'Hadar will detect our transporter beam," Riker said to Vaughn. "They may not notice it immediately, but they will before long, and then they could home in on the resistance stronghold."

"Can't be helped," Vaughn said. "And the way things are going down there, tactical projections are that the Jem'Hadar will find the resistance inside of forty-eight hours anyway."

Deanna took a deep breath and steeled herself. "Do you have confidence in the beam-in coordinates?"

"They were contained in the original resistance message the *Nautilus* received asking for Tevren. However, because the Jem'Hadar are expected to overrun that position at any time, we'll go in with phasers drawn." Vaughn stepped onto the platform and nodded to the transporter chief. "Be prepared to yank us out at a second's notice."

"Aye, sir."

"Ready when you are, Commanders."

Readying their own weapons, Deanna and Will joined him on the transporter pad, and Vaughn ordered, "Energize."

The next instant Deanna glanced around, finding herself on a rocky ledge at night, a dark wilderness spread out below her.

Vaughn, phaser ready, did a three-hundred-and-sixty-degree visual sweep of their beam-in location. "If the resistance was here, looks like they've left."

Deanna started to agree, then felt the gentle probe of a highly adept telepath brush her mind. A man stepped out of what appeared to be a solid wall of rock with his hands raised in a nonthreatening gesture.

"You're Starfleet, aren't you?" He made no effort to hide the jubilation in his voice. "We had almost given up hope."

The commander lowered his phaser. "I'm Commander Elias Vaughn. This is Commander William Riker and—"

"Deanna Troi. I'm Cort Enaren, and I've known Deanna since she was a little girl." Enaren glanced past them. "You're alone?"

"The *Enterprise* is in orbit." Deanna sensed Enaren's disappointment. "Were you expecting someone else?"

"My son, Sark."

"We received his message," Vaughn explained. "That's why we're here."

"And Sark?" Enaren's desperate hope was evident in his voice. "You left him on the ship?"

Vaughn shook his head. "I'm sorry."

Enaren's face momentarily crumpled with sorrow, and grief stabbed Deanna. The casualties of Betazed had taken on a familiar face. She had played with Sark Enaren as a child, and they had attended school together. Her former classmate had apparently given his life to deliver the resistance's message to Starfleet. How many more of the people she knew and loved had died?

Enaren quickly regained his composure and pointed to the rock face. "Come with me."

Vaughn motioned Deanna ahead of them, and she followed Enaren through a fissure in the cliff wall and down a rock-strewn trail. They had progressed only a few meters when approaching footsteps hammered on the path ahead of them. Another mind reached out to touch hers, and happiness flooded through her. She raced past Enaren and ran straight into Lwaxana's arms.

"Oh, Little One, I thought I'd never see you again!" After a fierce, brief hug, Lwaxana tugged Deanna through an aperture in the mountainside and down a short tunnel that opened into a large chamber filled with people. After the midnight darkness, the bright light and smoke of the torches burned Deanna's eyes, and the smell of unwashed bodies assaulted her nose.

Most distressing of all, however, was her mother's appearance. Deanna couldn't remember ever seeing her mother when she wasn't elegantly dressed or didn't have her hair perfectly coiffed, but the woman in front of her was a shambles. If Lwaxana's mind had not already touched hers, Deanna wouldn't have recognized her. Her clothes were tattered, her hair windblown and knotted, and dark circles ringed her eyes. Her formerly voluptuous figure was skin and bones. Underneath her happiness at reuniting with her daughter lay desolation and grief.

"Barin?" Deanna asked, afraid to hear the answer.

Before Lwaxana could reply, a small body launched itself out of the crowd and latched onto her knees.

"D'anna! You bring me chocolate?"

Deanna knelt and gathered her brother in her arms. "Not this time, Barin, but I will the next, I promise you."

Someone detached herself from the group and picked up Barin. Deanna realized with a start that the young woman who looked more like a scarecrow was her cousin Chaxaza. She, too, had obviously suffered from the privations caused by the conquering armies.

"Chaxaza, it's good to see you." Guilt flooded through Deanna. She had fought the Dominion, losing friends and crewmates in the process, but she hadn't experienced the deprivation these people had. At the end of every battle, she had always had her shower, her clean uniforms, and her replicator.

"Will!" her mother cried, interrupting her thoughts. "And Elias, is that you?" Lwaxana ran forward and immediately apprised the officers of a terrible outbreak of Rigelian fever among the children in the resistance stronghold.

Riker turned to Enaren. "We'll need to gather all the children and any noncombatants together immediately," the first officer told him as he tapped his combadge. "Riker to *Enterprise*, prepare to beam up sick and injured, mostly children. Inform sickbay to expect numerous cases of Rigelian fever, malnutrition, and assorted injuries. Stand by to transport on my signal. Riker out." Riker gestured for Enaren to lead the way deeper into the tunnels of the stronghold.

"Elias," Deanna said, "if you don't mind, I'd like a few moments alone with my mother."

Vaughn nodded. "It's good to see you, Lwaxana," he said sincerely, and moved off to confer with the other resistance members about their tactical status.

Chaxaza, still holding Barin, also moved away as Deanna followed Lwaxana down another passage and into a small alcove. Her mother drew back a drape over the opening, and Deanna stepped inside.

"Not very spacious, but it's been home for the past four months." Lwaxana settled on a pillow-strewn ledge carved out of the rock wall. Deanna sat beside her.

First tell me, Lwaxana began. *Did you bring him?*

There was no misunderstanding what her mother meant. *It was your idea, wasn't it, Mother? Using Tevren?* Deanna found it impossible to suppress her disappointment.

The involuntary feeling seemed to provoke anger in her mother. *Don't you dare presume to judge me. Not until you've spent four months living under the Jem'Hadar, waiting and waiting for Starfleet to do something while children die all around you, and then realizing the salvation you put your hope in just isn't coming. We're* desperate, *Little One. And I won't toler-ate your condemnation of that!*

The irony of hearing her own speech to Lanolan echoed by her mother didn't escape Deanna.

"Mother," she said aloud, "Tevren is dead."

Lwaxana flinched as if Deanna had struck her. "That can't be. Tell me that isn't true, Deanna."

With exacting detail, Deanna related how the away team had released Tevren from prison, how Beverly had removed his inhibitor, the horrific deaths of the Jem'Hadar patrols Tevren had wiped out, and his even-tual demise. "And before he died, Mother, he emptied his mind into mine."

Deanna felt herself shaking at the memory, and Lwaxana wrapped her arms around her daughter. Deanna drew back, her jaw set, her eyes blazing. "Let me tell you how Tevren killed people. He drew all a person's bioelectrical energy to the pain receptors in the brain and literally fried the synapses there. The re-sulting deaths were slow and excruciatingly painful, with prolonged and indescribable suffering. I wouldn't wish such an end on anyone, Mother, *anyone,* not even Jem'Hadar. To say Tevren's method is sadistic and cruel doesn't begin to explain it."

Lwaxana listened without expression. "If you're going to try to convince me that I should care how the Jem'Hadar die—"

"My God, Mother, can you hear yourself?" Deanna cried. "Your entire life has been devoted to *peace,* to working against barbarism and needless bloodshed. You're turning into the very thing you hate!"

She could see her mother shaking, feel the raw emotions raging inside, and for the first time in her life, Deanna looked at her mother with fear.

"We have our backs to the wall, Deanna," she said. "What else can we do? How many ships came with the *Enterprise?* How many Starfleet officers can beam down to Betazed? Can they arm every Betazoid? Can they do enough against fifty thousand Jem'Hadar? Are you really going to withhold from us what Tevren gave you?"

"No," Deanna said. "If you tell me this is what you want me to do, then I'll do it. But before you answer, I need you to tell me something, truthfully."

Lwaxana met her daughter's gaze, waiting.

"Have you truly thought about what going down this road will mean for us, as a people? Do you really want to live in the kind of world the use of Tevren's powers may create?"

Lwaxana said nothing, and the silence stretched on, mother and daughter simply staring into each other's eyes.

Then Deanna's combadge beeped. *"Picard to Troi."*

"Troi here."

"Counselor, have you revealed Tevren's knowledge to the resistance yet?"

"No, sir," she answered, still looking at her mother. "But I may have to very soon."

"Belay that. You and Commander Vaughn must return to the Enterprise *immediately. Commander Riker has already beamed up with his charges. I'll explain when you get here. Picard out."*

Lwaxana simply stared straight ahead. Deanna stroked her cheek gently. "I'll return as quickly as I can."

"No," Lwaxana said firmly, and for the first time since Deanna had arrived on Betazed, her voice had all the energy and authority of the elder daughter of the Fifth House, Holder of the Sacred Chalice of Rixx, and the one true Heir to the Holy Rings of Betazed. "If Jean-Luc has something to say that will affect the resistance, then I'm going to be there to represent them. Tell your transporter secretary or whatever he's called it's three to boom up."

Deanna smiled at the deliberate flub. "Beam up, Mother."

"As if I care," Lwaxana said impatiently. "Come, Little One. Let's find Elias."

"Lwaxana," Picard said. "This is a delightful surprise."

Lwaxana snorted as she, Vaughn, and Deanna took their places around the observation lounge table, where Riker, Dr. Povron, and Dr. Crusher were already seated. "I'm afraid I really have no interest in returning your advances this time, Jean-Luc. I suggest we get down to business."

Picard managed to keep a straight face, but doing so was a challenge. "Of course, Ambassador. My apologies. You're quite right. Time is of the essence. This is a bit complicated, but if you'll bear with me, I believe you'll welcome what I have to say." He took his place at the head of the table. "When Commander Vaughn first came to us with this mission, Counselor Troi related to me her experiences with Tevren. In explaining how he had developed his abilities to kill with his mind, she described the first telepathic skill that he learned, the ability to project extreme emotion into the mind of another. Am I remembering correctly, Counselor?"

"Yes, sir. He said that the emotion projection had no value to him except as a parlor trick, and held little interest for him, especially since it produced a debilitating drain on the telepath who employed it."

Picard nodded. "I've spent the last several hours interrogating Crell Moset. By appealing to the man's enormous ego, I've convinced him to share results of his experiments on the Jem'Hadar."

A visible shiver of revulsion passed over Nerissa Povron, and Picard guessed she was thinking how close she'd come to being the subject of one of Moset's experiments.

"Moset succeeded in creating telepathic Jem'Hadar," Picard said, "but they contained a fatal flaw. Because the Jem'Hadar mind processes emotions very differently from other humanoids, the ones that were made telepathic suddenly found themselves bombarded empathically, with no way to close off their new perceptions. Immediate, fatal seizures were invariably the result."

"You found a chink in the Jem'Hadar armor," Vaughn said.

Picard smiled. "I think so, yes. Using Moset's information, I've developed a theory. Telepathic Jem'Hadar can't handle an empathic overload. What if *normal* Jem'Hadar can't handle it either?"

Riker leaned forward. "That would explain why there were no mature Jem'Hadar on the station," he realized.

"Precisely, Number One. Neither the altered soldiers nor unaltered Jem'Hadar in close proximity could tolerate the empathic fallout of Moset's procedure."

Lwaxana frowned. "Are you suggesting, Jean-Luc, that my people learn to project emotions the way Tevren did and give all our enemies brain seizures?"

"Not exactly." Picard glanced around the room. "What I'm suggesting is that normal Jem'Hadar won't die from the overload of emotions, but if hit hard enough they will become seriously disoriented, perhaps enough to make their capture relatively effortless."

For the first time since the mission began, Deanna felt a surge of hope. "If that proves true, then Betazoids would be able to defeat the Jem'Hadar without wholesale slaughter."

"*If,*" the captain said, "is the operative word. I've had three Jem'Hadar beamed from the planet into the brig. Counselor, how quickly can you teach Tevren's emotion projection method to some of the stronger telepaths we rescued from the Cardassian freighter?"

"It shouldn't take long at all," Troi said. "They're among the strongest telepaths on Betazed."

"Make it so. When the telepaths are ready, assemble them in the brig. Dr. Crusher, you will monitor the responses of the Jem'Hadar."

Crusher inclined her head in agreement.

"Dr. Povron," Picard continued, "will you keep a close eye on the effects of the emotion projection technique on your people?"

The Betazoid doctor nodded. "I'll be happy to assist, Captain."

Chapter Eighteen

AFTER BEVERLY CRUSHER and Nerissa Povron completed their evaluations of the Betazoids and Jem'Hadar who had tested the emotion projection theory, Deanna, Lwaxana, Riker, and Dr. Povron transported to the resistance stronghold. Sorana Xerix, Cort Enaren, and the rest of the council were waiting for them in the meeting room.

Lwaxana faced the group. "We don't have much time, so we'll get right to the point. Deanna will explain what we've learned about an alternative to Tevren's killing method."

Deanna sensed the council's quickened interest as well as an unspoken sense of relief. The Betazoids would welcome another option, but the only other choice she could offer had its own horrible consequences. She was glad the decision wasn't hers. She would present the council with the facts and let them make the hard choices.

After explaining what Tevren did to her before he died and the brutal component to his killing method, Deanna told them, "You have another option. Tevren also had the ability to project intense emotions into people's minds."

"What good would that do us?" Sorana asked with impatience. "Do you expect us simply to scare the enemy to death?"

Deanna shook her head. "Thousands of Betazoids died on Sentok Nor, but as a result of the horrible experiments performed on them, we've learned something crucial about the Jem'Hadar. These soldiers have a flaw that telepaths can use to their advantage."

Enaren folded his arms over his chest, his face tight with concentration. Sorana and several other council members leaned forward, intent on Deanna's explanation. Lwaxana observed her daughter with undisguised pride.

"When Crell Moset succeeded in creating telepathic Jem'Hadar," Deanna continued, "his subjects all died from horrific seizures. Their minds were overwhelmed by the tremendous influx of emotions and sensations that a natural telepath learns to control over time. This is what killed them."

"Are you saying the Jem'Hadar on Betazed are telepathic?" Enaren asked in alarm.

"No," Deanna said, "but even without telepathic abilities, they don't process emotions as most humanoids do. When Captain Picard learned about this unique characteristic from Moset, the captain had several Jem'Hadar transported onto the *Enterprise*. In an experiment, I taught my mother and a group of telepaths we rescued from Sentok Nor how to project emotions into the Jem'Hadar's minds."

"What kind of emotions?" Sorana asked.

Deanna nodded to her mother to continue.

"We tapped into the whole gamut," Lwaxana explained. "Hate, guilt, apprehension, fear, anger, hope, despair, longing, sadness, surprise, resolve, annoyance, confusion, contentment, desire, grief, disapproval, even forgiveness and love. Our group bombarded the Jem'Hadar with these feelings, and Dr. Crusher monitored their responses."

"Did the Jem'Hadar die?" Enaren asked.

Deanna shook her head. "They became catatonic, as if overwhelmed."

"I don't understand," Sorana said with a shake of her head but a glint of hope in her eyes.

"Their minds shut down," Povron explained, "like a computer protecting itself from a power surge."

"They're permanently impaired?" Enaren asked.

"The Jem'Hadar on the *Enterprise* recovered in less than an hour," Povron said, "but during that hour they were helpless."

"So we don't have to kill them to conquer them?" Enaren said.

"That's the upside of this method," Lwaxana said. "We don't have to reduce ourselves to murderers."

"What's the downside?" Sorana asked.

"There are several disadvantages," Deanna said. She glanced at Will, who nodded in support. He more than anyone, besides her mother, knew how difficult presenting Tevren's information was for Deanna.

"First," Deanna said, "we don't know if the laboratory experiment can be duplicated over an entire planet."

"The Jem'Hadar are spread out," Lwaxana explained. "Reaching every soldier in every enemy encampment to overpower them empathically may prove difficult or even impossible."

Deanna nodded. "And we can't be sure how long the affected Jem'Hadar will remain catatonic. We need them incapacitated long enough to round them up and secure them behind force fields."

"We could imprison most of them in the prisons they built for us," Enaren suggested. "Poetic justice."

Sorana sighed. "So if we choose this method, we're taking a huge chance."

"The greatest stumbling block," Deanna admitted, "is that we don't know how much harm this invasive empathy will do to those who employ it."

Picking up on Deanna's hesitation, Enaren frowned. "What happened to the telepaths on the ship?"

Deanna asked Povron to explain.

"In our limited experiment," the doctor said, "the telepaths became extremely weak. The distance between the participants and the Jem'Hadar was only a few feet, and there were only three soldiers. I anticipate the sustained planetwide effort necessary to overcome fifty thousand troops will exhaust many of our people to the point of death."

There was a sharp intake of breath from Sorana, and several of the council exchanged long looks of horror.

Deanna had to tell them what she and Povron suspected. "Each telepath we lose will make it that much harder for the remaining ones to finish the task."

Will spoke for the first time. "Whichever method of ridding your planet of Jem'Hadar you choose, the *Tulwar, Scimitar,* and the *Enterprise* will remain in orbit to help coordinate communications and distribute weapons and portable force field generators. However, since either method requires telepathic skills, your people will be the ones on the front lines."

Sorana held up her hand. "We need more facts before we can make an informed decision. Would the original plan, teaching our people to kill with their minds, risk their lives?"

Lwaxana looked as if she wished to speak, but for once, her forceful mother held her tongue and motioned for her daughter to answer.

"Killing the way Tevren did," Deanna said, "causes no physical harm to the telepath. However, one needs tremendous telepathic strength, much more than I have, to accomplish such a task."

Deanna had inherited strong telepathic genes from her mother, but her father's human genes had diluted her skills. She was thankful that if the council chose to use Tevren's killing method, she would be unable to participate.

"If murdering others isn't what killed Tevren, how did he die?" Sorana pressed.

"Tevren died from the removal of his psionic inhibitor," Deanna explained. "He had become dependent on it."

"Does the invasive empathy affect Cardassians?" Enaren asked.

Deanna answered his question with certainty. "Projecting intense emotions in this manner won't harm other humanoids, not even Cardassians or Vorta. To overcome the few thousand Cardassian support troops, we'll need to use conventional weapons." She swept the council with her gaze. "Using invasive empathy to defeat the Jem'Hadar will cause the deaths of many Betazoids. But if we can succeed using this method, we won't become the heirs of Tevren's legacy."

Lwaxana joined Deanna at the front of the room. "As I stated earlier, time is of the essence. Unless someone has more questions, it's time for us to vote."

Swayed by Lwaxana's influence, the council, after heated debate, voted to attack the Jem'Hadar by invasive empathy. With the help of Commander Vaughn and the *Enterprise* senior staff, the planetwide assault was quickly planned. Deanna had requested and received permission to fight on the surface with the resistance movement.

On a path in the Loneel wilderness, she hefted her phaser rifle, hoping she'd never have to fire it. Relying on her rifle would mean their empathic efforts against the Jem'Hadar had failed. Her government-in-exile's decision not to use Tevren's killing techniques relieved her. That her people were willing to risk death to preserve their way of life filled Deanna with hope for Betazed's future—if their plan succeeded.

After the council vote, Deanna, Lwaxana, and Povron had trained the three dozen telepaths rescued from the Cardassian freighter in the invasive empathy technique. The trained telepaths from that group were then transported to each resistance cell on the surface to teach the members of that group and to set up communications with the *Enterprise* to coordinate efforts. The planetwide battle strategy was based on information gleaned from reconnaissance missions by resistance cells in every province of Betazed. All over the world, every resistance cell would execute the plan in a simultaneous effort.

Vaughn's strategy entailed encircling each encampment of Jem'Hadar with Betazoids, who traveled to the sites in small groups in order to attract less interest from Jem'Hadar patrols. Breaking up the Betazoid attack force into groups also insured they were less likely to set off Jem'Hadar sensors. If one group was detained, at least the others would make it through.

Every cell on the planet had a Starfleet officer and several security personnel responsible for protecting the telepaths. Each small group had to be in position, ready to project their emotions at the Jem'Hadar by the designated attack time. Other Betazoids, those less telepathically adept, would be responsible for placing the catatonic Jem'Hadar into force fields and prisons and taking out any remaining patrols that escaped the initial empathic assault. Timing and the element of surprise would be critical to the plan's success.

With Lwaxana beside her, Deanna marched along the wilderness path toward the Jem'Hadar encampment, comfortable with her decision to join the unconventional battle. Captain Picard and the *Enterprise* would target Cardassian centers of communication from orbit, and keep watch for Dominion reinforcements. Will and Vaughn would have their hands full subduing the Cardassian troops, against whom the invasive empathy wasn't expected to work.

Nerissa Povron and Enaren brought up the rear of Lwaxana's group. Povron seemed lost in her own thoughts, Enaren cloaked in grief for his son.

We're almost there, Lwaxana announced.

I remember all too well. Enaren's mind was heavy with sorrow for the loss of Sark and Okalan, the friend he'd had to kill at this very encampment. He had lost much in this war, and he'd been the first to volunteer for this mission.

Lwaxana, a stronger telepath than Deanna, must have been weighed down by Enaren's anguish. She directed strong encouragement to her fellow council member and old friend. *Gather up your emotions. Soon you can put your feelings to good use.*

In the burgeoning dawn, Lwaxana stopped the group behind a copse of trees. Line of sight to the Jem'Hadar troops wasn't necessary. The telepaths needed simply to approach close enough, a distance of over a hundred meters for the strongest among them.

Using her phaser rifle, Deanna checked their location. Its targeting scope, capable of detecting and tracking life-forms, indicated short-range biological scans of a concentrated group of Jem'Hadar, too many for a patrol, dead ahead. Her group had reached the encampment. *We are in position.*

Take cover, Lwaxana ordered.

Concealed by a row of evergreens, Deanna settled on the floor of the forest between Lwaxana and Povron. Enaren crouched behind a nearby thicket. Aiming her rifle in the direction of the encampment, ready for rapid fire if needed, Deanna closed her eyes and felt the presence of other groups in the surrounding woods, just as across her homeworld, other cells encircled other Jem'Hadar encampments and duplicated their efforts.

We have two minutes, Lwaxana announced. *Relax. Meditate. Focus every emotion and prepare to release it as Deanna taught us.*

I'm ready. Grief, hostility, and sadness emanated from Enaren.

I, too. Povron's hatred for the enemy, clear and polished, had a razor-sharp edge.

One minute to go. Lwaxana warned. She thought of Ian, of Kestra, of Deanna and Barin. *Breathe deeply. Relax. Focus on the Jem'Hadar.*

Deanna watched as the three telepaths breathed in through their noses, out through their mouths, and drew energy from deep inside themselves.

Ten seconds, Lwaxana counted.

Five.

Now!

Deanna could feel the emotions being hurled into the nearest Jem'Hadar. In her mind, she pictured them grasping their heads in shock, confusion, and fear. She felt wave after wave of anger and despair. It almost sent her reeling, and she was just getting the backwash. She peered through the phaser rifle sight and saw that some of the Jem'Hadar stumbled. Others stopped in their tracks. Seconds lengthened into minutes, and minutes seemed to last forever. All around her, the air grew thick with bitterness and hope, hatred of the enemy and love of hearth and home, and the sensation of a growing weariness among the telepaths.

Keep at them, Lwaxana urged her companions. *Our friends to the left of us . . . are gone.*

All around Deanna, Betazoids were falling, some dying. Like a weakened swimmer tugged under by a riptide, she fought to keep from succumbing to the wave of lethargy that threatened to engulf her. She grieved for the lost group. Resisting the weakness that threatened to drown her, she remembered her people, the many who had already died and those who would perish this day. Fighting to keep from tumbling down into blackness, she stubbornly fired off her anger at the possibility of losing this war—

Imzadi . . .

—until the blackness won and sucked her under.

Chapter Nineteen

WHEN GUL LEMEC ESCAPED the doomed Sentok Nor, he had sent a subspace message, requesting reinforcements for Betazed. The reply was not to his liking. Cardassian and Dominion reinforcements had been intercepted by a Federation fleet. No help was coming.

Within hours of his arrival on Betazed, Luaran had appeared at Lemec's headquarters. She'd tracked him down immediately to inform him of her escape from Sentok Nor. She could not, however, confirm or deny Moset's survival. If the doctor hadn't perished in the destruction of the station, he had possibly fallen captive.

Confronting the Vorta in his office, the gul didn't bother to conceal his delight at the doctor's plight. If not for Moset, the space station would never have been compromised.

"We face bigger problems than the loss of Sentok Nor," Lemec told her.

Luaran's face remained serene, in spite of the displeasure in her voice. "The Founders will not be pleased if Federation forces have captured Moset. The loss of his research is bad enough, without losing the man as well."

"Moset's research was worthless." Lemec's blood boiled at the memory of the doctor's lowering the shields and making the station vulnerable to attack. "Instead of enhancing Jem'Hadar, he succeeded only in killing them."

"True," Luaran agreed, "but in time, he might have made a breakthrough."

"Time is something we don't have. Sensors have picked up Starfleet transporter signals all over the planet. We must assume the *Enterprise* has contacted the resistance cells."

The Vorta shrugged. "Our latest reports indicate the remaining resistance members are hungry, without medical resources or weapons, and—"

"They could be mounting a united campaign in an effort to drive us off their planet."

Luaran smiled. "Good."

"Good?" Lemec couldn't believe he'd heard correctly. "Our enemies could be ready to attack, and you think that's good?"

"To fight, they must come out of hiding," the Vorta said. "These unmilitaristic people are no match for Jem'Hadar, and once they attack, we'll defeat them and maintain our complete control of this world."

"The Betazoids are desperate and have nothing left to lose but their lives." Lemec, recalling the Bajoran resistance, feared the fanaticism such circumstances evoked. And the Bajorans weren't telepathic. "Now Starfleet is helping them, probably supplying weapons and tactical and communications support. It would be a mistake to underestimate them. An assault could be far more intense—"

"If we lose Jem'Hadar," Luaran said in the same placid tone, "we'll breed more. I don't see a problem."

Lemec shook his head. "I hope you're right. This is one time I'll be happy to be proved wrong."

A glinn barged into Lemec's office, so obviously rattled he forgot to salute. "Sir, you asked me to notify you if . . ."

The glinn hesitated, and Lemec snapped, "Yes? What's happened?"

"It's the Jem'Hadar, sir. They have gathered for their supply of white and . . . they're acting . . . odd."

Lemec frowned. "Odd?"

"Jem'Hadar can't act odd," Luaran stated matter-of-factly.

"You'd better see for yourselves."

Lemec and Luaran followed the glinn from Lemec's office into the headquarter's operations center. Cardassians manned their stations, but their attention was clearly concentrated on a viewscreen showing the adjacent Jem'Hadar barracks and grounds.

Despite the glinn's claim, Lemec expected to see Jem'Hadar queuing in their usual lines, accepting their ration of white from a Vorta and repeating their ritual words of thanks. Instead, most of the Jem'Hadar stood as if frozen, barely breathing, eyes unblinking. A few wrestled each other in the dirt in brutal hand-to-hand combat. Several others had drawn their weapons and were firing on one another. Oblivious to the total chaos around them, the immobile ones didn't flex a muscle. Some fell without flinching when the erratic weapons fire struck them.

"Is this some kind of drill?" Lemec asked Luaran.

"Jem'Hadar don't kill one another in drills. The Founders don't appreciate the unnecessary waste of soldiers."

"Maybe the white's contaminated," Lemec suggested. "The resistance could have poisoned it."

The glinn shook his head. "Most of them haven't received their allotment yet."

"Send in the Cardassian troops," Luaran demanded. "This unacceptable behavior must cease at once."

An officer at communications spoke up. "I'm receiving reports of similarly bizarre Jem'Hadar activity from every outpost. Do you have orders, sir?"

"Seal our perimeter with Cardassian troops," Lemec ordered. "Order the others to do the same."

The communications officer shook his head. "I can't get through now. Someone's jamming our signals."

"It must be the *Enterprise*. Keep trying."

Luaran frowned at the soldiers fighting on the viewscreen. "What about the Jem'Hadar?"

"You said yourself they're replaceable."

The Vorta had no chance to reply. A huge explosion rocked their headquarters, showering dust and debris and knocking several of the operations staff to the floor. Computer stations sparked and ignited. Lights flickered and went out.

Lemec shoved himself to his feet. The officer at

communications would never rise again. A fallen ceiling beam had caved in his chest.

The loss of several of his staff was the least of Lemec's concern. Where were the rest of his soldiers? Had they received his order to guard the perimeter? With the viewscreen blank, Lemec grabbed a phase-disruptor rifle and staggered outside to assess the situation, leaving Luaran to find her own way.

Shouted orders and the screams of wounded and dying greeted him. His headquarters was under attack and sustaining phaser fire from all sides. From the number of Cardassian bodies on the ground, he concluded that his troops had suffered heavy losses in the initial assault. Smoke from burning barracks and supply warehouses clouded the air, filled his nose, and obscured his vision. Stunned, he caught sight of Betazoid and Starfleet troops advancing on his position through the haze.

Beside him, Luaran doubled over and gasped for air. "You must do something."

Before Lemec could issue an order, Starfleet forces overran the compound and surrounded him and Luaran. A tall human with dark hair and a dark beard pointed his phaser at Lemec. The pips on his collar identified him as a Starfleet commander. Upon seeing the gul, his eyes narrowed. "I remember you. Stand down, Lemec."

Lemec remembered the commander as well: Riker of the *Enterprise,* who had been on hand for the gul's last great humiliation when he'd faced Starfleet's Captain Jellico. Out of options, Lemec dropped his rifle.

"What are your terms?" Luaran asked.

The commander smiled. "Unconditional surrender."

Resigned to defeat, Lemec raised his hands above his head. Luaran did not. She simply stood there, which puzzled him.

The gul whispered, "Isn't this when I get the pleasure of watching you activate your voluntary termination implant?"

Luaran's calm was unshattered. "Not when I can still escape. Good luck, Lemec." And with that, the Vorta pressed a contact on her gauntlet, became enveloped in a Dominion transporter effect, and was gone.

Riker fired his phaser, but it was too late. "Damn," he muttered.

"Problem?" someone asked, and Lemec saw another Starfleet commander stride toward them, only this one had white hair and a white beard.

"The Vorta beamed out," Riker said.

The second commander regarded Lemec with what looked like sympathy. "Can't say I'm surprised. She obviously knows a lost cause when she sees one." Looking at Riker, the white-haired commander continued, "The force field enclosures around the Jem'Hadar barracks are almost all up. They'll contain both the Jem'Hadar and the Cardassians we've captured."

Riker gestured with his phaser toward the stockade where Lemec had housed and tortured Betazoid prisoners. "Your cell is waiting."

Lemec lowered his hands. All his hopes for advancement had evaporated. By blaming the destruction of Sentok Nor on Moset, he might have salvaged his career from the ashes of that disaster. Losing Betazed, however, was a blow from which he'd never recover.

He met the unwavering gaze of his Starfleet captor. "I don't suppose you could just shoot me instead?"

Riker hit the panel beside the Cardassian cell with his fist, raising the force field on Gul Lemec, who sat with his head in his hands. After posting security guards at the door of the stockade, Riker strode across the dusty grounds of the enemy encampment toward Lemec's former office and surveyed the ongoing activities with satisfaction.

Teams composed of Betazoids and members of the Starfleet task force's crews moved efficiently throughout the area, aiding the wounded and tagging the dead for the burial detail that would follow. Both Jem'Hadar and Cardassian troops were securely contained behind force fields or incarcerated in the stockade. If their plan had worked as smoothly across the rest of the planet as it had here, Betazed was effectively free of Dominion rule.

Riker shook his head, recalling the morning's battle. It had been one of the strangest he'd ever taken part in. The assault had begun not to the roar of weapons, but with the silent empathic attack of the Betazoid telepaths. Once observers had signaled that the Jem'Hadar had been disabled, the armed Starfleet and Betazoid teams had opened fire. Caught by surprise and unable to count on the Jem'Hadar for backup, the Cardassian troops had quickly conceded.

Imzadi.

At that point in the battle, Riker had heard Deanna's thought, had felt her mind reaching out to his. Although he wasn't telepathic, his relationship with Deanna had deepened over the years to the point that she could sometimes touch his mind, and he could sense her presence. With that one word, he'd felt her love—and her withdrawal. He quickened his steps, eager to complete his mission so he could locate her and assure himself that she was all right.

Without warning, the hair on the back of his neck suddenly rose. The conquest had been *too* easy, and he couldn't shake an uneasy feeling that a second shoe was going to drop. Anxious for a full report, he hurried into Gul Lemec's old office, which Vaughn had commandeered as a temporary command post.

The older commander stood at the window, hands clasped behind his back, but with a hint of fatigue in the set of his shoulders. Vaughn turned when Riker entered, and Will was taken aback by the pain mirrored in the commander's eyes.

"Have you received a situation report yet?" Riker asked.

"Captain Picard just informed me the *Enterprise* has received accounts from the other Betazoid resistance cells. Every group was successful in subduing the Jem'Hadar and Cardassians. Betazed is free."

Vaughn's voice held no jubilation in imparting his news, however, and his expression remained grim. Riker felt a chill down his spine.

"That's good news, isn't it?" he asked warily.

With a heavy sigh, Vaughn settled into the chair at Lemec's desk. "It should be."

"Why wouldn't it be?"

Vaughn scrubbed his face with his hands as if trying to wash away his exhaustion. "Because contained in those situation reports are the casualty stats for the telepaths who fought the Jem'Hadar empathically."

"Casualties," Riker said. "You mean wounded?"

The commander shook his head. "The people have their planet back, but at a terrible price. On average, four out of every ten telepaths lost their lives."

Riker reeled at the news. "Forty percent dead," he whispered.

Vaughn lifted his head, and in his eyes Riker could read the history of too many battles, too many deaths. "We have reports on the telepaths from every cell but this one. We haven't managed to locate all of ours yet."

"Deanna?" Riker asked through a mouth gone dry.

"No word," Vaughn answered with a fearful heaviness in his voice.

Riker tapped his combadge. "Riker to Troi. Report."

Vaughn pushed himself to his feet, approached Will, and placed his hand on the younger officer's shoulder.

"It's no use. I've been trying to raise her for the last five minutes. She doesn't answer."

Chapter Twenty

SOUNDS RETURNED TO DEANNA FIRST. Into the all-encompassing blackness trickled the soft murmur of voices, muted footsteps, and the mechanical tones of biofunction monitors.

"She's coming around, Dr. Crusher," an unfamiliar voice announced quietly.

Swimming upward through the gloom that enveloped her, Deanna opened her eyes to meet Beverly's bright blue ones.

"Welcome back," the doctor said.

A quick peripheral glance informed Deanna she was in the *Enterprise* sickbay, where every bed seemed filled. "Is it over?" she asked.

With a reassuring smile, Beverly squeezed her hand. "It's over. We won."

Relief washed through Deanna. "Tell me what happened."

"There's someone you should see first. If I don't let him talk to you soon, he's going to force his way in. He's been hovering outside ever since we transported you here. He can fill you in on the details."

"Wait, please. Do you know if my mother is all right?"

Beverly nodded to the next bed, and Deanna turned to find Lwaxana, lying pale and strangely quiet.

"She's still unconscious," the doctor said, "but her vital signs are strong. With rest, she'll recover quickly."

Beverly left and returned seconds later with Will. When he saw Deanna, his grin lit his face like the sun. "Hey," he said softly. "You gave us quite a scare. How are you feeling?"

"Tired," Deanna replied, "and a little embarrassed. I didn't realize the effect being around all those emotions would have on me. I never should have volunteered."

"As though any of us could've stopped you."

Giving Will a tired smile at the good-natured barb, she asked, "So the Jem'Hadar are really defeated?"

Will nodded with grim satisfaction. "Fifteen thousand died. The others are prisoners, along with the Cardassians."

His statistics shocked her, and she feared she had taught her people a killing technique after all. "The invasive empathy killed that many?"

"Not exactly. Just as we anticipated, the majority turned catatonic long enough for us to disarm them and erect force fields. But a small percentage went berserk and turned their weapons on themselves and others. Their behavior accounts for the high death toll."

His face darkened, and she sensed he was withholding bad news. "There's more, isn't there?"

He grasped her hand in both of his. "The Betazoid death toll was also high."

"How many?"

"Over twelve hundred."

"Killed by Dominion forces?"

Will shook his head. "From the strain of the empathic assault."

Stunned, Deanna looked to the doctor. "Twelve hundred dead. How could that happen?"

"I could give you a long lesson in Betazoid physiology to explain what occurred," Beverly said, "but essentially, they pushed themselves past their limits and burned out their telepathic cortex. The weaker ones died first. Only the very strongest, like your mother, survived."

Deanna blinked away tears. To drive the enemy from their soil while preserving the integrity of their society, her people had sacrificed themselves. She had never been more proud of her Betazoid heritage than at that moment.

"Tell me who died," Deanna said to Will.

He hesitated and glanced at Beverly, as if asking her consent. Crusher nodded.

"In your mother's cell," Riker said softly, "Sorana Xerix. Nerissa Povron. Too many others. You should wait until you've recovered to hear the rest."

"Enaren?" Deanna asked.

Beverly pointed across the room. "He's here. It was touch and go for a while, but we expect him to make a full recovery. And speaking of a full recovery, if you want me to release you soon, I can't do it. You need rest. I'll give you something to help you sleep."

The last thing Deanna remembered before losing consciousness was Will's lips brushing her forehead. When she awoke again, he was gone. Beverly glanced her way, and when she noticed Deanna was awake, she approached her. "You're looking better already."

"I am better."

Deanna felt physically stronger, but her spirit grieved for the loss of so many of her people. In the greater scheme of things, twelve hundred lives seemed a small price to pay for the liberation of an entire world—until she put names and faces and personalities to those people. For those who loved them, the loss of even one was too dear.

Are you all right, Little One?

Deanna lifted herself on her elbows and looked at her mother in the next bed.

We did it, Mother. Betazed is free.

Dr. Crusher told me.

Deanna sensed the sadness emanating from her mother and guessed that Lwaxana also knew how many of their people had died.

Barin, Deanna asked, *is he okay?*

He's fine. He and Chaxaza have been given quarters on the Enterprise *until I'm released from sickbay.*

The doors to the corridor opened, and Captain Picard entered with Commander Vaughn.

"Jean-Luc," Lwaxana said with the brightest smile she could manage. "How lovely to see you again. I knew we could count on your help, and you've come through admirably, as usual. Perhaps when Dr. Crusher releases me, I can thank you over an intimate dinner."

Deanna watched the captain assume what Will had once described in old Earth terms as a deer-caught-in-the-headlights expression. She exchanged an amused look with Commander Vaughn, who apparently was well acquainted with her mother's flirtatious ways.

Picard, however, recovered quickly, and, while keeping his distance, acknowledged her mother's invitation with a gracious nod. "An intimate dinner would be delightful, Lwaxana." She seemed pleased at Picard's acceptance, until he spoke again. "I'll invite the entire council, so we can discuss the continued defense of Betazed and an exchange of your captives for Starfleet prisoners of war."

Vaughn, blue eyes curiously warm, stepped to Deanna's side.

"I came to thank you for your help—and to say good-bye."

The older man's imminent departure filled her with regret. She'd grown fond of Elias, and with their mission accomplished, she'd looked forward to his sharing more about his days with her father. Like so many other things, their talk would have to wait until the war ended. "Where are you headed?"

He shrugged. "I go where they send me."

Deanna wanted to tell him to stay in touch, but knew better than to believe that was an option. "Keep safe, Elias."

"You, too, Deanna."

Epilogue

ON HOLODECK FOUR, Deanna lay on her stomach in the warm sand and let the simulated sun of Risa bake the weariness from her bones.

"Still brooding?" Will asked, basking in the sun's rays on the blanket beside her.

"Is it that obvious?"

"As a matter of fact, yes. You've been somber for days. Is it because of what happened on Betazed?"

"No, I've come to terms with the fact that it turned out as well as it could have, given the circumstances."

"It's too bad the invasive empathy had such a high mortality rate. Otherwise, the Federation could use Betazoid teams to knock out Jem'Hadar installations all over the quadrant."

"I doubt my people will ever use it again," Deanna said, "now that they know the cost."

Will propped himself on his elbow and studied her. "Then what's troubling you?"

She shrugged. "I guess I just feel guilty, lounging on a holodeck while there's still a war going on."

"Doctor's orders," Will reminded her. "But after all you've been through, I find it hard to believe you have reason to feel guilty about anything. Try again."

Deanna didn't answer at first, and they lay there in silence for long minutes, the sound of simulated waves against the holographic shore a dull roar. Then she sat up, facing Will cross-legged, staring into her open hands as she tried to find the words for what she needed to say. She wasn't sure how to begin, and she feared to give voice to it.

Finally she looked at him, feeling tears streaming down her cheeks.

"He's still in my head, Will," she whispered.

Riker looked into her eyes, and the anguish he saw there cut into him. He wanted to say something, but didn't know what.

"I still remember everything," Deanna went on. "Everything he knew, everything he did, everything he felt. He's still in my head, and I truly don't know if I'll ever get him out."

"Yes, you will," Will said quietly.

She almost laughed through the tears. "You know that for a fact, do you?"

"Yeah," he said, sitting up. "I do. I know it because in every way that counts, you're stronger than he was. I know it because no matter how bad things get, you always manage to hold it together, not just for yourself, but for everyone around you. And I know it because after all the difficult times in my life you've helped me through, there's no way I'm not gonna be there to help you through yours."

She smiled then, a ray of light through the dark cloud of her anguish, and slowly, with a few deep, cathartic breaths, the tears faded.

"Are you all right?" Will asked.

"No," she said honestly. "But I will be."

"Never doubted it." He grinned.

She embraced him tightly then. His arms reached around her in return, and Will suddenly felt tears welling up in his own eyes. In silence they continued to hold each other, long after the tears faded, and long after the holographic sun went down, each one knowing they'd never let go.

About the Authors

After teaching writing and communications at the college level, **Charlotte Douglas** now writes full-time. A graduate of the University of North Carolina at Chapel Hill, she is working on her nineteenth novel. She lives on Florida's West Coast with her husband and two cairn terriers.

Susan Kearney used to set herself on fire four times a day. While she no longer performs her signature fire dive (she's taken up figure skating), she never runs out of ideas for characters and plots. A business graduate of the University of Michigan, Susan has sold twenty-three novels and writes full-time. She resides in a small town outside Tampa, Florida, with her husband, children, and a spoiled Boston terrier. Visit her web site at www.SusanKearney.com.

Special Sneak Preview of

STARGAZER: BOOK ONE

Gauntlet

by
Michael Jan Friedman

Coming in May from Pocket Books!

Captain's personal log, supplemental.

We have arrived at Starbase 32, where Commander Gilaad Ben Zoma and I are to attend a convocation of starship captains and their executive officers. While such gatherings have rarely taken place before, our newly minted Admiral McAteer seems intent on closely coordinating the activities of all ships in his sector.

Ben Zoma thinks the entire meeting will be a waste of time—particularly the cocktail party the admiral is hosting this evening. I, on the other hand, am looking forward to the opportunity to rub elbows with my fellow captains.

No doubt there is a great deal I can learn from

them . . . considering I have officially been on the job less than a week now.

JEAN-LUC PICARD, captain of the Federation starship *Stargazer,* surveyed the imposing dome-shaped room that opened before him. It was filled with a sea of crimson uniforms and gold-barred sleeves, along with several matching crimson-draped tables bearing pale bowls of Andorian punch and piles of dark brown finger sandwiches.

Glancing at his first officer, Picard said, "I don't think I've ever seen so many command officers in one place."

Ben Zoma, a man with dark good looks and a mischievous glint in his eye, smiled at the remark. "One well-placed photon torpedo and you'd wipe out half the fleet."

"Perhaps not *half,* Number One."

"Close enough," Ben Zoma insisted.

"Think of it as a unique opportunity," Picard told him. He regarded a knot of a half-dozen men and women gathered around the nearest punch bowl. "A chance to pick the brains of those more experienced at this than you or I."

Ben Zoma, like Picard, had been promoted only recently. Before being named first officer of the *Stargazer,* he had served as the vessel's chief of security.

"Follow me," the captain said, meaning to take his own advice.

Joining the group by the punch bowl, he smiled at the glances that came his way. Then, as he helped himself to some punch, he listened in on the conversation.

"Of course," said a man with red hair that had begun graying at the temples, "I had never done anything like that before. But the circumstances seemed to call for it."

A large-boned woman with dark features nodded. "I've been in that situation myself."

A second woman grunted. She didn't look like the type who smiled much, despite the youthful scattering of freckles on her face. "I think we all have," she said soberly.

"I hate to interrupt," Picard chimed in, "but what are we talking about exactly? An encounter with a hostile force? A brush with some undiscovered phenomenon?"

He sounded more gung ho than he had intended. But then, he was *feeling* rather gung ho.

That is, until the others looked at him as if he had placed his hindquarters in the punch bowl. There was an awkward silence for what seemed a long time. Then one of the officers, the man with the red hair, offered a response.

"I was talking," he said, "about putting my dog to sleep."

Picard felt his cheeks grow hot. "Yes. Yes, of course you were. How silly of me to assume otherwise."

No one replied. They just stood there, looking at him. Finally, he took the hint.

"If you'll excuse me . . ." he said rather lamely.

When no one objected to his doing so, Picard separated himself from the group and strolled to the other side of the room. Ben Zoma walked beside him, a look of bemusement on his face.

"Gilaad," Picard said to his first officer, "is it my imagination or was I just snubbed?"

Ben Zoma looked back at the group they had just left. "I'd like to tell you that it's your imagination, Jean-Luc, but I don't think I can do that."

"What I said was admittedly a bit inappropriate, given the tenor of the conversation. But it wasn't deserving of that kind of response. Someone else might even have laughed at it."

Ben Zoma nodded. "True enough."

"Then why did they react that way?" Picard asked. He looked down at his newly replicated dress uniform. "Did I put my trousers on backward this evening?"

"Your trousers are fine," his friend said. "I have a feeling it has more to do with the age of the person inside them. You *are* the greenest apple ever to take command of a Starfleet vessel."

Picard couldn't argue the point. "So I am."

At the tender age of twenty-eight, he was the youngest captain yet in the history of the fleet. Even younger than the legendary James T. Kirk, and that was saying something.

"And it's not just your age," Ben Zoma said, ticking off the strikes against the captain on his fingers. "You've never had the experience of serving as first officer. You would never have gotten your commission so quickly if Captain Ruhalter hadn't been killed in the course of a battle with hostile aliens. And—because an inexperienced whippersnapper like you couldn't *possibly* have gotten a captaincy on merit—it was probably a political appointment."

Picard grunted. "Thank you, Number One. I was beginning to actually feel capable of commanding a starship for a moment there, but you have managed to completely disabuse me of that notion."

"My pleasure," his friend told him archly. "What's a

first officer for if not to deflate his captain's ego from time to time?"

"Indeed," Picard said thinly, sharing in the joke at his own expense.

He looked around the domed room again and noticed a few sidelong glances being cast in his direction. They didn't exactly look like expressions of admiration.

Perhaps Ben Zoma was right, the captain reflected. Perhaps his colleagues were looking at him differently because of his age and relative inexperience.

But if the looks on their faces were any indication, he wasn't just an object of curiosity. He was an object of disdain.

It hurt Picard to think so—even more than he would have guessed. After all, they had no firsthand observations to go on. They could only know what they had heard.

Yet these were starship captains and first officers—men and women who represented the finest the Federation had to offer. Picard would have expected them to be more welcoming of a fledgling colleague, more sensitive to his situation.

Apparently, he would have been wrong in that regard.

As was often the case, Ben Zoma seemed to read his thoughts. "All in all, not the friendliest-looking group I've ever seen."

"Nor I," Picard said. "I get the feeling I'm running a gauntlet."

"If you are, it's undeserved. You've earned your command, Jean-Luc." He jerked his head to include the other captains in the room. "Maybe more so than *they* have."

Picard didn't want to appear to feel sorry for himself, even if it was just in front of Ben Zoma. However, his colleagues' doubts weren't all that was bothering him. If they were, he could have taken the situation in stride.

Unfortunately, the glances they sent his way underlined a much more troublesome and insidious fact: the captain harbored some doubts *himself*.

Weeks earlier, when Admiral Mehdi called him into his office, he had expected the admiral to lay into him—to chew him out for the chances he had taken against the Nuyyad. Instead, Mehdi had ordained him Captain Ruhalter's successor.

Picard had been too stunned at the time to question the admiral's judgment. He had been too excited by the challenge to consider the wisdom of such a move.

But was he *qualified* to be a captain?

He had seized the reins in an emergency and brought his crew out of it alive, no question about it. But did he have the ability to command a starship over the long haul? Was he a long-distance runner . . . or just a sprinter?

"You're not saying anything," Ben Zoma pointed out. "Should I send for a doctor?"

The captain chuckled. "No, I don't think that will be necessary." He caught sight of a waiter with a tray of food. "Perhaps an hors d'oeuvre will brighten up the evening for me. I've always been partial to pigs in blankets."

His first officer looked skeptical. "Really?"

Picard smiled at him. "No. But they'll do in a pinch."

He had already embarked on an intercept course with the waiter when he felt a hand on his arm. Turning, he saw a tall fellow with a seamed face and a crew cut the color of sand.

Like Picard, he wore a captain's uniform. "Pardon

me," the fellow said. "You're Jean-Luc Picard, aren't you?"

Picard nodded. "I am."

The man extended his hand. "My name's Greenbriar. Denton Greenbriar."

Picard recognized the name. Anyone would have. "The captain of the *Cochise,* isn't it?"

Greenbriar grinned, deepening the lines in his face. "I see my reputation's preceded me."

In fact, it had. Denton Greenbriar was perhaps the most decorated commanding officer in Starfleet.

Picard pulled Ben Zoma over. "Captain Greenbriar, Gilaad Ben Zoma—my executive officer."

The two shook hands. "A pleasure to meet you," Greenbriar said. He turned back to Picard. "And a pleasure to meet *you,* sir. I've heard good things about you."

"You have?" Picard responded, unable to keep from sounding surprised. Embarrassed, he smiled. "Sorry, Captain. It's just that I feel like a bit of an oddity here."

"Why's that?" asked Greenbriar. "Just because you're the youngest man ever to command a starship?"

"Well," said Picard, "yes."

"People are often not what they seem, Jean-Luc." Greenbriar took in the other men and women in the room with a glance. "Looks to me like our colleagues here have forgotten that."

"I appreciate the vote of confidence," Picard told him.

Greenbriar shrugged his broad shoulders. "Admiral Mehdi is a sharp cookie. Always has been. If he has confidence in you, I'm certain it's well deserved."

"It is," Ben Zoma agreed.

Picard felt his cheeks turn hot. He cleared his throat and said, "I'm not sure what I find more uncomfortable—the cold shoulder or the company of flatterers."

Greenbriar laughed. "That's the last bit of flattery you'll get from *me,* Captain. I promise."

And with that, he left to refill his glass.

Ben Zoma turned to Picard. "That was refreshing."

"Unfortunately," the captain replied, "it's not likely to happen again this evening."

"What do you say we find something else to do?"

Picard frowned. It was a tempting suggestion. He said as much. "Nonetheless," he continued, "I feel obliged to stick it out here a while longer."

"Your duty as a captain?" Ben Zoma asked.

Picard nodded. "Something like that, yes."

So they stayed. But, as he had predicted, no one else came near them the rest of the evening.

Not even Admiral McAteer. In fact, Picard couldn't find the man the entire evening.

Carter Greyhorse, chief medical officer on the *Stargazer,* watched Gerda Asmund advance on him in her tight-fitting black garb. The navigation officer's left hand extended toward him while her right remained close to her chest, her slender fingers curled into nasty-looking claws.

"Kave'ragh!" she snarled suddenly, and her beautiful features contorted into a mask of primal aggression.

Then her right hand lashed out like an angry viper, her knuckles a blur as they headed for the center of his face. Greyhorse flinched, certain that Gerda had finally miscalculated and was about to deal him a devastating, perhaps even lethal blow. But as always, her attack fell short of its target by an inch.

Looking past Gerda's knuckles into her merciless, ice-blue eyes, Greyhorse swallowed. He didn't want to contemplate the force with which she would have driven her flattened fist into his mouth. Enough, surely, to cave in his front teeth. Enough to make him choke and sputter on his own blood.

But she had exercised restraint and pulled her punch. After all, it wasn't a battle in which they were engaged, or even a sparring session. It was just a lesson.

"Kave'ragh?" he repeated, doing his best not to completely mangle the Klingon pronunciation.

"Kave'ragh," Gerda repeated, having no trouble with the pronunciation. But then, she had been speaking the Klingon tongue from a rather early age.

The navigator stayed where she was for a moment, allowing Greyhorse to study her posture. Then she took a slow step back and retracted her fist, as if reloading a medieval crossbow.

"Now you," Gerda told him.

Greyhorse bent his knees and drew his hands into the proper position. Then he curled his fingers under at the first knuckle, exactly as she had taught him.

Gerda's eyes narrowed, but she didn't criticize him. It was a good sign. During their first few lessons, she had done nothing *but* criticize him—his balance, his coordination, even his desire to improve.

To be sure, Greyhorse wasn't the most athletic individual and never had been. When the other kids had chosen sides to play parisses squares, he had invariably been the last to be picked.

But he was big. And strong. Gerda seemed to know how to tap the power he possessed but had never made use of.

"Kave'ragh!" he bellowed, trying his best to duplicate his teacher's effort.

She spoiled his attack with an open-handed blow to the side of his wrist. It sent his fist wide of her face, where it couldn't do any harm. But at least he didn't stumble, as he had in their first few sessions. Maintaining his balance, he pulled back and reloaded.

"Kave'ragh!" he snapped again, determined to get past Gerda's defenses.

This time she hit the inside of his wrist and redirected the force of his attack upward, leaving the right side of his body woefully unguarded. Before he could move to cover the deficiency, Gerda drove her knuckles into his ribs.

Hard.

The pain made him recoil and cry out. Seeing this, Gerda shot him a look of disdain.

"Next time," she told him, "you'll do better."

He would too. And not because she had nearly cracked a rib with her counterattack. He would do better because he bitterly hated the idea of disappointing her.

The first time they had fought, in one of the *Stargazer*'s corridors, he had surprised her by getting in a lucky punch, and she had gazed at him with admiration in her eyes. It was to resurrect that moment that he endured this kind of punishment.

He didn't do it in order to become an expert in Klingon martial arts—he had no aspirations in that regard. He came to the gym three times a week and suffered contusions and bone bruises for one reason only: to force Gerda to see him as an equal. To see him as a warrior.

And eventually, if he was very diligent and very fortunate, to see him as a lover.

With this in mind, Greyhorse again assumed the basic position. Knees bent, he reminded himself. One hand forward, one hand back. Knuckles extended, so.

More important, he focused his mind. He saw himself driving his fist into his opponent's face, once, twice, and again, so quickly that his blows couldn't be parried. And he ignored the fact that it was Gerda's face he was pounding.

"Kave'*ragh!*" growled the doctor, a man who had never growled at anything in his life.

This time Greyhorse's attack was more effective. Gerda was unable to knock it off-line. In fact, it was only by moving her head at the last moment that she avoided injury.

He was grateful that she had. He didn't want to hurt her. He only wanted to prove to her that he could.

It was an irony he found difficult to accept—that he could only hope to win Gerda's love by demonstrating an ability to maim her. But then, the woman had been raised in a culture that made aggression a virtue. She had, to say the least, an *unusual* point of view.

Again, Greyhorse roared, *"Kave'ragh!"* and moved to strike her. Again, Gerda was unable to deflect his blow. And again, she managed to dodge anyway.

Getting closer, he told himself. She knew it, too. He could see it in her gaze, hard and implacable, demanding everything of him and giving away nothing.

Not even hope.

Yet Gerda knew how much he wanted her. She *had* to. He had blurted it out that day in the corridor.

She hadn't acknowledged it since, of course, and Greyhorse hadn't brought it up again. All they did was show up at their appointed time in the gym, teacher and pupil, master and enslaved.

"Kave'ragh!" he cried out.

Then he put everything into one last punch—too much, as it turned out, because he leaned too far forward and Gerda took painful advantage of the fact.

She didn't just elude Greyhorse's attack. She sidekicked him in the belly, knocking the wind out of him and doubling him over. Then she hit him in the back of his head with the point of her elbow, driving him to his knees.

Stunned, gasping for breath and dripping sweat, he remained on all fours for what seemed like a long time. Finally, he found the strength to drag himself to his feet.

Gerda was waiting for him with her arms folded across her chest, a lock of yellow hair dangling and a thin sheen of perspiration on her face. He had expected to find disapproval in her expression, maybe even disgust at the clumsiness he had exhibited.

But what he saw was a hint of the look she had given him in the corridor. A hint of *admiration.*

It made Greyhorse forget how Gerda had bludgeoned him, though his throat still burned and his ribs still throbbed and there was a distinctly metallic taste of blood in his mouth. In fact, it made him eager for more.

"Tomorrow?" she asked.

He nodded, inviting waves of vertigo even with that modest gesture. "I'll be here."

Gerda tilted her head slightly, as if to appraise him better. She remained that way for a moment, piercing his soul with her eyes. Then she turned her back on him, pulled a towel off the rack on the wall, and left the gym.

Greyhorse watched her go. She moved with animal grace, each muscle working in perfect harmony with all the others. When the doors hissed closed behind her, he felt as if he had lost a part of himself.

How he loved her.

Look for STAR TREK fiction from Pocket Books

Star Trek®: The Original Series

#16 • *Invasion! #3: Time's Enemy* • L.A. Graf
#17 • *The Heart of the Warrior* • John Gregory Betancourt
#18 • *Saratoga* • Michael Jan Friedman
#19 • *The Tempest* • Susan Wright
#20 • *Wrath of the Prophets* • David, Friedman & Greenberger
#21 • *Trial by Error* • Mark Garland
#22 • *Vengeance* • Dafydd ab Hugh
#23 • *The 34th Rule* • Armin Shimerman & David R. George III
#24-26 • *Rebels* • Dafydd ab Hugh
   #24 • *The Conquered*
   #25 • *The Courageous*
   #26 • *The Liberated*

Books set after the Series
   The Lives of Dax • Marco Palmieri, ed.
   Millennium • Judith and Garfield Reeves-Stevens
      #1 • *The Fall of Terok Nor*
      #2 • *The War of the Prophets*
      #3 • *Inferno*
A Stitch in Time • Andrew J. Robinson
Avatar, Book One • S.D. Perry
Avatar, Book Two • S.D. Perry
Section 31: Abyss: • David Weddle & Jeffrey Lang
Gateways #4: Demons of Air and Darkness • Keith R.A. DeCandido
Gateways #7: What Lay Beyond: "Horn and Ivory" • Keith R.A. DeCandido

Star Trek: Voyager®

Mosaic • Jeri Taylor
Pathways • Jeri Taylor
Captain Proton: Defender of the Earth • D.W. "Prof" Smith
Novelizations
   Caretaker • L.A. Graf
   Flashback • Diane Carey
   Day of Honor • Michael Jan Friedman
   Equinox • Diane Carey
   Endgame • Diane Carey & Christie Golden

#1 • *Caretaker* • L.A. Graf
#2 • *The Escape* • Dean Wesley Smith & Kristine Kathryn Rusch
#3 • *Ragnarok* • Nathan Archer
#4 • *Violations* • Susan Wright
#5 • *Incident at Arbuk* • John Gregory Betancourt
#6 • *The Murdered Sun* • Christie Golden
#7 • *Ghost of a Chance* • Mark A. Garland & Charles G. McGraw
#8 • *Cybersong* • S.N. Lewitt

Star Trek®: Starfleet Corps of Engineers (eBooks)

Have Tech, Will Travel • John J. Ordover, ed.
  #1 • *The Belly of the Beast* • Dean Wesley Smith
  #2 • *Fatal Error* • Keith R.A. DeCandido
  #3 • *Hard Crash* • Christie Golden
  #4 • *Interphase, Book One* • Dayton Ward & Kevin Dilmore
Miracle Workers • John J. Ordover, ed.
  #5 • *Interphase, Book Two* • Dayton Ward & Kevin Dilmore
  #6 • *Cold Fusion* • Keith R.A. Decandido
  #7 • *Invincible, Book One* • Keith R.A. Decandido and David Mack
  #8 • *Invincible, Book Two* • Keith R.A. Decandido and David Mack
  #9 • *The Riddled Post* • Aaron Rosenberg
  #10 • *Gateways Epilogue: Here There Be Monsters* • Keith R.A. DeCandido
  #11 • *Ambush* • Dave Galanter & Greg Brodeur
  #12 • *Some Assembly Required* • Scott Ciercin & Dan Jolley
  #13 • *No Surrender* • Jeff Mariotte
  #14 • *Caveat Emptor* • Ian Edginton

Star Trek®: Invasion!

#1 • *First Strike* • Diane Carey
#2 • *The Soldiers of Fear* • Dean Wesley Smith & Kristine Kathryn Rusch
#3 • *Time's Enemy* • L.A. Graf
#4 • *The Final Fury* • Dafydd ab Hugh
Invasion! Omnibus • various

Star Trek®: Day of Honor

#1 • *Ancient Blood* • Diane Carey
#2 • *Armageddon Sky* • L.A. Graf
#3 • *Her Klingon Soul* • Michael Jan Friedman
#4 • *Treaty's Law* • Dean Wesley Smith & Kristine Kathryn Rusch
The Television Episode • Michael Jan Friedman
Day of Honor Omnibus • various

Star Trek®: The Captain's Table

#1 • *War Dragons* • L.A. Graf
#2 • *Dujonian's Hoard* • Michael Jan Friedman
#3 • *The Mist* • Dean Wesley Smith & Kristine Kathryn Rusch
#4 • *Fire Ship* • Diane Carey

#5 • *Once Burned* • Peter David
#6 • *Where Sea Meets Sky* • Jerry Oltion
The Captain's Table Omnibus • various

Star Trek®: The Dominion War

#1 • *Behind Enemy Lines* • John Vornholt
#2 • *Call to Arms...* • Diane Carey
#3 • *Tunnel Through the Stars* • John Vornholt
#4 • *...Sacrifice of Angels* • Diane Carey

Star Trek®: Section 31™

Rogue • Andy Mangels & Michael A. Martin
Shadow • Dean Wesley Smith & Kristine Kathryn Rusch
Cloak • S. D. Perry
Abyss • Dean Weddle & Jeffrey Lang

Star Trek®: Gateways

#1 • *One Small Step* • Susan Wright
#2 • *Chainmail* • Diane Carey
#3 • *Doors Into Chaos* • Robert Greenberger
#4 • *Demons of Air and Darkness* • Keith R.A. DeCandido
#5 • *No Man's Land* • Christie Golden
#6 • *Cold Wars* • Peter David
#7 • *What Lay Beyond* • various

Star Trek®: The Badlands

#1 • Susan Wright
#2 • Susan Wright

Star Trek®: Dark Passions

#1 • Susan Wright
#2 • Susan Wright

Star Trek® Omnibus Editions

Invasion! Omnibus • various
Day of Honor Omnibus • various

The Captain's Table Omnibus • various

Star Trek: Odyssey • William Shatner with Judith and Garfield Reeves-
Stevens

Millennium Omnibus • Judith and Garfield Reeves-Stevens

Starfleet: Year One • Michael Jan Friedman

Other Star Trek® Fiction

Legends of the Ferengi • Ira Steven Behr & Robert Hewitt Wolfe

Strange New Worlds, vols. I, II, III, and IV • Dean Wesley Smith, ed.

Adventures in Time and Space • Mary P. Taylor

Captain Proton: Defender of the Earth • D.W. "Prof" Smith

New Worlds, New Civilizations • Michael Jan Friedman

The Lives of Dax • Marco Palmieri, ed.

The Klingon Hamlet • Wil'yam Shex'pir

Enterprise Logs • Carol Greenburg, ed.

STAR TREK®

STICKER
BOOK

MICHAEL OKUDA
DENISE OKUDA
DOUG DREXLER

POCKET BOOKS
A VIACOM COMPANY

isbn: 0-671-01472-2

STKR

Ever wonder what to serve at a
Klingon Day of Ascension?

Just can't remember if you bring a gift
to a *Rumarie* celebration?

You know that Damok was on the
ocean, but you can't recall just what
that means?

Have no fear! Finally you too
can come prepared to any
celebration held anywhere in
Federation space.

Laying out many of the complex and compelling rituals
of *Star Trek*'s varied cultures, this clear and handy guide
will let you walk into any celebration with assurance.
Plus: in a special section are the celebrations that have
become part of the traditions of Starfleet.

From shipboard promotion to the Klingon coming-of-age
to the joyous exchange of marriage vows, you can be a
part of it all with

STAR TREK®
Celebrations

Pocket Books
A VIACOM COMPANY

3116

STAR TREK
SECTION 31

BASHIR
Never heard of it.

SLOAN
We keep a low profile....
We search out and identify
potential dangers to the
Federation.

BASHIR
And Starfleet sanctions
what you're doing?

SLOAN
We're an autonomous
department.

BASHIR
Authorized by whom?

SLOAN
Section Thirty-One was
part of the original
Starfleet Charter.

BASHIR
That was two hundred years
ago. Are you telling me
you've been on your own
ever since? Without specific
orders? Accountable to
nobody but yourselves?

SLOAN
You make it sound so
ominous.

BASHIR
Isn't it?

No law. No conscience. No stopping them.
A four book, all <u>Star Trek</u> series beginning in June.

Excerpt adapted from *Star Trek:Deep Space Nine*®
"Inquisition" written by Bradley Thompson & David Weddle.